W9-BAV-432

PETRONIUS

made the Seven Deadly Sins fashionable and amusing. A scientist of pleasure, a master of debauchery, he spent his days in sleep, his nights at official duties—or amusements. By his dissolute life, he became the most famous voluptuary—next to Nero himself—of the decadent Roman Empire.

History also immortalizes Petronius on another score: as the author of that penetrating satire of high and low Roman life, *The Satyricon.*

William Arrowsmith's brilliant unexpurgated translation recaptures all the rowdy humor of Petronius' classic. Here is the entire dubious world of Nero's Rome—the fools, the hypocrites, the fatuous philosophers, the pompous rhetoricians, the new rich . . . all in passionate pursuit of pleasure.

"One of the comic masterpieces in the literature of the Western world."   THE NEW YORK TIMES

WILLIAM ARROWSMITH is a former Rhodes Scholar and Guggenheim Fellow, and a winner of the Prix de Rome. He has taught at Princeton and Wesleyan universities and at the University of Texas. He is well known for his translations of Euripides, as general editor of New American Library's Greek comedy series, and as the pre-eminent translator of Aristophanes.

·⚜ The ⚜·
SATYRICON
PETRONIUS

TRANSLATED, WITH AN INTRODUCTION,
BY
WILLIAM ARROWSMITH

A MERIDIAN CLASSIC
NEW AMERICAN LIBRARY
NEW YORK AND SCARBOROUGH, ONTARIO

For Saul Bellow

NAL BOOKS ARE AVAILABLE AT QUANTITY DISCOUNTS
WHEN USED TO PROMOTE PRODUCTS OR SERVICES. FOR
INFORMATION PLEASE WRITE TO PREMIUM MARKETING DIVISION,
NEW AMERICAN LIBRARY, 1633 BROADWAY,
NEW YORK, NEW YORK 10019.

Copyright © by William Arrowsmith 1959
Copyright © renewed 1987 by William Arrowsmith

All rights reserved

Library of Congress Catalog Card Number: 83-61421

The Satyricon previously appeared in a Signet Classic ediiton.

MERIDIAN CLASSIC TRADEMARK REG. U.S. PAT. OFF. AND FOREIGN COUNTRIES
REGISTERED TRADEMARK—MARCA REGISTRADA
HECHO EN WINNIPEG, CANADA

SIGNET, SIGNET CLASSIC, MENTOR, ONYX, PLUME,
MERIDIAN and NAL BOOKS are published *in the United States* by
NAL PENGUIN INC., 1633 Broadway, New York, New York 10019,
in Canada by The New American Library of Canada Limited,
81 Mack Avenue, Scarborough, Ontario M1L 1M8

First Medidian Classic Printing, November, 1983

4 5 6 7 8 9 10 11 12

PRINTED IN CANADA

INTRODUCTION

Few literary fragments are more tantalizing than the pitifully small portion that remains to us of Petronius' great satirical masterpiece, the *Satyricon*. Now read for the most part either as a surreptitious classic, for amusement or titillation, or as one of the earliest examples of the novel, it is nonetheless, even in its mutilated state, one of the finest achievements of the Roman imagination, everywhere remarkable for a vigor and vividness and glorious candor that make it unique in both Greek and Latin literature. There is literally nothing like it. Apparently a bewildering hodgepodge of genres and subjects, relentlessly blending the comic, the mock-heroic and the satirical, the realistic and the poetic, it is nonetheless a triumph in its own right. Clearly in the mainstream of ancient satire, it is also something recognizably apart and utterly original; visibly a novel, it is yet somehow not a novel at all. What was it intended to be and what sort of man wrote it?

PETRONIUS

Unfortunately we know next to nothing of the author of the *Satyricon* and nothing at all with certainty. If his very name is still in question,* his period has equally been the subject of long and inconclusive disagreement. † Despite this, there is now something like a consensus among scholars that the Petronius who wrote the *Satyricon* is probably to be identified with Petronius Arbiter, the consul and intimate of the emperor Nero. What little we know of Petronius Arbiter comes, of course, from the famous

---

* In antiquity we find Petronius referred to as Petronius Arbiter or even as Arbiter alone. In Tacitus' passage, he bears the name Gaius, and *elegentiae arbiter* appears as a kind of title rather than as an integral part of his name. In Pliny (*Hist. Nat.* xxxvii, 8, 20), he is called Titus. In essence, the question centers on whether Arbiter is a cognomen or an agnomen, and this is, of course, impossible to decide.

† For discussion, see Sage's edition of the *Satyricon* and also Gilbert Bagnani's *Arbiter of Elegance*. The latest advocate of a later date for Petronius is E. Marmorale (*La Questione Petroniana*).

description given us by Tacitus. The notice deserves to be quoted in its entirety:

The case of Gaius Petronius deserves further brief mention. He spent his days in sleeping, his nights in work and the enjoyment of life. That success which most men achieve by dint of hard work, he won by laziness. Yet unlike those prodigals who waste themselves and their substance alike, he was not regarded as either a spendthrift or a debauchee, but rather as a refined voluptuary. Indeed, his words and actions displayed such apparent casualness and unconventional freshness that people found them all the more charming. Nonetheless, as governor of Bithynia and soon afterwards as consul, he proved himself a capable and energetic administrator. Upon later reverting to a life of vice (or of apparent vice), he was admitted as effective arbiter of taste into the select circle of Nero's intimates. No imperial pastime or entertainment which lacked Petronius' approval could be regarded as either elegant or luxurious. And so Tigellinus, jealous of a rival whose expertise in the science of pleasure far surpassed his own, appealed to the emperor's cruelty (Nero's dominant passion) and accused Petronius of friendship with the conspirator Scaevinus. A slave was bribed to incriminate Petronius; no defense was permitted and most of the prisoner's household was placed under arrest.

At that time the emperor was in Campania. Petronius had gone as far as Cumae when he was apprehended. The prospect of temporizing, with its attendant hopes and fears, seemed intolerable; equally he had no desire to dispatch himself hastily. So he severed his veins and then bound them up as the fancy took him, meanwhile conversing with his friends, not seriously or sadly or with ostentatious courage. And he listened while they talked and recited, not maxims on the immortality of the soul and philosophical reflections, but light and frivolous poetry. He then rewarded some of his slaves and assigned beatings to others. He dined and then dozed so that his death, even though compulsory, might still look natural. Nor did he adopt the conventional deathbed routine of flattering Nero, Tigellinus, and the other worthies. Instead, he wrote out a list of the emperor's debaucheries, citing by name each of his sexual partners, male and female, with a catalogue of his sexual experi-

*ments, and sent it off to Nero under seal. He then
destroyed his signet ring so that it could not be used
later for the purpose of incriminating others.**

Unconventionality, charm, courage, refinement, an appetite
for pleasure, a dislike of heroic postures and an understanding of others: if we had to imagine for ourselves the probable character of the Petronius who wrote the *Satyricon*, it
is exactly these qualities we should be compelled to select.
Which is to say that a sound principle of economy supports the claim of Tacitus' Petronius to be the author
of the *Satyricon*. Such a man would have been a rarity in
any age, and those who reject Gaius Petronius' authorship
of the *Satyricon* must accept the responsibility for finding a more likely candidate.

THE WORK

If we know little of Petronius, we know almost as little
about the nature of the *Satyricon* as a whole: its genre,
its theme, its size, even its title, are in dispute. True, at-
tached to the famous manuscript of the work found at
Trau in Dalmatia by Petit in 1663 there is a note which
tells us that the contents are fragments "from the fifteenth
and sixteenth books." But this evidence is late and unreliable and needs to be treated with reserve, all the more since
—even on the assumption that the *Satyricon* contained
sixteen rather than, say, twenty or twenty-four books—
the result would be a work of almost unprecedented
length. What we have, in fact, is a tantalizing fragment
from a whole of uncertain length, and even the parts we
do possess are not continuous but are everywhere marred
by lacunae of greater or lesser length. Equally, however,
the very length of the *Satyricon* even in its present fragmentary state allows us almost certainly, I think, to reject
the once fashionable view that the work is to be identified
with the famous catalogue of debaucheries which the dying Petronius sent off to Nero. Again, even the title of the
work is of uncertain authenticity. *Satyricon* seems to be
formed from a Greek genitive plural, though it is impossible to decide whether we should read *Satyricon* or
Satiricon, and perhaps it hardly matters. For it may be
that the author was punning off both *satura* (i.e., "satire"
in its specifically Roman sense—a potpourri or farrago of
mixed subjects in a variety of styles) and *saturika* (that is,
concerned with satyrs, which is to say, lecherous, randy).

---

* *Annals*, xvi, 18 ff.

On this interpretation, the *Satyricon* (or *Satiricon*) would mean a book of randy satires, of satyr-things satirically treated, and it is precisely this that the extant fragments seem to show us.

Formally, of course, the *Satyricon* (like Boethius' *On the Consolation of Philosophy*) belongs to that genre we call Menippean satire, the curious blending of prose with verse and philosophy with realism invented by the Cynic philosopher Menippus of Gadara and continued by his Roman disciple, Varro. But this tells us very little, for apart from its use of alternate prose and verse, Petronius' work is as far removed from the humble, homespun moralizings of Menippus as Shakespeare's histories are from the chronicles they used. Moreover, though recognizably satirical, the *Satyricon* in general shows very little resemblance to that form of satire which the Romans thought was their own distinctive contribution to the history of literature. Compare Petronius to the major Roman satirists and the differences are immediately apparent. But the crucial difference is surely that the *Satyricon* is unmistakably comic, everywhere shot through with a gusto and a verve and a grace of humor that is almost totally absent from the tolerant strictures of Horace or the gentle, crabbed austerity of Persius or the enormous savagery of Juvenal. After all, one *laughs* with Petronius; the effect of the *Satyricon* is neither scorn nor indignation, but the laughter appropriate to good satire enlarged by the final gaiety of comedy; the comic completes the satire and gives the whole randy work that effortless rightness of natural gaiety that makes it so improbably wholesome. Thus Trimalchio may very well be a satirical portrait of the *nouveau riche*, but he is also, like Falstaff and Don Quixote, a comic creation in his own right, vulgarity at once so vast and so vivid that he easily survives his own satirical role. And it is this wonderful blending of satire and comedy that makes Petronius, to my mind, unique among Roman satirists and the *Satyricon* a genre of its own.*

---

* The latest example of the genre is, I suspect, Nabokov's *Lolita*. At least it seems to me that Nabokov is attempting a satire along Petronian lines and the comparative failure is instructive. Unlike the *Satyricon*, that is, *Lolita* almost never succeeds in rising from satire to comedy and therefore finally rides unhappily suspended at some level between the two, pulled down again and again by a sad prurience and cleverness of sophistication that prevent comedy. Almost everything is there but the gaiety which would have redeemed the strategy of perversion.

But as a farrago, a potpourri, the *Satyricon* splendidly satisfies at least one sense of ancient satire (*satura:* a medley, a mixed dish), for it is literally one great continuous mélange of genres and styles, incongruously blending verse with prose, the fabulous with the realistic, grafting pompous epic onto doggerel or lyric, setting high speech against low speech in endless profusion of parody and mockery. Variety and the deliberate variety of incongruity: these are everywhere and they need to be noticed for what they are—the source of Petronius' satirical comedy. For if the characters are realistic, they also reach out for the fabulous; if they mock one another, they are in turn mocked by what they are or by their placement in a narrative situation. And the condition of these ironies is the crisscrossing of crucial perspectives and incongruous styles: if we see how the realistic undercuts the fabulous, we should also see how the fabulous sometimes emerges from the realistic. Trimalchio, for instance, is satirized superbly and fully, but the very grossness and scale of his own humanity also mock in turn the sophisticated narrator and his friends. So too we see a wretched old hag suddenly burst into the magnificent Vergilian hexameters of the true witch, or the courtesan Circe set off, in a moment of poetry, in the figure of "the true Danae." Similarly Encolpius typically begins a stale rhetorical set-piece on the vicissitudes of human fortune only to come upon the unmistakable high language of passionate conviction. And invariably when the perverted lovers reach their peak of anguish or happiness, we find them talking in the cheap melodramatic lines of contemporary farce or the sentimental rhetoric of Greek romance, their whole unreal perverse passion exposed and ridiculed by irony and parody.

The *Satyricon*, then, is a satirical comedy based upon a fictional narrative both episodic and recognizably picaresque in nature. It also freely and gaily mixes and parodies half a dozen other genres, and these parodied genres are in turn central to the comedy at the same time that they provide scope to the satirist. Thus we find several Milesian tales (the famous story of the matron of Ephesus in Chapter xi is a good example of the genre) as well as a continuous running inversion of the sentimental Greek romance* with its stereotyped lovers and melodramatic

---

* Cf. for instance, *Leucippe and Cleitophon* by Achilles Tatius or the *Ethiopica* of Heliodorus. The genre is typically rhetorical and sentimental, consisting for the most part of the trials and tribulations (as well as the final reunion) of separated lovers.

situations. The allusions to farce and mime and tragedy are everywhere and also overtly insisted upon so that the audience will not miss its cues. Alternatively, the whole work could be (and has been) described as a kind of burlesque or mock-epic, an *Odyssey buffa* or satyr's *Aeneid*, in which Encolpius like an anti-hero suffers the wrath of an outraged Priapus. And yet the *Satyricon*, by reason of its very variety and its originality, is clearly something very different from any one of these component genres.

Can we perhaps cut through this scholarly thicket of genres by declaring the *Satyricon* to be a satirical or comic novel and leaving it at that? There is no reason why we should not, though given the vagueness which usually attends any definition of the novel, this hardly seems very helpful. Besides, in at least one crucial respect, the *Satyricon* is utterly unlike such later picaresque novels as, say, *Gil Blas* or *Roderick Random*. That respect is rhetoric, the fact of oral presentation. For unless I am badly mistaken, the *Satyricon* was clearly written not to be read silently but to be recited aloud by a trained artist with a voice and virtuosity capable of registering the enormous variety of the work, its typically Roman relish for high sound, its sudden shifts of pace, every nuance of parody and inversion, every variation of subject and style. Indeed the episodic structure of the *Satyricon* is itself determined and clarified by this fact of oral presentation (a fact which also doubles the translator's difficulty). Variety is central, and so we see the work again and again separate itself into discrete episodes, each episode bounded by a subject or a tone or a style—erotic tales, the familiar Menippean symposium behind Trimalchio's dinner, a stream of virtuoso invective, a lecture on the decline of the arts, a harangue on education or how to write an epic, a showpiece on the vicissitude of fortune, a rhetorician's shipwreck, etc. Showpiece upon showpiece, parody upon parody—particularly parody of those genres that depended upon or normally required oral presentation: epic, mime, tragedy, the rhetorical set-piece. Wherever one looks, the work suggests, and suggesting seems to require, the mediation of a voice.

If we try to imagine the *Satyricon* being read aloud, we can immediately see, I think, how the variety and virtuosity are sustained and enlarged by the actor's voice and how the prose sections can, without unnaturalness or jarring, leap suddenly into poetry. We understand, that is, how the voice of the reader by tone and emphasis guides the individual sections into place in the general design, interpreting as he goes. In prose that is merely read to one-self, for instance, the strategy of perversion is a ticklish one (just how ticklish the failure of Nabokov's *Lolita* clearly shows); the slightest error, overstatement or under-statement, is fatal. And with Petronius the tone of irony that everywhere attends the lovemaking and crises of Encolpius and Giton is often missed by modern readers precisely because the voice that once sustained it and shaped it is no longer heard. But in the Latin the sound of the irony is unmistakable, a melodramatic inflation, a stagey overblown diction that completely undercuts these perverse lovers with the bathos of Greek romance turned inside out and makes them, as lovers, unreal or figures of parody-fun. So, too, elsewhere we *hear* Eumolpus and Aga-memnon beautifully hoisted with their own petard, that frigid thumping rhetoric of theirs. And in the dinner scene the vividness is almost doubled if we hear the actor's voice informing Trimalchio's tantrums or lectures and emphasizing the contrast of styles: the correct sophisticated Latin of Encolpius against the crackling, racy vigor of Trimalchio and his friends, each style mocking the other, correctness set against ignorance, but also warmth and colorful humanity exposing the superior mocker. No translation can do such a spoken narrative justice, for it requires a third dimension. And it is just this third dimen-sion that distinguishes the ancient novel—all of it, Apuleius and Petronius and Greek romance as well—from the modern novel as a whole. Rhetoric, the sound of the human voice, is its distinction and also its curse.

Is there a visible theme or unity in the *Satyricon*? Ob-viously the extremely fragmentary state of the work for-bids certainty or even probability, but there is one in-teresting clue which seems to me amply supported by our present fragment. At first glance the *Satyricon* looks like a loose episodic series of raffish amatory adventures which takes us from a locale somewhere in the Bay of Naples by sea and shipwreck to Croton and closes probably at Mar-seilles. These mock-epic wanderings allow Petronius, of course, to satirize Roman society at length: the parvenu freedman of great wealth, illiteracy and superstition, the professional rhetorician, the legacy hunters, and so forth. Binding these wanderings together, it has been proposed, is a picaresque Wrath: just as Odysseus suffered the wrath of Poseidon and was driven over land and sea to learn the customs of men and their ways, so here Encolpius (his name means roughly "The Crotch") is persecuted by the heavy anger of the lord of lust, Priapus. Encolpius directly compares himself with Odysseus and tells how he, too, is hounded endlessly by Priapus' wrath: *Hellespontiaci sequitur gravis ira Priapi*. From Priapus (and his own perverse or ambiguous Priapic nature) all his troubles spring. Because he sees the secret rites of Priapus, he must undergo the orgy of Priapus' priestess, Quartilla. He is struck with impotence and prays to Priapus to release him, just as he later offends again by killing Priapus' pet goose. With the courtesan Circe he adopts the Homeric pseudonym of Polyaenos (i.e., "the much-praised," one of Odysseus' epithets) and he meets his Cyclops in Lichas. Further, if I read the remaining fragments correctly, the whole adventure ends with a homecoming and perhaps even with a Penelope.* Beyond this point the interpretation cannot be pushed, and should not: what needs to be seen is merely the way in which such a mock-heroic parallel supports the action and informs the parody, the figure of Priapic comic man set against his heroic prototype.

A word about obscenity. Like Rabelais' *Gargantua* and Apuleius' *Golden Ass*, the *Satyricon* is commonly read (and translated) with that gingerly, lubricous, slightly guilty respect we accord to the surreptitious classic. But in the *Satyricon* the conflict between the moral decencies of the conventional reader and the work has deliberately, I think, been made as sharp as possible. No moralizing veil intervenes between the reader and the work; nothing here corresponds either to Rabelais' thin pretense of monkish edification and moral mystery or to that moving religious conversion which in Apuleius serves to explain and redeem the sexual misadventures of the ass-man Lucius. It is simple realism and nothing more, Petronius declares in a rare aside, that defends his work from the attacks of prudery:

> Then why in heaven's name
> must every nagging prude
> of Cato's ilk cry shame,
> denounce my work as lewd,

* For the homecoming, see fragment 84 in Baehrens' *Poetae Latini Minores*: *O litus vita mihi dulcius, O mare! Felix/ cui licet ad terras ire subinde meas* . . . For the suggestion of an Odysseus returning to his Penelope, see fragment 87: *Naviget et fluctus lasset mendicus Ulixes,/ in terris vivet candida Penelope.*

> damning with a look
> my guileless, simple art,
> this simple, modern book?
> To prudes I now assert—
> my purity of speech;
> such candor in my pen
> as will not stoop to teach.
> I write of living men,
> the things they say and do,
> of every human act
> admitted to be true.
> And where's the shame in that,
> if loving men enjoy
> the pleasures of the night
> whereby each girl and boy
> experience delight?

No one familiar with Petronius' ironic habits will miss the deliberate disingenuousness of that defense, but equally an awareness of the irony should not obscure what Petronius is saying. For though the *Satyricon* is anything but the product of a "guileless simple art," its author is nonetheless a convinced and passionate hedonist and his art proceeds from the very special vantage point of the professional voluptuary and the sophisticated worldly satirist.

But sophistication is central, and the *Satyricon* clearly presupposes a sophisticated and even an intellectual response. Its satire, that is, is subtle and also deeply literary, everywhere requiring a genuine susceptibility to nuance and shade in language and an ability to detect at what point language and situation turn false and so create incongruity and a reciprocal flow of ironies. One looks in vain for the crude overexposed targets and the stock jeremiads of the professional moralist. If Eumolpus, for instance, in his epic on the civil wars appears as a standard *laudator temporis acti* with his stale denunciation of a Rome turned rotten and effeminate through the loss of homely Republican virtues, Petronius' point is not what Eumolpus says but the contrast between his pretensions here and his practices elsewhere. The ferocity of the satire, that is, lies in the eye and the perception and the composition, not in the language of denunciation. And this ferocity of perception, combined with an effortless easy tolerance of the obvious moral lapses of men and a hard realism about human nature in general, makes Petronius' satire an instrument of wonderful delicacy, compared to which the saeva indignatio of Juvenal seems clumsy and obtuse.

Partly as a consequence of this subtlety, the Satyricon is sometimes treated as though it were merely the story of the misadventures of a trio of picaresque perverts told by a pornographer of genius. And given the author's brio of sensuality and his unconventional voluptuary precision, this misunderstanding was almost inevitable. Petronius will doubtless always be read by those whose end is titillation, and perhaps, given his frank hedonism, it is right that he should be. But despite its patent concern with the erotic and the perversely erotic in particular, the Satyricon is not, I think, either mere pornography or (as some of its apologists have thought) a gay debunking of prudery and sexual shibboleths (nor, for that matter, let it be said, is it a manual of pederasty for adepts in search of classic precedents). But the voluptuary element is deeply there, a verve, a zest, a style in the texture of the work and the author's sensibility, and we do Petronius a wrong by ignoring it or explaining it away historically. For though it may be true that homosexuality was more overt and more leniently regarded in Petronius' time than in our own, Petronius' concern with perversion is not (as the Pergamene episode in Chapter VII so clearly shows) merely a matter of social and sexual realism, but a way of telling a certain kind of a story.

And, improbable or not, the story is finally a wholesome one, composed with wonderful candor and sensual gusto by a man of exquisite taste and observation, combining in one person the comic realist, the satirist, and the poet. In his candor of detachment as well as in his worldly tolerance and knowing sensuality, Petronius is, of course, typically Roman—ancient or modern, for the Romans have not changed much. And for that mind sexuality is a fact of conduct and behavior, a matter for personal taste, not moral judgment; if the taste happens to be a queer one, you watch it with detached amusement much as you might watch a pair of crocodiles copulating: after all, it is odd in a familiar sort of way. And if you happen to be a satirist (and a satyrist into the bargain), what better way of reporting the lovely, natural, human chaos of this vivid world's insanity than through the prejudiced eyes of a first-person pederast? For in this way the mocker is mocked in return, his pretensions exposed in his own rhetorical passion and his cool raffish eye clouded by what he cannot see: his own absurdity.

And so Petronius with deliberate, spoofing detachment shows us everything through Encolpius' fastidious eyes: the pompous ranting academics; the rich businessmen who kill you with their bounty, read their wills aloud and sob over their own graves; the posturing poets with their empty-hearted denunciations of their own age and their hypocritical loyalty to a society that never was; the simple freedman's sentimental nostalgia for Republican simplicity and morality. The comedy comes, of course, in the crossing of perspectives and the dramatizing of the satirical: between Encolpius and Trimalchio or Eumolpus and Philomela's daughter what is there to choose? The wholesomeness, on the other hand, lies in the wonderful comprehensiveness of Petronius' comic vision. For finally it is all there, his world and ours too: the mockers and the mocked, Mammon everywhere muddled with death, the everyday reality of pimps, businessmen, professors, pederasts, whores, poets, and slaves in that fabulous world where witches talk in poetry, Circe inhabits the whore and Odysseus the rogue, a landscape "so infested with divinity that one might meet a god more easily than a man."

THE TRANSLATION

This translation is intended to be both a contemporary version and an American one. Because the original is written in a lucid, lively, flowing contemporary Latin, I have everywhere tried to eschew both archaism and gratuitous stylistic flourishes and to avoid as the very plague that neutral, lifeless Anglo-American idiom that seems to me to vitiate so much contemporary translation from the classical languages. More than most writings in Latin, the *Satyricon* requires the context and vigor of a *particular* language, a language at once vividly colloquial and vigorously literary, and no contemporary idiom of English seems to me to supply that particularity in such ripe fullness as American English. At the same time, I have tried to the best of my ability to make my version an accurate one, without, however, allowing myself to be unduly cramped by the scholar's notion of accuracy. I should not like this to be understood as a confession of having taken unwarranted liberties or of having tampered with my text.

Wherever possible, I have kept before me the translator's ideal of being loyal to two different languages at the same time. But where loyalty to Latin would have involved me in disloyalty to English, I have invariably come down firmly on the side of English. For a translation is, after all, a transfer of experience from one language to another, and unless it lives in the language to which it has been transferred, it has finally no life at all. Or so I see it. Which is to say merely that I have been as loyal as possible to Latin, but a little more loyal to English.

Thus, for instance, I have not hesitated to invent new English puns when the Latin puns proved to be impossible of literal translation (as they almost invariably are, since nowhere does the genius of a language preside more stubbornly than over those adventitious similarities that make punning possible). Further, since translation to be complete usually involves a transference of culture as well as language, I have tried to create a recognizably contemporary version of the *Satyricon*, without, however, wholly modernizing it. This meant that it was frequently impossible for me to reproduce the literal intent of some of Petronius' satires and parodies. For all too frequently the genre or style or sentiment that Petronius is satirizing either possesses no contemporary equivalent or none that can be effectively parodied. Eumolpus' long epic effusion on the civil wars (Chapter XIV) is an obvious instance. Presumably this poem is Petronius' parody of the epic manner and structure of his contemporary Lucan, but Lucan's style and genre is one which nowadays has no prominent exponents. (Who, one wonders, would be our contemporary Lucan?) In the circumstances, I have tried to shape the parody in such a way that it should at least be recognizable as a parody of a directly contemporary style, though the cost of that attempt has been to obscure the specific target of Petronius' satire. To scholars this may seem an indefensible procedure (and I am prepared to admit that it is less than satisfactory), but the only feasible alternative was to attempt a parody of Elizabethan or Miltonic epic (which would have turned Petronius' satire into a dull academic exercise) or a straightforward rendering (which would have had no point as a parody).

Again, it may perhaps be objected that I have now and then oversimplified the variety of spoken Latin or reduced its range. For though the text employs three or four different varieties of Latin speech, the reader will find in my version essentially only two: the vivid colloquial speech of Trimalchio and his freedmen friends and the more sophisticated and "literary" style of Encolpius, Ascyltus, Agamemnon, Eumolpus, and so forth. This reduction was intentional. For it would have been, I think, an intolerable anachronism to attempt to reproduce the varieties of spoken Latin with an equivalent variety of realistic American dialects: a Southern drawl for Ganymedes, Brooklynese for Echion, and so forth. Somewhere, that is, I felt that the line had to be drawn. And rightly or wrongly, I have drawn my line just short of the point where I think I would have invited the reader's reluctance to accept a convention (an ancient classic in contemporary idiom) already strained to the maximum. Roman banquets and ruthlessly realistic American accents simply will not mix without shattering that crucial and delicate convention by which the translator works. It is not, I sometimes think, generally recognized just how much effective translation depends upon the maintenance of this precarious convention, the illusion of contemporaneity. Just as the dramatist requires the assistance of his audience in coping with a convention that flouts all probability, so too the translator must persuade the willing reader to forget for a little while that Rome is dead and that Trimalchio spoke Latin (more or less). But if he stretches his convention too far and strains his reader's credulity, he must forfeit his illusion and lose his labor. Thus I too dislike translationese and archaism and avoid them (for they trouble the illusion of reality), but equally a ruthless realism, the precise realism of a particular place and an unmistakable time, seem to me no less jarring and destructive. Hence the reader will find that though my freedmen speak a colloquial American idiom, it is colloquial by convention and not the real speech of a particular region or city. Only so, I thought, could I maintain the crucial illusion.

But in general my major effort has been to realize what seemed to me the central facts of Petronius' style and narrative: its speed, its liveliness, its versatility and imaginative color. Even at the risk of apparent disloyalty to Latin now and then, I wanted to find credible English equivalents for Petronius' mercurial shifts from one style to another: from low Latin to educated Latin, from bathetic or frivolous parody-doggerel to flatulent epic to sheer lyric loveliness; from the rhetorical fustian of set-pieces to the sudden discovery of a true passion in language. I may on some occasions have gone too far; on others I may have been too timid. But the scholar who is tempted to judge my practices severely should bear in mind his own happy exemption from the translator's necessity, the anguish of having at times to choose between the letter and the spirit. I too read Latin and teach it, and I know from experience the cost of the translator's choice between evils. But like politics, translation is an art of the possible, never of perfection. And if translators are by definition traitors, their treachery is defined by the necessities of their profession, not their natural inclinations—as who should love two women at the same time and yet be forced to choose.

THE TEXT

The basis of this translation has been primarily the brilliant edition of Alfred Ernout (Paris, 1950), though I have also made use of E. T. Sage's edition and commentary (New York, 1929) and the *Cena Trimalchionis* of W. D. Lowe (Cambridge, 1905). The Latinless reader should perhaps be aware that the chapter headings employed in this translation are not to be found in the text of Petronius, but have been devised by me as a means of dividing the work into episodes and preserving continuity between large lacunae. Similarly I have felt free to introduce paragraphs according to the norms of modern prose. Elsewhere, in order to maintain continuity and reduce the reader's dependence upon footnotes, I have deliberately intruded short glosses. Readers who desire more detailed commentary on difficult passages, historical or topographical allusions or justifications of the translation, are directed to the notes on pages 166-92. The translation itself is unexpurgated. The bracketed numbers in the text indicate the original chapters.

For the time to complete this translation I am deeply indebted to both the Guggenheim Memorial Foundation and the American Academy in Rome (though I should in honesty confess that this translation was not the project for the completion of which both of those institutions awarded me fellowships).

WILLIAM ARROWSMITH

Austin, Texas, 1958

CONTENTS

I

AMONG THE RHETORICIANS

[*1*] "But look here," I protested, "aren't you professors*
hounded by just these same Furies of inflated language
and pompous heroics? How else can you account for all
that wretched rant:

> Nay, but gentle sirs, mark ye well these wounds I
> suffered in the struggle to preserve our common liberties.
> 'Twas on thy behalf I made the supreme sacrifice of
> this eye. Vouchsafe me, therefore, a helping hand.
> Guide me to my children, for my withers are unwrung
> and support my frame no more . . .

And so on.
"No one would mind this claptrap if only it put our
students on the road to real eloquence. But what with
all these sham heroics and this stilted bombast you stuff
their heads with, by the time your students set foot in
court, they talk as though they were living in another
world. No, I tell you, we don't educate our children at
school; we stultify them and then send them out into the
world half-baked. And why? Because we keep them utterly
ignorant of real life. The common experience is something
they never see or hear. All they know is pirates trooping
up the beach in chains, tyrants scribbling edicts compelling sons to chop off their fathers' heads or oracles condemning three virgins—but the more the merrier—to be
slaughtered to stop some plague. Action or language, it's
all the same: great sticky honeyballs of phrases, every
sentence looking as though it had been plopped and rolled
in poppyseed and sesame. [*2*] A boy gorged on a diet like
this can no more acquire real taste than a cook can stop
stinking. What's more, if you'll pardon my bluntness, it
was you rhetoricians who more than anyone else strangled
true eloquence. By reducing everything to sound, you
concocted this bloated puffpaste of pretty drivel whose
only real purpose is the pleasure of punning and the thrill

---

* More detailed comments on certain words and passages will
be found in the notes on pp. 166-92.

of ambiguity. Result? Language lost its sinew, its nerve. Eloquence died.

"But in those great days when Sophocles and Euripides invariably found the exact word, talent had not yet been cramped into the mold of these set-speeches of yours. Long before you academic pedants smothered genius with your arrogance, Pindar and the nine lyric poets were still so modest that they declined even to attempt the grand Homeric manner. Nor are my objections based on poetry alone. What about Plato or Demosthenes? I never heard it said of them that they ever submitted to your sort of formal training. No, great language is chaste language—if you'll let me use a word like 'chaste' in this connection—not turgidity and worked-up purple patches. It soars to life through a natural, simple loveliness. But then, in our own time, that huge flatulent rhetoric of yours moved from Asia to Athens. Like a baleful star, it blighted the minds of the young; their talents shriveled at the very moment when they might have taken wing and gone on to greatness. And once the standards of good speech were corrupted, eloquence stopped dead or stuttered into silence. Who, I ask you, has achieved real greatness of style since Thucydides and Hyperides? Poetry herself is sick, her natural glow of color leached away. All the literary arts, in fact, cloyed with this diet of bombast, have stunted or died, incapable of whitening naturally into an honest old age. And in painting you see the same decay: on the very day when Egyptian arrogance dared to reduce it to a set of sterile formulas, that great art died."

[3] Agamemnon, however, refused to let me rant on an instant longer than it had taken him to sweat out his declamation in the classroom. "Young man," he broke in, "I see that you are a speaker of unusual taste and, what is even rarer, an admirer of common sense. So I shan't put you off with the usual hocus-pocus of the profession. But in all justice allow me to observe that we teachers should not be saddled with the blame for this bombast of which you complain. After all, if the patients are lunatics, surely a little professional lunacy is almost mandatory in the doctor who deals with them. And unless we professors spout the sort of twaddle our students admire, we run the risk of being, in Cicero's phrase, 'left alone at our lecterns.' Let me offer you by way of analogy those professional sponges in the comic plays who scrounge their suppers by flattering the rich. Like us, they must devote their entire

22

attention to one end—the satisfaction of their audience;
for unless their little springes con their listeners' ears, they
stand to lose their quarry. We are, that is, rather in the
position of a fisherman: unless he baits his hook with
the sort of tidbit the little fishes like, he is doomed to
spend eternity sitting on his rock without a chance of a
bite.

[4] "So what should the verdict be? In my opinion,
those parents who refuse to impose a stern discipline upon
their sons must bear the blame. As with everything else,
even their children are sacrificed on the altar of their
ambition. Then, in their haste and greed to reap a harvest,
they shove these callow, newborn babies into the public
arena, and eloquence—that same eloquence which they
profess to honor as the crown of a liberal education—is
chopped down in size to fit a fetus. If, however, our students' lessons could be graded by order of difficulty; if
the minds of the young could be molded and shaped by
long years of intimacy with the minds of great thinkers;
if these crude attempts to form a style could be ruthlessly
chastened and these budding talents steeped in the study
of great models, then, and only then, might our great lost
art of oratory recover her old magnificence. But what do
we find instead? The schoolrooms packed with children
wasting their time and playing at learning; our recent
graduates disgracing themselves in public life and, what is
worst of all, the very things that they mislearned when
young, they are reluctant to confess in old age. And lest
you think I despise the simplicity and spontaneity of old
Lucilius, let me extemporize my sentiments in verse:

[5] ADVICE TO A YOUNG POET

If greatness, poet, is your goal,
the craft begins with self-control.
For poems are of the poet part,
and what he is decides his art.
With character true poems begin.
Poet, learn your discipline.

Avoid ambition as the blight
of talent. If the rich invite
you out to dine, be proud; decline.
Don't snuff your genius in your wine
nor pin your Muse to clique or claque.
Avoid the postures of the hack.

23

Whether Athena, poet, from her Parthenon smiles down
upon your youth, or Spartan homestead gave you birth,
or African Cyrene where the lovely Sirens sang,
dedicate, I say, your early years to verse. Drink deep
at the great Homeric font and satisfy your thirst.
But when you've drunk your fill, then discipline your
        soul
by study with the wise: let logic and the laws of
        thought
be your curriculum and curb. And when at last
the great Socratic troupe admits you as their friend,
shake loose your reins and give your passions room to
        run:
wield a free man's prose, those weapons forged in war
by great Demosthenes. Then let the Roman writers
guide you home from Greece; transform your borrowed
        taste
and build a native style. Meanwhile, withdraw from
        court,
and let the epic, martial Muse run proud and free
to make such clangor as she, by lightning march
and sudden ambush, may unloose. Make war your feast;
sing such clamor you unleash the thundered verse
of epic Cicero, bloody but unbowed.

                                        O poet,
gird yourself with every goodness you can get,
until the Muse herself usurps your swelling tongue
and sets your name beside the great on Helicon!

❧

II

GITON, ASCYLTUS, AND I

[6] But while I was concentrating on Agamemnon's
poem, I failed to see Ascyltus slink away . . .

❧

Some time later, while we were strolling through the
garden, still hot in argument, a great crowd of students
came pouring out into the portico, just leaving, I sup-

posed, the speech of the professor who had followed Agamemnon. But while they were jeering away at the speaker's ideas and criticizing the whole structure of his speech, I seized my chance and quickly slipped away in pursuit of Ascyltus. But I had forgotten where our rooms were and kept losing my way. Worse, whichever road I took, I somehow kept coming back to the place where I had started. Finally, drenched with sweat and completely limp from running around in circles, I went up to a little old woman who was selling vegetables beside the road.

[7] "Excuse me, ma'am," I asked, "but would you happen to know where I live?"

Apparently charmed by this genteel stupidity, she said, "But I of course I do." With that, she rose to her feet and started off while I tagged tamely at her heels, thinking she must be a prophetess. A few minutes later, in a much shabbier section of town, she stopped before a door, pulled back the curtain and said, "This must be where you live." I was saying that I'd never seen the place before when I suddenly saw several women walking suggestively to and fro and a number of large posters, each stating a price. Slowly, much too slowly, it dawned on me that the treacherous old hag had led me to a whorehouse. I cursed the old bitch out, covered my head in my robes and sprinted straight through the whorehouse in the direction of the entrance on the next street. There in the doorway, just coming in, who should I meet but Ascyltus himself, looking half-dead and every bit as exhausted as myself. In fact, for an instant I wondered whether the same old woman had brought him there too. Then, with a great laugh of relief, I threw myself into his arms and asked him what in the world he was doing in a place like that.

[8] "Gods," he gasped, mopping away the sweat, "if you only knew what I've been through!"

"But what happened?" I asked.

He was still panting so furiously he could barely speak. "I've been running around like crazy. I must have covered the whole city, but I couldn't find our rooms anywhere. Then a man came up, respectable family-man type, or so I thought, and very kindly offered to lead me to my rooms. Well, he steered me through a lot of back alleys and finally brought me here. Then he pulled out his wallet and began to proposition me. He'd already paid the Madam of the house for a room. The next thing I knew he was feeling me up, and if I hadn't been stronger than he was, I'd have been damn well raped by now."

❦

Every person in the place seemed to be completely drunk on aphrodisiacs . . .

❦

But by uniting our forces, we managed to repel the invaders' attack . . .

❦

[9] Dimly, as through a thick fog, I caught sight of Giton standing at the corner of an alley and I raced over . . .

❦

When I asked the boy whether he had made our supper, he suddenly burst into tears, collapsed on the bed and lay there wiping his eyes with his thumb. Frantic at seeing him in such a state, I begged him to tell me what had happened. Only much later, after my pleas had turned into threats, did he speak, and even then with great reluctance. "It's that man," he sobbed, "the one you call your brother, your friend Ascyltus. He ran up to my garret a little while ago and tried to take me by force. When I screamed for help, he pulled out his sword. 'If you want to play Lucretia, boy,' he cried, 'you've met your Tarquin.'"

Furious at such treachery, I rushed across to Ascyltus and shook my fist in his face. "What do you say to that?" I yelled. "You male whore, you! You bugger! Even your breath stinks of buggery!"

At first he pretended to be insulted. Then he started throwing his fists around and yelling at the top of his voice. "Shut up!" he bellowed. "You stinking gladiator! Even in the arena you were a washout! Shut up! Thief! You cheap burglar! When were you ever man enough to take on a real woman? No, first it was me in the garden. Now it's this boy in the inn."

"What's more," I said bitterly, "you sneaked away when the professors were debating."

[10] "What the hell was I supposed to do, sap?" he

26

shrieked. "Die of hunger? Stand there and listen to that drivel, that rhetoric of broken bottles and cheap dream-analysis? By god, you're ten times worse! Trying to scrounge a meal by buttering a poet!"

Finally, however, the squalid argument ended and we soon found ourselves laughing and at peace with each other once more and went on to other things . . .

❦

But the memory of what Ascyltus had done kept coming back and rankling. Finally, I decided to have it out. "Ascyltus," I said, "let's face it: we're not compatible any more. Let's divide our few possessions and strike out for ourselves, each one on his own. You're an educated man, and so am I. But just so we don't tread on each other's toes, I'll arrange to take a different tutoring job. Otherwise we'll have a thousand run-ins every day and get ourselves gossiped about all over town."

He agreed. "However, for today," he added, "let's keep together, since our position as professors is worth an invitation to dinner and we don't want to lose it. Then tomorrow, if that's what you want, I'll start looking for another bed and a little friend of my own."

"But it's silly," I objected, "to postpone our decision." . . .

❦

It was sex, of course, that made us part ways so brusquely. For a long time now I had been anxious to remove this obstacle in the way of resuming my old relationship with Giton . . .

❦

[11] After wandering all over town in a fruitless search for work, I returned to the room. At last I was free to make love to Giton without restraint, and wrapping the boy in the closest of embraces, I took my fill of a bliss that even happy lovers might envy. We were still at it, however, when Ascyltus came tiptoeing up to the door. Finding it locked, he banged so violently that the bolts rattled loose, the door swung open, and he walked in and discovered us at our games. Amused at first, he clapped

27

his hands and roared with laughter till the whole room shook. Then he snatched away the cloak I had thrown over Giton and myself. "Well, well," he sneered, "what's going on here, my saintly friend? Are you sharing something with our little friend?" And not content with sarcasm, he pulled a leather thong from his pack and began to flog me mercilessly, punctuating every blow with fresh sneers: "So that's your notion of sharing with your friends, is it?"

✿

III

LOST TREASURE RECOVERED

[*12*] It was just turning dark when we came into the market in the main square. There we saw a great deal of merchandise laid out for sale, most of it worthless stuff, but its shoddiness or suspect provenance now decently obscured in the half-light. Happening to have the stolen mantle with us, we took advantage of the time and place and unrolled a small strip of it in a dark corner, hoping that the richness and color of the material might attract a buyer. We did not have long to wait. After a few minutes, a peasant—whose face seemed somehow familiar to me—came up, accompanied by a girl, and began to finger the mantle very closely. Ascyltus, for his part, could not keep his eyes off the shoulder of our peasant customer, and then I suddenly saw him blanch and gasp with astonishment. With growing excitement, I began to stare too, for the peasant was strikingly like the man who had found our tunic in the deserted place where we had left it. Finally there could be no doubt: it was the same man. Ascyltus, not daring to believe his eyes and terrified of alarming the man, went up closer and, lifting the hem of the tunic off his shoulder, started to scrutinize it like a prospective buyer.

[*13*] By some absolutely incredible stroke of luck, the peasant had not yet stuck his meddling fingers into the seam; in fact, he was condescendingly offering the tunic for sale as though it were some beggar's cast-off. Seeing

28

that our cache was intact and that we were dealing with a fool, Ascyltus motioned me aside. "Friend," he whispered, "do you realize that our treasure has come back to us? That's the same tunic, the one I was so upset at having lost. And, so far as I can tell, the gold is still there in the seams, intact. But what should we do? Should we bring a formal complaint against him in court for the recovery of our property?"

Enormously pleased, not only because we had recovered our lost cache, but because our stroke of luck had relieved me of a very ugly suspicion, I told Ascyltus that we should not beat around the bush, but take our complaint directly to the authorities and obtain a court order if the peasant refused to return our property.

[14] Ascyltus, having little faith in the authorities, disagreed. "Who can vouch for us here?" he objected. "Who knows us? If you ask me, I think we ought to buy it back, even though it's our own property, rather than risk a chancy lawsuit:

What good are the laws where Money is king,
    where the poor are always wrong,
and even the mockers who scoff at the times
    will sell the truth for a song?

The courts are an auction where justice is sold;
    the judge who presides bangs a gavel of gold."

But except for one small coin which we had put aside to buy lupins and chickpeas, we had literally nothing. So to keep our quarry from leaving with our cache, we decided to sell the mantle cheap, thinking that our profit on the tunic would lighten the loss on the cloak. Acting quickly, we unrolled the mantle completely and the veiled girl who had come with the peasant began a minute inspection of the design. Suddenly she grabbed the cloak with both hands and started to scream "Thief! Thief!" We, of course, panicked, but rather than do nothing, we started tugging away at our filthy tattered tunic and screamed "Thief!" too. But the discrepancy in what we were claiming was so great that even the tradesmen who had come running up at the outcry burst out in guffaws. Not without justice, I must admit, since we were struggling for a set of rags that couldn't even have been used for patches, while they were claiming a cloak worth a good sum of money.

Finally Ascyltus succeeded in silencing them. [15] "It is obvious," he declared, "that each party prefers his own property. Let them give us back our tunic and we'll give them the cloak." This suggestion proved perfectly acceptable to the peasant and the girl, but some local shysters—or better, sneak-thieves—anxious to clear a profit on the mantle, demanded that the articles in dispute should be deposited with them and the whole matter referred to the judge on the following day. Their concern, they said, was less the goods in dispute than the fact that both parties clearly fell under suspicion of theft, a much graver matter. Those in favor of impounding the articles were a majority, and one of the tradesmen, a bald fellow with a hideously splotched forehead who used to plead cases now and then, confiscated the cloak and said that he would produce it in evidence the next day. By now it was perfectly clear what their game was: they would make off with the cloak, while we, of course, would not dare appear in court for fear of being charged with theft.

❦

The suggestion was quite agreeable to us, and a lucky incident served both parties. For our peasant, livid with rage when we demanded that his tattered tunic be publicly exhibited, threw it in Ascyltus' face. Then, since we now had nothing to complain of, he demanded the return of the mantle, the sole article still under dispute.

❦

Having recovered our cache, or so we thought, we hurried back to our room, locked the door securely and burst out laughing both at the tradesmen whose sharp dealing had restored us our property and the naïveté of our country opponent.

> Too easy victory I find
>   repugnant to my pride.
> I like the savor of desire
>   before I'm satisfied.

❦

IV

THE PRIESTESS OF PRIAPUS

[*16*] We had barely finished the supper prepared for
us by Giton's kindness when there came a sudden imperi-
ous pounding at the door.

The blood drained from our faces. "Who is it?" we
managed to quaver in chorus.

"Open the door and see for yourselves," said a voice.
At that moment, of their own accord, the bolts on the
door slid back and the door swung wide before the in-
truder. It was the veiled girl whom we had seen with the
peasant in the market only an hour before.

"So you thought you'd made a fool of me, did you?"
she cried. "Listen. I am the maid of Quartilla, the lady
whose secret rites in the grotto of Priapus you disturbed.
My mistress has come here in person and asks to be allowed to speak with you. You needn't be alarmed. Far
from having come to reproach you or punish you, she
would like to know what god has brought two such charming young men into her vicinity."

[*17*] To all this we said not a single word, neither yes
or no. An instant later, Quartilla, followed by a little girl,
made her entrance. Then, throwing herself down on my
bed, she promptly burst into a flood of tears. For a considerable time she sat there sobbing away, while we looked
on, too dumfounded by her sobs and this obviously prearranged display of grief to say a word. By degrees the
melodramatic storm began to abate and the gusts of
sobbing came less frequently. Proudly lifting her head, she
removed her veil. Then, twisting her fingers until the
knuckles cracked, she spoke:

"I confess, gentlemen, I do not know what name to
give to this incredible audacity of yours. Where have you
learned this daring in which you surpass even the great
rogues of mythology? Heaven knows, I pity you. No man
on earth may look on forbidden things as you have done
and escape punishment. Especially here, a land so infested with divinity that one might meet a god more
easily than a man. You must not think I have come here

31

for vengeance. No, the spectacle of your innocent youth moves me far more deeply than any wrong you have done me. Moreover, I believe that your terrible crime was done in youthful ignorance. But all night afterwards, I tossed in terror, shivering so horribly that I felt an attack of malaria coming on. So I asked for a cure in my dreams, and was commanded by a vision to track you down and cure my malaria by a certain stratagem. But it is not the cure that troubles me most; a greater grief ravages my heart and hurries me down to inevitable death. I am afraid that in your youthful indiscretion you may be led to reveal the things you saw in the chapel of Priapus and divulge our mysteries to the world. And so I kneel before you now with outstretched hands and I beg you, I beseech you, not to make a mockery of our nocturnal rites or reveal a secret so jealously guarded over the centuries, a secret which scarcely a thousand men have ever known."

[18] She concluded this appeal to our pity by bursting into tears again, buried herself in my bed and lay there, shaken by protracted sobs. Torn as much by fear as pity, I tried to reassure her. On neither score, I said, need she feel concern. No one would betray her rites; as for her malaria, if some god had shown her a cure for it, we would do everything in our power to assist the will of heaven, even if it cost us our lives. Relieved by these promises, she began to brighten up, kissed me several times and ran a caressing hand through the long curls that tumbled down about my ears. "Very well," she laughed, "I'll make my peace with you and settle my case out of court. However, if you had refused to help me with my cure, I would have come here tomorrow with a whole regiment prepared to avenge my honor and wipe out my wrongs:

> The shame of defeat, the victor's disdain:
> I'd rather with neither live.
> The wise will fight when honor's at stake;
> the victors are those who forgive."

Then suddenly clapping her hands, she burst out with such an explosive peal of laughter that we were terrified. The maid who had announced her promptly followed suit and even the little girl joined in. [19] For some time the whole room rang with shrieks of theatrical laughter, while

32

we looked first at each other and then at the women, utterly bewildered by the abrupt change in their mood.

❦

"I have given strict orders," Quartilla announced, "that no man is to be allowed to set foot inside this inn today. I am determined to receive my malaria treatments in complete and uninterrupted privacy." At this announcement, Ascyltus went white, while I turned colder than a French winter and couldn't say a word. But on reflection the fact that there were three of us relieved me of my worst fears. After all, if it came to an attempt on our honor, three weak women were hardly a match for us. If nothing else, we had the strength of our sex in our favor and we were not hampered, as they were, by long billowing dresses. In fact, if matters came to a fight, I had already paired us off. I would take on Quartilla, Ascyltus would break a lance with the maid, and the little girl could be left to Giton.

❦

At this unexpected blow, we lost all determination to resist, and the shadow of certain death was already falling on our eyes . . .

❦

[20] "If you have anything worse than this in store for us, madam," I cried, "for god's sake, despatch us quickly. Our crime is surely not so terrible that we deserve to die in agony.".

❦

The maid, whose name was Psyche, carefully spread a blanket on the floor . . .

❦

With her hand she began to stroke that part of me which by now was cold as ice, shriveled with a thousand deaths . . .

❦

Thoroughly convinced by now of the dangers of meddling in the secrets of others, Ascyltus buried his head in his robes . . .

❦

Drawing two straps from her dress, Psyche proceeded to bind us hand and foot.

❦

The conversation was languishing when Ascyltus broke out: "Hey, don't I deserve a drink too?" Psyche, her little plan betrayed by my snickers, clapped her hands with amazement. "Young man," she said to me, "I put the glass beside you. Have you drunk all that medicine by yourself?"

"Did he really?" cried Quartilla. "Encolpius drank all our aphrodisiac?"

❦

She shook all over with a wonderful rippling laugh . . .

❦

In the end even Giton could not keep from laughing too, especially when the little girl threw her arms around his neck and kissed the unresisting boy on the lips at least a thousand times . . .

❦

[21] In our misery we wanted to scream for help, but there was no one there to come to our aid. Worse, every time I tried to shout, Psyche gouged my cheek with a hairpin, while the little girl stood over poor Ascyltus with a sponge dipped in aphrodisiac . . .

❦

As the crowning touch to our miseries, in waddled a eunuch dressed in a robe of myrtle-green bound up with a sash . . . Springing at us again and again, he slobbered our faces with filthy kisses and ground away at us with his buttocks until Quartilla, holding her dress up above her knees, drove him off with a whale-bone-cane and ordered him to leave us poor wretches alone.

❧

We both of us swore the most solemn oaths that this terrible secret would die with us both . . .

❧

Several masseurs arrived next. After a generous rubdown with oil, we slowly began to revive. Then, feeling more or less ourselves again, we put on dinner-clothes and were conducted into the next room where we found three couches drawn up and a table, very luxuriously laid out, awaiting us. We were invited to take our seats, and the meal began with some sumptuous *hors d'oeuvres.* As for wine, we were fairly swimming in it, and it was fine Falernian at that. After several more courses we had begun to doze sleepily off, when Quartilla said: "No sleeping, gentlemen. Must I remind you again that the whole night has been consecrated to Priapus?"

❧

[22] Ascyltus, utterly exhausted by his ordeal, had just dozed off when the little maid whom he had driven off so rudely tiptoed up to him while he slept and smeared his face with soot and painted his lips and shoulders a bright scarlet. By this time my own exhaustion was beginning to tell, and I must have dozed off briefly. The servants in both rooms had already fallen asleep. Some were slumped on the floor at the feet of the guests, others stood propped against the wall, while several lay sprawled, head to head, in the doorway. Meanwhile the oil-lamps had burnt low and gave out only a feeble dying flicker.

Suddenly I woke with a start to see two Syrian slaves come gliding stealthily into the room and start to pocket the silver. In their greed, however, they began to fight over a large two-handled pitcher, each one tugging at a handle. Without warning the handles snapped and the pitcher landed with a crash on the table. The table promptly collapsed, showering silver and glassware in every direction, and one heavy goblet landed on the head of a maid who was lying curled up on the couch. The cut was deep, and she screamed with pain, alarming the two thieves and waking the rest of us from our drunken stupor. The Syrians, realizing that they had been discovered, threw themselves on the end of a couch and with great aplomb started to snore away as though they had been asleep for hours.

The butler, awakened by the hubbub, rose and refilled the flickering lamps, while the servants, sleepily rubbing their eyes, returned to their posts at our elbows. Then with a great crash of cymbals a girl-musician strode in, woke up the remaining sleepers [23] and the party began all over again. Quartilla kept urging us to drink up, while the girl with the cymbals went marching around the room banging away to get us all back to the proper festive mood.

❧

At this point a second eunuch arrived, so incredibly insipid that he seemed a fitting representative of the whole menage. Clapping his hands for attention, he cleared his throat, grunted, and gave vent to the following:

> O fairies, O buggers,
>   O eunuchs exotic!
> Come running, come running,
>   ye anal-erotic!
>
> With soft little hands,
>   with flexible bums,
> Come, O castrati,
>   unnatural ones!

Having finished his effusion, he promptly started to slobber me with his loathsome kisses, and before I knew it, he had straddled me on the couch and, despite my resistance, pulled off my clothes. Then, for what seemed hours, he worked on me but without the slightest success. Meanwhile a river of sweat and perfume was streaming down his face, leaving his wrinkled cheeks so creviced with powder that he looked like some cracked wall standing desolate under a pelting rain.

[24] Finally I was reduced to tears and in my agony cried out to Quartilla, "For god's sake, madam, help me. Even your passive support would be appreciated."

At this she clasped her hands with delight. "Oh, what

36

a funny little man it is! What a fountain of wit!" she cried. "But I'm giving you exactly what you want. Didn't you know we call these fellows passives?"

But misery wants company, and so did I. "Madam, I protest," I cried. "Is Ascyltus the only man in the room who gets a holiday?"

"That seems only fair," she said. "We must see that Ascyltus has his share of our passive support."

The eunuch immediately changed horses and mounted Ascyltus, kissing him so furiously and battering him so hard with his buttocks that he almost murdered him. Giton, meanwhile, had come up closer to get a better view and was splitting with laughter at Ascyltus' plight. Eying him narrowly, Quartilla asked to whom he belonged. When I told her that he was a friend of mine, she said, "Well, doesn't your little friend have a kiss for me?" With that she called him over, pawed him and kissed him a bit and then reached her hand inside his tunic and playfully fondled that poor novice tool of his for some time. "Tomorrow," she laughed, "this will make a fine antipasto for my lechery. But today's *entrée* stuffed me so full, I couldn't swallow even this little tidbit now."

[25] Suddenly Psyche sidled up giggling, and whispered something into Quartilla's ear. "A splendid idea," said Quartilla, "I can't imagine a more opportune time for deflowering our little Pannychis." Immediately a rather pretty little girl—the same one who had come with Quartilla to our rooms—was led out. I doubt that she could have been more than seven, but with the exception of myself everybody present applauded the idea and demanded that the marriage be consummated instantly. I was shocked, however, and pointed out that Giton, a very bashful boy, could hardly be expected to undergo such drudgery yet. Besides, I protested, the girl was much too young to be assuming a woman's position.

"Pish," snorted Quartilla. "Is she any younger than I was when I had my first man? May Juno strike me dead if I can ever remember being a virgin. When I was a little girl, I played ducks and drakes with the little boys; as I got bigger, I applied myself to bigger boys, until I reached my present age—whence I think the proverb arose, she'll bear the bull that bore the calf." Fearing that Giton might suffer something still worse if I refused, I rose reluctantly to help with the ceremony. [26] Psyche placed a saffron veil on the little girl's head, while a whole troop of drunken women, led by the eunuch with a blazing torch, marched off to prepare the room for this travesty of marriage. Quartilla, flushed and excited by the gross obscenity of the whole affair, took Giton by the hand and led him into the bedroom.

In point of fact the boy made no objection and even the little girl appeared quite unmoved by the notion of being a bride. Finally the door was shut, the bolts shot, and we all took up our positions around the door. Then Quartilla, standing in the front row, treacherously cut a slit in the panel and peeked with lecherous curiosity at their innocent childish play. With a gentle caress she drew me to the chink to watch too, and since our faces were often close together, kept turning her lips to me and stealing kisses.

❧

We threw ourselves into bed and spent the remainder of the night unmolested ...

❧

V

DINNER WITH TRIMALCHIO

At last the third day had come with its prospect of a free meal and perhaps our last meal on this earth. But by now our poor bodies were so bruised and battered that escape, even if it cost us a meal, seemed preferable to staying where we were. While we were gloomily wondering how we could avoid the orgy in store for us with Quartilla, one of Agamemnon's slaves came up and dispelled our despair. "What's eating you?" he asked. "Have you forgotten where you're going tonight? Trimalchio's giving the meal. He's real swank. Got a great big clock in his dining room and a uniformed bugler who blows a horn every hour so the old man won't forget how fast his time is slipping away." Needless to say, we forgot our troubles fast when we heard this. We slipped into our best clothes, and when Giton very sweetly offered to act as our servant, we told him to attend us to the baths.

[27] There we wandered around at first without getting undressed. Or rather we went joking around, mixing with various groups of bathers at their games. Suddenly we caught sight of an old, bald man in a long red undershirt, playing ball with a bunch of curly-headed slave boys. It wasn't so much the boys who took our eyes—though they were worth looking at—as the old man himself. There he stood, rigged out in undershirt and sandals, nothing else, bouncing a big green ball the color of a leek. When he dropped one ball, moreover, he never bothered to stoop for it, but simply took another from a slave who stood beside him with a huge sack tossing out fresh balls to the players. This was striking enough, but the real refinement was two eunuchs standing on either side of the circle, one clutching a chamber pot of solid silver, the other ticking off the balls. He was not, however, scoring the players' points, but merely keeping count of any balls that happened to drop on the ground. While we were gawking at these elegant gymnastics, Menelaus came rushing up. "That's him!" he whispered, "that's the fellow who's giving the meal. What you're seeing now is just the prelude to the show." These words were hardly out when Trimalchio gave a loud snap with his fingers. The eunuch came waddling up with the chamber pot, Trimalchio emptied his bladder and went merrily on with his game. When he was done, he shouted for water, daintily dipped the tips of his fingers and wiped his hands in the long hair of a slave.

[28] But the details of his performance would take too long to tell. We quickly undressed, went into the hot baths, and after working up a sweat, passed on to the cold showers. There we found Trimalchio again, his skin glistening all over with perfumed oil. He was being rubbed down, not with ordinary linen, but with cloths of the purest and softest wool. During this rubdown, right before his eyes, the three masseurs were guzzling away at the finest of his rare Falernian wines. In a minute, moreover, they were squabbling and in the next second the wine had spilled all over the floor. "Tut, a mere trifle," said Trimalchio, "they were merely pouring me a toast." He was then bundled into a blazing scarlet wrapper, hoisted onto a litter and trundled off. Before him went four runners in spangled harness and a little wheelbarrow in which the old man's favorite rode, a little boy with a wrinkled face and bleary, crudded eyes, even uglier than his master. A

musician with a miniature flute trotted along at Trimalchio's head and during the entire trip played into his master's ear as though whispering him little secrets.

Drunk with admiration, we brought up the rear and Agamemnon joined us when we reached Trimalchio's door. Beside the door we saw a sign:

ANY SLAVE LEAVING THE PREMISES
WITHOUT AUTHORIZATION FROM THE MASTER
WILL RECEIVE ONE HUNDRED LASHES!

At the entrance sat the porter, dressed in that same leek-green that seemed to be the livery of the house. A cherry-colored sash was bound around his waist and he was busily shelling peas into a pan of solid silver. In the doorway hung a cage, all gold, and in it a magpie was croaking out his welcome to the guests.

[29] I was gaping at all this in open-mouthed wonder when I suddenly jumped with terror, stumbled, and nearly broke my leg. For there on the left as you entered, in fresco, stood a huge dog straining at his leash. In large letters under the painting was scrawled:

BEWARE OF THE DOG!

The others burst out laughing at my fright. But when I'd recovered from the shock, I found myself following the rest of the frescoes with fascination. They ran the whole length of the wall. First came a panel showing a slave market with everything clearly captioned. There stood Trimalchio as a young man, his hair long and curly in slave fashion; in his hand he held a staff and he was entering Rome for the first time under the sponsorship of Minerva. In the next panel he appeared as an apprentice accountant, then as a paymaster—each step in his career portrayed in great detail and everything scrupulously labeled. At the end of the portico you came to the climax of the series: a picture of Mercury grasping Trimalchio by the chin and hoisting him up to the lofty eminence of the official's tribunal. Beside the dais stood the goddess Fortuna with a great cornucopia and the three Fates, busily spinning out Trimalchio's life in threads of gold, while in the background a group of runners were shown working out with their trainer. In the corner at the end of the portico was a huge wardrobe with a small built-in shrine. In the shrine were silver statuettes of the household gods, a Venus in marble, and a golden casket containing, I was told, the clippings from Trimalchio's first beard. I began questioning the attendant about some other frescoes in the middle. "Scenes from the *Iliad* and the *Odyssey*," he explained, "and the gladiator games given by Laenas." [30] But there was far too little time to ask about everything that took my eye.

We approached the dining room next where we found the steward at the door making up his accounts. I was particularly struck by the doorposts. For fixed to the jamb were fasces, bundles of sticks with axes protruding from them; but on the lower side the bundles terminated in what looked like the brass ram of a ship, and on the brass this inscription had been engraved:

TO GAIUS POMPEIUS TRIMALCHIO,
OFFICIAL OF THE IMPERIAL CULT,
FROM HIS STEWARD
CINNAMUS.

Hanging from the ceiling on a long chain was a two-bracket lamp with the same inscription, and on each of the doorposts a wooden tablet had been put up. On one of these, if I remember rightly, this memo was written:

"The Master will be dining in town
on the 30th and 31st of December."

On the other tablet was a diagram of the orbits of the moon and the seven planets, with the lucky and unlucky days all indicated by knobs of different colors.

We duly noted these refinements and were just about to step into the dining room when suddenly a slave—clearly posted for this very job—shouted, "RIGHT FEET FIRST!" Well, needless to say, we froze. Who wants to bring down bad luck on his host by walking into his dining room in the wrong way? However, we synchronized our legs and were just stepping out, right feet first, when a slave, utterly naked, landed on the floor in front of us and implored us to save him from a whipping. He was about to be flogged, he explained, for a trifling offense. He had let

41

someone steal the steward's clothing, worthless stuff really, in the baths. Well, we pulled back our right feet, faced about and returned to the entry where we found the steward counting a stack of gold coins. We begged him to let the servant off. "Really, it's not the money I mind," he replied with enormous condescension, "so much as the idiot's carelessness. It was my dinner-suit he lost, a birthday present from one of my dependents. Expensive too, but then I've already had it washed. Well, it's a trifle. Do what you want with him." [*31*] We thanked him for his gracious kindness, but when we entered the dining room up ran the same slave whom we'd just begged off. He overwhelmed us with his thanks and then, to our consternation, began to plaster us with kisses. "You'll soon see whom you've helped," he said. "The master's wine will prove the servant's gratitude."

At last we took our places. Immediately slaves from Alexandria came in and poured ice water over our hands. These were followed by other slaves who knelt at our feet and with extraordinary skill pedicured our toenails. Not for an instant, moreover, during the whole of this odious job, did one of them stop singing. This made me wonder whether the whole menage was given to bursts of song, so I put it to the test by calling for a drink. It was served immediately by a boy who trilled away as shrilly as the rest of them. In fact, anything you asked for was invariably served with a snatch of song, so that you would have thought you were eating in a concert-hall rather than a private dining room.

Now that the guests were all in their places, the *hors d'oeuvres* were served, and very sumptuous they were. Trimalchio alone was still absent, and the place of honor—reserved for the host in the modern fashion—stood empty. But I was speaking of the *hors d'oeuvres*. On a large tray stood a donkey made of rare Corinthian bronze; on the donkey's back were two panniers, one holding green olives, the other, black. Flanking the donkey were two side dishes, both engraved with Trimalchio's name and the weight of the silver, while in dishes shaped to resemble little bridges there were dormice, all dipped in honey and rolled in poppyseed. Nearby, on a silver grill, piping hot, lay small sausages, while beneath the grill black damsons and red pomegranates had been sliced up and arranged so as to give the effect of flames playing over charcoal.

[*32*] We were nibbling at these splendid appetizers when

42

suddenly the trumpets blared a fanfare and Trimalchio was carried in, propped up on piles of miniature pillows in such a comic way that some of us couldn't resist impolitely smiling. His head, cropped close in a recognizable slave cut, protruded from a cloak of blazing scarlet; his neck, heavily swathed already in bundles of clothing, was wrapped in a large napkin bounded by an incongruous senatorial purple stripe with little tassels dangling down here and there. On the little finger of his left hand he sported an immense gilt ring; the ring on the last joint of his fourth finger looked to be solid gold of the kind the lesser nobility wear, but was actually, I think, an imitation, pricked out with small steel stars. Nor does this exhaust the inventory of his trinkets. At least he rather ostentatiously bared his arm to show us a large gold bracelet and an ivory circlet with a shiny metal plate.

[33] He was picking his teeth with a silver toothpick when he first addressed us. "My friends," he said, "I wasn't anxious to eat just yet, but I've ignored my own wishes so as not to keep you waiting. Still, perhaps you won't mind if I finish my game." At these words a slave jumped forward with a board of juniper wood and a pair of crystal dice. I noticed one other elegant novelty as well: in place of the usual black and white counters, Trimalchio had substituted gold and silver coins. His playing, I might add, was punctuated throughout with all sorts of vulgar exclamations.

We, meanwhile, were still occupied with the *hors d'oeuvres* when a tray was carried in and set down before us. On it lay a basket, and in it a hen, carved from wood, with wings outspread as though sitting on her eggs. Then two slaves came forward and, to a loud flourish from the orchestra, began rummaging in the straw and pulling out peahen's eggs which they divided among the guests. Trimalchio gave the whole performance his closest attention. "Friends," he said, "I ordered peahen eggs to be set under that hen, but I'm half afraid they may have hatched already. Still, let's see if we can suck them." We were handed spoons—weighing at least half a pound apiece—and cracked open the eggs, which turned out to be baked from rich pastry. To tell the truth, I had almost tossed my share away, thinking the eggs were really addled. But I heard one of the guests, obviously a veteran of these dinners, say, "I wonder what little surprise we've got in here."

So I cracked the shell with my hand and found inside a fine fat oriole, nicely seasoned with pepper.

[34] By this time Trimalchio had finished his game. He promptly sent for the same dishes we had had and with a great roaring voice offered a second cup of mead to anyone who wanted it. Then the orchestra suddenly blared and the trays were snatched away from the tables by a troupe of warbling waiters. But in the confusion a silver side dish fell to the floor and a slave quickly stooped to retrieve it. Trimalchio, however, had observed the accident and gave orders that the boy's ears should be boxed and the dish tossed back on the floor. Immediately the servant in charge of the dishware came pattering up with a broom and swept the silver dish out the door with the rest of the rubbish. Two curly-haired Ethiopian slaves followed him as he swept, both carrying little skin bottles like the circus attendants who sprinkle the arena with perfume, and poured wine over our hands. No one was offered water.

We clapped enthusiastically for this fine display of extravagance. "The god of war," said Trimalchio, "is a real democrat. That's why I gave orders that each of us should have a table to himself. Besides, these stinking slaves will bother us less than if we were all packed in together."

Glass jars carefully sealed and coated were now brought in. Each bore this label:

GENUINE FALERNIAN WINE
GUARANTEED ONE HUNDRED YEARS
OLD!
BOTTLED
IN THE CONSULSHIP
OF
OPIMIUS.

While we were reading the labels, Trimalchio clapped his hands for attention. "Just think, friends, wine lasts longer than us poor suffering humans. So soak it up, it's the stuff of life. I give you, gentlemen, the genuine Opimian vintage. Yesterday I served much cheaper stuff and the guests were much more important." While we were commenting on it and savoring the luxury, a slave brought in a skeleton, cast of solid silver, and fastened in such a way that the joints could be twisted and bent in any direction. The servants threw it down on the table in front of us and pushed it into several suggestive postures by twisting its joints, while Trimalchio recited this verse of his own making:

> Nothing but bones, that's what we are.
> Death hustles us humans away.
> Today we're here and tomorrow we're not,
> so live and drink while you may!

[35] The course that followed our applause failed, however, to measure up to our expectations of our host, but it was so unusual that it took everybody's attention. Spaced around a circular tray were the twelve signs of the zodiac, and over each sign the chef had put the most appropriate food. Thus, over the sign of Aries were chickpeas, over Taurus a slice of beef, a pair of testicles and kidneys over Gemini, a wreath of flowers over Cancer, over Leo an African fig, virgin sowbelly on Virgo, over Libra a pair of scales with a tartlet in one pan and a cheesecake in the other, over Scorpio a crawfish, a lobster on Capricorn, on Aquarius a goose, and two mullets over the sign of the Fishes. The centerpiece was a clod of turf with the grass still green on top and the whole thing surmounted by a fat honeycomb. Meanwhile, bread in a silver chafing dish was being handed around by a black slave with long hair who was shrilling in an atrocious voice some song from the pantomime called Asafoetida. With some reluctance we began to attack this wretched fare, but Trimalchio kept urging us, "Eat up, gentlemen, eat up!"

[36] Suddenly the orchestra gave another flourish and four slaves came dancing in and whisked off the top of the tray. Underneath, in still another tray, lay fat capons and sowbellies and a hare tricked out with wings to look like a little Pegasus. At the corners of the tray stood four little gravy boats, all shaped like the satyr Marsyas, with phalluses for spouts and a spicy hot gravy dripping down over several large fish swimming about in the lagoon of the tray. The slaves burst out clapping, we clapped too and turned with gusto to these new delights. Trimalchio, enormously pleased with the success of his little tour de force, roared for a slave to come and carve. The carver appeared instantly and went to work, thrusting with his knife like a gladiator practicing to the accompaniment of a water-organ. But all the time Trimalchio kept mumbling in a low voice, "Carver, carver, carver carver . . ." I suspected that

this chant was somehow connected with a trick, so I asked my neighbor, an old hand at these party surprises. "Look," he said, "you see that slave who's carving? Well, he's called Carver, so every time Trimalchio says 'Carver,' he's also saying 'Carve 'er!' and giving him orders to carve."

[37] This atrocious pun finished me: I couldn't touch a thing. So I turned back to my neighbor to pick up what gossip I could and soon had him blabbing away, especially when I asked him about the woman who was bustling around the room. "Her?" he said, "why, that's Fortunata, Trimalchio's wife. And the name couldn't suit her better. She counts her cash by the cartload. And you know what she used to be? Well, begging your Honor's pardon, but you wouldn't have taken bread from her hand. Now, god knows how or why, she's sitting pretty: has Trimalchio eating out of her hand. If she told him at noon it was night, he'd crawl into bed. As for him, he's so loaded he doesn't know how much he has. But that bitch has her finger in everything—where you'd least expect it too. A regular tightwad, never drinks, and sharp as they come. But she's got a nasty tongue; get her gossiping on a couch and she'll chatter like a parrot. If she likes you, you're lucky; if she doesn't, god help you.

"As for old Trimalchio, that man's got more farms than a kite could flap over. And there's more silver plate stuffed in his porter's lodge than another man's got in his safe. As for slaves, whoosh! So help me, I'll bet not one in ten has ever seen his master. Your ordinary rich man is just peanuts compared to him; he could knock them all under a cabbage and you'd never know they were gone.

[38] "And buy things? Not him. No sir, he raises everything right on his own estate. Wool, citron, pepper, you name it. By god, you'd find hen's milk if you looked around. Now take his wool. The home-grown strain wasn't good enough. So you know what he did? Imported rams from Tarentum, bred them into the herd. Attic honey he raises at home. Ordered the bees special from Athens. And the local bees are better for being crossbred too. And, you know, just the other day he sent off to India for some mushroom spawn. Every mule he owns had a wild ass for a daddy. And you see those pillows there? Every last one is stuffed with purple or scarlet wool. That boy's loaded!

"And don't sneer at his friends. They're all ex-slaves, but every one of them's rich. You see that guy down there on the next to last couch? He's worth a cool half-million.

Came up from nowhere. Used to tote wood on his back. People say, but I don't know, he stole a cap off a hobgoblin's head and found a treasure. He's the gods' fairhaired boy. That's luck for you, but I don't begrudge him. Not so long ago he was just a slave. Yes sir, he's doing all right. Just a few days ago he advertised his apartment for rent. The ad went like this:

APARTMENT FOR RENT AFTER THE FIRST OF JULY.
AM BUYING A VILLA. SEE G. POMPEIUS DIOGENES.

"And you see that fellow in the freedman's seat? He's already made a pile and lost it. What a life! But I don't envy him. After the first million the going got sticky. Right now I'll bet he's mortgaged every hair on his head. But it wasn't his fault. He's too honest, that's his trouble, and his crooked friends stripped him to feather their own nests. One thing's sure: once your little kettle stops cooking and the business starts to slide, you get the brushoff from your friends. And, you know, he had a fine, respectable business too. Undertaking. Ate like a king: boars roasted whole, pastry as tall as buildings, pheasants, chefs, pastrycooks—the whole works. Why, he's had more wine spilled under his table than most men have in their cellars. Life? Hell, it was a dream! Then when things started sliding, he got scared his creditors would think he was broke. So he advertised an auction:

GAIUS JULIUS PROCULUS
WILL HOLD
AN AUCTION
OF HIS
SPARE FURNITURE!"

[39] By now the astrological course had been removed, the guests were gaily attacking the wine, and there was a loud hubbub of laughing and chatter. My neighbor's pleasant prattle, however, was interrupted by Trimalchio. Lounging back on his elbow, he burst out: "Gentlemen, I want you to savor this good wine. Fish must swim, and that's a fact. But I'd like to know if you were really taken in by that stuff you saw on the top tray. Is that what you think of me? What does our Vergil say?

Is this what men report of great Ulysses?

Not on your life. At dinner, I say, there should be culture as much as food. My old master—may his bones rest

47

in peace—wanted me to be a man of the world and a gentleman of culture. And I think that last course will show you there isn't much that I don't know. Listen now, and I'll explain to you about the zodiac. This heaven, which is where the twelve gods live, changes into twelve signs. Now sometimes it turns into the Ram, that is, Aries. Everyone who gets himself born under the Ram owns heaps of sheep and lots of wool; besides, his head is hard, his forehead like brass and his horns like swords. That's why many professors and also muttonheads are born under the sign of the Ram."

We all applauded our droll astrologer and he continued. "After the Ram, the Universe switches over to the Bull, who's sometimes called Taurus. The people who are born under the Bull include bullies and cowboys and people who lie down in soft pastures. Under the Twins, old Gemini, you get two-horse teams, yokes of oxen, lechers who are led around by their balls, and two-faced politicians. Cancer, or the Crab, is my sign; therefore I walk on many legs and my possessions stretch over land and sea, for the crab is at home in both those elements. That's why I avoided putting anything on my sign for a long time: I didn't want my birth-sign queered. Under Leo the Lion you get gluttons and big shots; under Virgo the Virgin you get useless women, deserters, and those who wear chains on their ankles, fetters for men, bracelets for women. Stinger Scorpio has poisoners and murderers. Under Archer Sagittarius you get cross-eyed thieves who cock an eye at the beets but snitch the ham. Under Capricorn, because it means goat-horn, come men who have horns or corns; corn-men are workers who sweat for their wages and horn-men are cuckolds all. Aquarius is a water carrier, so under him you find innkeepers who water the wine and people who are all wet. But Pisces is for Fishes and he gives us the fishier types of men: gape-mouthed lawyers or just plain fish peddlers. That's why things are as they are. The universe goes whizzing around like a millwheel and is always up to some mischief and people are either dying or just getting born. As for the hunk of earth you saw sitting in the middle, that was packed with meaning too. For dead in the center of everything sits old Mother Earth, as fat as an egg, and loaded with goodies like a honeycomb."

[40] We all cheered and cried "Bravo" and swore that Aratus and Hipparchus were mere amateurs, not to be compared with our host. But while we were flattering

him, servants came and draped our couches with special covers, each one entirely embroidered with hunting scenes —nets, hunters with spears lying in ambush, and all the rest. We were wondering what all this was leading up to, when suddenly there came a hideous uproar outside the room and then huge Spartan mastiffs came bounding in and began to gallop around the table. Following the dogs came servants with a tray on which we saw a wild sow of absolutely enormous size. Perched rakishly on the sow's head was the cap of freedom which newly freed slaves wear in token of their liberty, and from her tusks hung two baskets woven from palm leaves: one was filled with dry Egyptian dates, the other held sweet Syrian dates. Clustered around her teats were little suckling pigs made of hard pastry, gifts for the guests to take home as it turned out, but intended to show that ours was a brood-sow. The slave who stepped up to carve, however, was not our old friend Carver who had cut up the capons, but a huge fellow with a big beard, a coarse hunting cape thrown over his shoulders, and his legs bound up in cross-gaiters. He whipped out his knife and gave a savage slash at the sow's flanks. Under the blow the flesh parted, the wound burst open and dozens of thrushes came whirring out! But bird-catchers with limed twigs were standing by and before long they had snared all the birds as they thrashed wildly around the room. Trimalchio ordered that a thrush be given to each guest, adding for good measure, "Well, that old porker liked her acorns juicy all right." Then servants stepped forward, removed the baskets hanging from the sow's nose, and divided the dry and sweet dates out equally among the guests.

[41] Meanwhile I was desperately trying to figure out why the sow had been brought in with that freedom cap on her head. One after another, I tried all kinds of crazy, far-fetched ideas; finally I mustered up my courage and asked my neighbor. "Why, gods alive," he snorted, "even your slave could have figured that one out. It's no riddle at all, clear as day. Look: yesterday this sow was served for dinner, but the guests were so stuffed they let it go. Get it? They *let it go*. So today naturally she comes back to the table as a free sow." I cursed myself for being so slow and decided to ask no more questions. Altogether it was beginning to look as though I'd never dined in good company before.

During this exchange a pretty little boy came into the

room, wearing a wreath of vine leaves and ivy in his hair
like a little Bacchus or Father Liber. He did us a number
of imitations of Bacchus under various forms: as Lyaeus,
Bromius, Evius, and so on. Then, warbling some of
Trimalchio's poetry in a shrill soprano, he went around
offering the guests grapes from his basket. Finally Trimalchio took notice of the boy's efforts and called him
over. "Come here, you baby Dionysus. Little Father Liber,
I hereby liberate you." At this the boy snatched the freedom cap from the boar's head and stuck it on his own.
Trimalchio wheeled back, laughing. "Well, gentlemen,
how did you like that? I've liberated Liber. I've set the
wine-god free. So let it flow. And drink up, gentlemen.
It's all on me!" We clapped our approval of his elaborate
pun and kissed the little boy soundly as he made the
round of the couches to be congratulated on his new
freedom.

At this point Trimalchio heaved himself up from his
couch and waddled off to the toilet. Once rid of our table
tyrant, the talk began to flow more freely. Damas called
for larger glasses and led off himself. "What's one day?
Bah, nothing at all. You turn round and it's dark. Nothing
for it, I say, but jump right from bed to table. Brrrr.
Nasty spell of cold weather we've been having. A bath
hardly warmed me up. But a hot drink's the best overcoat
of all; that's what I always say. Whoosh, I must have
guzzled gallons. I'm tight and no mistake. Wine's gone
right to my head . . ."

[42] "As for me," Seleucus broke in, "I don't take a
bath every day. Your bath's a fuller; the water's got teeth
like a comb. Saps your vital juices. But once I've had a
slug of mead, then bugger the cold. Couldn't have had a
bath today anyway. Had to go to poor old Chrysanthus'
funeral. Yup, he's gone for good, folded his tent forever.
And a grand little guy he was; they don't make 'em any
better these days. I might almost be talking to him now.
Just goes to show you. What are men anyway but balloons
on legs, a lot of blown-up bladders? Flies, that's what we
are. No, not even flies. Flies have something inside. But
a man's a bubble, all air, nothing else. And, you know,
Chrysanthus might still be with us if he hadn't tried that
starvation diet. Five days and not a crumb of bread, not a
drop of water, passed his lips. Tch, tch. And now he's
gone, joined the great majority. Doctors killed him. Maybe
not doctors, call it fate. What good's a doctor but for

peace of mind? But the funeral was fine, they did it up proper: nice bier, fancy drapes, and a good bunch of mourners turned out too. Mostly slaves he'd set free, of course. But his old lady was sure stingy with the tears. Not that he didn't lead her a hard life, mind. But women, they're a race of kites. Don't deserve love. You might as well drop it down a well. And old love's a real cancer . . ."

[43] He was beginning to be tiresome and Phileros shouted him down. "Whoa there," he cut in, "let's talk about the living. He got what was coming to him. He lived well, he died well. What the hell more did he want? And got rich from nothing too. And no wonder, I say. That boy would have grubbed in the gutter for a coin and picked it out with his teeth too. God knows what he had salted away. Just got fatter and fatter, bloated with the stuff. Why, that man oozed money the way a honeycomb oozes honey. But I'll give you the lowdown on him, and no frills either. He talked tough, sure, but he was a born gabber. And a real scrapper too, regular pair of fists on legs. But you take his brother: now that's a real man for you, friendly and generous as they come, and what's more, he knows how to put on a spread. Anyway, as I was saying, what does our boy do but flop on his first big deal and end up eating crow? But come the vintage and he got right back on his feet and sold his wine at his own figure. What really gave him a boost was some legacy he got. And I don't mind telling you, he milked that legacy for all it was worth and then some. So what does the sap do next but pick a fight with his own brother and leave everything to a total stranger? I mean, it just shows you. Run from your kin and you run a damn long ways, as the saying goes. Well, you know, he had some slaves and he listened to them as though they were a lot of oracles, so naturally they took him in the end. It's like I always say, a sucker gets screwed. And that goes double when a man's in business. But there's a saying, it isn't what you're given, but what you can get that counts. Well, he got the meat out of that one all his life. He was Lady Luck's fair-haired boy and no mistake. Lead turned to gold in his hand. Of course, it's easy when the stuff comes rolling in on its own. And you know how old he was when he died? Seventy and then some. But carried it beautifully, hard as nails and his hair as black as a crow. I knew him for ages, and he was horny, right to the end. By god, I'll bet he even pestered the dog. Boys were what

51

he really liked, but he wasn't choosy: he'd jump anything with legs. I don't blame him a bit, you understand. He won't have any fun where he's gone now."

[44] But Ganymedes struck in, "Stuff like that doesn't matter a bit to man or beast. But nobody mentions the real thing, the way the price of bread is pinching. God knows, I couldn't buy a mouthful of bread today. And this damn drought goes on and on. Nobody's had a belly-ful for years now. It's those rotten officials, you take my word for it. They're in cahoots with the bakers: you scratch me and I'll scratch you. So the little people get it in the neck, but in the rich man's jaws it's jubilee all year. By god, if we only had the kind of men we used to have, the sort I found here when I arrived from Asia. Then life was something like living. Man, milk and honey day in and day out, and the way they'd wallop those blood-sucking officials, you'd have thought old Jupiter was having himself a tantrum. I remember old Safinius now. He used to live down by the old arch when I was a boy. More peppercorn than man. Singed the ground wherever he went. But honest and square and a real friend! Why, you could have matched coins with him in the dark. And in the townhall he'd lay it right on the line, no frills at all, just square on the target. And when he made a speech in the main square, he'd let loose like a bugle blowing. But neat as a pin all the time, never ruffled, never spat: there was something Asiatic about him. And you know, he always spoke to you, even remembered your name, just as though he were one of us. And bread was dirt-cheap in his day. For a penny you got a loaf that two men couldn't finish. Nowadays bulls' eyes come bigger than bread. But that's what I mean, things are just getting worse and worse. Why, this place is running downhill like a heifer's ass. You tell me, by god, the good of this three-fig official of ours who thinks more of his graft than what's happening to us. Why, that boy's just living it up at home and making more in a day than most men ever inherit. If we had any balls, let me tell you, he'd be laughing out of the other side of his face. But not us. Oh no, we're big lions at home and scared foxes in public. Why, I've practically had to pawn my clothes and if bread prices don't drop soon, I'll have to put my houses on the market. Mark my words, we're in for bad times if some man or god doesn't have a heart and take pity on this place. I'll stake my luck on it, the gods have got a finger in what's

52

been happening here. And you know why? Because no one believes in the gods, that's why. Who observes the fast days any more, who cares a rap for Jupiter? One and all, bold as brass, they sit there pretending to pray, but cocking their eyes on the chances and counting up their cash. Once upon a time, let me tell you, things were different. The women would dress up in their best and climb barefoot up to the temple on the hill. Their hair was unbound and their hearts were pure and they went to beg Jupiter for rain. And you know what happened? Then or never, the rain would come sloshing down by the bucket, and they'd all stand there like a pack of drowned rats, just grinning away. Well, that's why the gods have stuffed their ears, because we've gotten unreligious. The fields are lying barren and . . ."

[45] "For god's sake," the ragseller Echion broke in, "cut out the damned gloom, will you? 'Sometimes it's good, sometimes it's bad,' as the old peasant said when he sold the spotted pig. Luck changes. If things are lousy today, there's always tomorrow. That's life, man. Sure, the times are bad, but they're no better anywhere else. We're all in the same boat, so what's the fuss? If you lived anywhere else, you'd be swearing the pigs here went waddling around already roasted. And don't forget, there's a big gladiator show coming up the day after tomorrow. Not the same old fighters either; they've got a fresh shipment in and there's not a slave in the batch. You know how old Titus works. Nothing's too good for him when he lets himself go. Whatever it is, it'll be something special. I know the old boy well, and he'll go whole hog. Just wait. There'll be cold steel for the crowd, no quarter, and the amphitheater will end up looking like a slaughterhouse. He's got what it takes too. When the old man died —and a nasty way to die, I'm telling you—he left Titus a cool million. Even if he spent ten thousand, he'd never feel it, and people won't forget him in a hurry either. He's already raked together a troupe of whirling dervishes, and there's a girl who fights from a chariot. And don't forget that steward that Glyco caught in bed with his wife. You just wait, there'll be a regular free-for-all between the lovers and the jealous husbands. But that Glyco's a cheap bastard. Sent the steward down to be pulled to pieces by the wild beasts, you know. So that just gave his little secret away, of course. And what's the crime, I'd like to know, when the poor slave is told to do it? It's

53

that piss-pot-bitch of his that ought to be thrown to the bulls, by god! Still, those who can't beat the horse must whop the saddle. But what stumps me is why Glyco ever thought old Hermogenes' brat would turn out well anyway. The old man would have pared a hawk's claws in mid-air, and like father, like daughter, as I always say. But Glyco's thrown away his own flesh and blood; he'll carry the marks of this mess as long as he lives and only hell will burn it away. Yes sir, that boy has dug his own grave and no mistake.

"Well, they say Mammaea's going to put on a spread. Mmmm, I can sniff it already. There'll be a nice little handout all around. And if he does, he'll knock old Norbanus out of the running for good. Beat him hands down. And what's Norbanus ever done anyway, I'd like to know. A lot of two-bit gladiators and half-dead at that: puff at them and they'd fall down dead. Why, I've seen better men tossed to the wild animals. A lot of little clay statues, barnyard strutters, that's what they were. One was an old jade, another was a clubfoot, and the replacement they sent in for him was half-dead and hamstrung to boot. There was one Thracian with some guts but he fought by the book. And after the fight they had to flog the whole lot of them the way the mob was screaming, 'Let 'em have it!' Just a pack of runaway slaves. Well, says Norbanus, at least I gave you a show. So you did, says I, and you got my cheers for it. But tot it up and you'll see you got as much as you gave. So there too, and tit for tat, says I.

[46] "Well, Agamemnon, I can see you're thinking, 'What's that bore blabbing about now?' You're the professor here, but I don't catch you opening your mouth. No, you think you're a cut above us, don't you, so you just sit there and smirk at the way we poor men talk. Your learning's made you a snob. Still, let it go. I tell you what. Someday you come down to my villa and look it over. We'll find something to nibble on, a chicken, a few eggs maybe. This crazy weather's knocked everything topsy-turvy, but we'll come up with something you like. Don't worry your head about it, there'll be loads to eat.

"You remember that little shaver of mine? Well, he'll be your pupil one of these days. He's already doing division up to four, and if he comes through all right, he'll sit at your feet someday. Every spare minute he has, he buries himself in his books. He's smart all right, and there's good stuff in him. His real trouble is his passion for birds.

54

I killed three of his pet goldfinches the other day and told him the cat had got them. He found some other hobby soon enough. And, you know, he's mad about painting. And he's already started wading into Greek and he's keen on his Latin. But the tutor's a little stuck on himself and won't keep him in line. The older boy now, he's a bit slow. But he's a hard worker and teaches the others more than he knows. Every holiday he spends at home, and whatever you give him, he's content. So I bought him some of those big red lawbooks. A smattering of law, you know, is a useful thing around the house. There's money in it too. He's had enough literature, I think. But if he doesn't stick it out in school, I'm going to have him taught a trade. Barbering or auctioneering, or at least a little law. The only thing that can take a man's trade away is death. But every day I keep pounding the same thing into his head: 'Son, get all the learning you can. Anything you learn is money in the bank. Look at Lawyer Phileros. If he hadn't learned his law, he'd be going hungry and chewing on air. Not so long ago he was peddling his wares on his back; now he's running neck and neck with old Norbanus. Take my word for it, son, there's a mint of money in books, and learning a trade never killed a man yet.'"

[47] Conversation was running along these lines when Trimalchio returned, wiping the sweat from his brow. He splashed his hands in perfume and stood there for a minute in silence. "You'll excuse me, friends," he began, "but I've been constipated for days and the doctors are stumped. I got a little relief from a prescription of pomegranate rind and resin in a vinegar base. Still, I hope my tummy will get back its manners soon. Right now my bowels are bumbling around like a bull. But if any of you has any business that needs attending to, go right ahead; no reason to feel embarrassed. There's not a man been born yet with solid insides. And I don't know any anguish on earth like trying to hold it in. Jupiter himself couldn't stop it from coming.—What are you giggling about, Fortunata? You're the one who keeps me awake all night with your trips to the potty. Well, anyone at table who wants to go has my permission, and the doctors tell us not to hold it in. Everything's ready outside—water and pots and the rest of the stuff. Take my word for it, friends, the vapors go straight to your brain. Poison your whole system. I know of some who've died from being too polite

55

and holding it in." We thanked him for his kindness and understanding, but we tried to hide our snickers in repeated swallows of wine.

As yet we were unaware that we had slogged only halfway through this "forest of refinements," as the poets put it. But when the tables had been wiped—to the inevitable music, of course—servants led in three hogs rigged out with muzzles and bells. According to the headwaiter, the first hog was two years old, the second three, but the third was all of six. I supposed that we would now get tumblers and rope dancers and that the pigs would be put through the kind of clever tricks they perform for the crowds in the street. But Trimalchio dispelled such ideas by asking, "Which one of these hogs would you like cooked for your dinner? Now your ordinary country cook can whip you up a chicken or make a Bacchante mincemeat or easy dishes of that sort. But my cooks frequently broil calves whole." With this he had the cook called in at once, and without waiting for us to choose our pig, ordered the oldest slaughtered. Then he roared at the cook, "What's the number of your corps, fellow?"

"The fortieth, sir," the cook replied.

"Were you born on the estate or bought?"

"Neither, sir. Pansa left me to you in his will."

"Well," barked Trimalchio, "see that you do a good job or I'll have you demoted to the messenger corps."

The cook, freshly reminded of his master's power, meekly led the hog off toward the kitchen, [48] while Trimalchio gave us all an indulgent smile. "If you don't like the wine," he said, "we'll have it changed for you. I'll know by the amount you drink what you think of it. Luckily too I don't have to pay a thing for it. It comes with a lot of other good things from a new estate of mine near town. I haven't seen it yet, but I'm told it adjoins my lands at Terracina and Tarentum. Right now what I'd really like to do is buy up Sicily. Then I could go to Africa without ever stepping off my own property.

"But tell me," he said, turning to Agamemnon, "what was the subject of your debate today? Of course, I'm no orator myself, but I've learnt a thing or two about law for use around the place. And don't think I'm one of those people who look down on learning. No sir, I've got two libraries, one Greek and the other Latin. So tell us, if you will, what your debate was about."

"Well," said Agamemnon, "it seems that a rich man and a poor man had gone to court . . ."

"A poor man?" Trimalchio broke in, "what's that?"

"Very pretty, very pretty," chuckled Agamemnon and then launched out into an exposition of god knows which of his debating topics.

But Trimalchio immediately interrupted him: "If that's the case, there's no argument; if it isn't the case, then what does it matter?" Needless to say, we pointedly applauded all of Trimalchio's sallies.

"But tell me, my dear Agamemnon," continued our host, "do you remember the twelve labors of Hercules or the story about Ulysses and how the Cyclops broke his thumb trying to get the log out of his eye? When I was a kid, I used to read all those stories in Homer. And, you know, I once saw the Sibyl of Cumae in person. She was hanging in a bottle, and when the boys asked her, 'Sibyl, what do you want?' she said, 'I want to die.'"

[49] He was still chattering away when the servants came in with an immense hog on a tray almost the size of the table. We were, of course, astounded at the chef's speed and swore it would have taken longer to roast an ordinary chicken, all the more since the pig looked even bigger than the one served to us earlier. Meanwhile Trimalchio had been scrutinizing the pig very closely and suddenly roared, "What! What's this? By god, this hog hasn't even been gutted! Get that cook in here on the double!"

Looking very miserable, the poor cook came shuffling up to the table and admitted that he had forgotten to gut the pig.

"You forgot?" bellowed Trimalchio. "You forgot to gut a pig? And I suppose you think that's the same thing as merely forgetting to add salt and pepper. Strip that man!"

The cook was promptly stripped and stood there stark naked between two bodyguards, utterly forlorn. The guests to a man, however, interceded for the chef. "Accidents happen," they said, "please don't whip him. If he ever does it again, we promise we won't say a word for him." My own reaction was anger, savage and unrelenting. I could barely restrain myself and leaning over, I whispered to Agamemnon, "Did you ever hear of anything worse? Who could forget to gut a pig? By god, you wouldn't catch me letting him off, not if it was just a fish he'd forgotten to clean."

Not so Trimalchio, however. He sat there, a great grin widening across his face, and said: "Well, since your memory's so bad, you can gut the pig here in front of us all." The cook was handed back his clothes, drew out his knife with a shaking hand and then slashed at the pig's belly with crisscross cuts. The slits widened out under the pressure from inside, and suddenly out poured, not the pig's bowels and guts, but link upon link of tumbling sausages and blood puddings.

[50] The slaves saluted the success of the hoax with a rousing, "LONG LIVE GAIUS!" The vindicated chef was presented with a silver crown and honored by the offer of a drink served on a platter of fabulous Corinthian bronze. Noticing that Agamemnon was admiring the platter, Trimalchio said, "I'm the only man in the world who owns genuine Corinthian bronze." I expected him to brag in his usual way that he'd had the stuff imported directly from Corinth, but he was way ahead of me. "Perhaps," he said, "you'd like to know why I'm the only man who owns genuine Corinthian. Well, I'll tell you. It's because I have it made by a craftsman of mine called Corinthus, and what's Corinthian, I'd like to know, if not something Corinthus makes? And don't think I'm just a stupid half-wit. I know very well how Corinthian bronze got invented. You see, when Troy was taken, there was this fellow called Hannibal, a real swindler, and he ordered all the bronze and gold and silver statues to be melted down in a pile. Well, the stuff melted and made a kind of mixture. So the smiths came and started carting it off and turning out platters and side dishes and little statues. And that's how real Corinthian began, a kind of mishmash metal, and nothing on its own. If you don't mind my saying so though, I like glass better. It doesn't stink like bronze, and if it weren't so breakable, I'd prefer it to gold. Besides, it's cheap as cheap.

[51] "But, you know, there was once a workman who invented a little glass bottle that wouldn't break. Well, he got in to see the emperor with this bottle as a present. Then he asked the emperor to hand it back to him and managed to drop it on the floor on purpose. Well, the emperor just about died. But the workman picked the bottle back up from the floor and, believe it or not, it was dented just a little, as though it were made out of bronze. So he pulled a little hammer out of his pocket and tapped it back into shape. Well, by this time he

58

thought he had Jupiter by the balls, especially when the emperor asked him if anyone else was in on the secret. But you know what happened? When the workman told him that nobody else knew, the emperor ordered his head chopped off. Said that if the secret ever got out, gold would be as cheap as dirt.

[52] "But silver's my real passion. I've got a hundred bowls that hold three or four gallons apiece, all of them with the story of Cassandra engraved on them: how she killed her sons, you know, and the kids are lying there dead so naturally that you'd think they were still alive. And there's a thousand goblets too which Mummius left my old master. There's pictures on them too, things like Daedalus locking up Niobe in the Trojan Horse. And on my cups, the heavy ones, I've got the fights of Hermeros and Petraites. No sir, I wouldn't take cash down for my taste in silver."

In the midst of this harangue, a slave dropped a goblet on the floor. Once he had finished talking, Trimalchio wheeled on him and said, "Why don't you go hang yourself? You're no damn good to me." The slave began to whimper and beg for mercy. But Trimalchio was stern: "Why come whining to me for pity? As if I got you into your mess. Next time tell yourself not to be so damn dumb." However, we interceded once more and managed to get the slave off. The instant he was pardoned, he began to scamper around the table . . .

❦

Then Trimalchio shouted, "Out with the water, in with the wine!" We dutifully applauded the joke, and particularly Agamemnon who was an old hand at wangling return invitations.

By now Trimalchio was drinking heavily and was, in fact, close to being drunk. "Hey, everybody!" he shouted, "nobody's asked Fortunata to dance. Believe me, you never saw anyone do grinds the way she can." With this he raised his hands over his forehead and did an impersonation of the actor Syrus singing one of his numbers, while the whole troupe of slaves joined in on the chorus. He was just about to get up on the table when Fortunata went and whispered something in his ear, probably a warning that these drunken capers were undignified. Never was a man so changeable: sometimes he would bow down to

Fortunata in anything she asked; at other times, as now, he went his own way.

[53] But it was the secretary, not Fortunata, who effectively dampened his desire to dance, for quite without warning he began to read from the estate records as though he were reading some government bulletin.

"Born," he began, "on July 26th, on Trimalchio's estate at Cumae, thirty male and forty female slaves.

"Item, five hundred thousand bushels of wheat transferred from the threshing rooms into storage.

"On the same date, the slave Mithridates crucified alive for blaspheming the guardian spirit of our master Gaius.

"On the same date, the sum of three hundred thousand returned to the safe because it could not be invested.

"On the same date, in the gardens at Pompeii, fire broke out in the house of the bailiff Nasta . . ."

"What?" roared Trimalchio. "When did I buy any gardens at Pompeii?"

"Last year," the steward replied. "That's why they haven't yet appeared on the books."

"I don't care what you buy," stormed Trimalchio, "but if it's not reported to me within six months, I damn well won't have it appearing on the books at all!"

The reading was then resumed. First came the directives of the superintendents on various estates and then the wills of the gamekeepers, each one excluding Trimalchio by a special clause. There followed a list of his overseers, the divorce of a freedwoman by a nightwatchman for being caught in flagrante with an attendant from the baths, and the banishment of a steward to Baiae. It closed with the accusation against a cashier and the verdict in a dispute between several valets.

At long last the tumblers appeared. An extremely insipid clown held up a ladder and ordered a boy to climb up and do a dance on top to the accompaniment of several popular songs. He was then commanded to jump through burning hoops and to pick up a big jug with his teeth. No one much enjoyed this entertainment except Trimalchio who claimed that the stunts were extremely difficult. Nothing on earth, he added, gave him such pleasure as jugglers and buglers; everything else, such as animal shows and concerts, was utter trash. "I once bought," he bragged, "several comic actors, but I used them for doing farces and I told my flutist to play nothing but Latin songs, the funny ones."

[54] Just at this point the ladder toppled and the boy on top fell down, landing squarely on Trimalchio. The slaves shrieked, the guests screamed. We were not, of course, in the least concerned about the boy, whose neck we would have been delighted to see broken; but we dreaded the thought of possibly having to go into mourning for a man who meant nothing to us at all. Meanwhile, Trimalchio lay there groaning and nursing his arm as though it were broken. Doctors came rushing in, Fortunata at their head, her hair flying, a goblet in her hand, and filling the room with wails of distress. As for the boy, he was already clutching us by the legs and begging us to intercede for him. My own reaction was one of suspicion. I was afraid, that is, that these pleas for pity were simply the prelude to one more hoax; for the incident of the slave who had forgotten to gut the pig was still fresh in my mind. So I started to examine the room rather uneasily, half expecting, I suppose, that the walls would split open and god knows what contraption would appear. And these suspicions were somewhat confirmed when they began flogging a servant for having bound up his master's wounded arm with white, rather than scarlet, bandages. Actually, as it turned out, I was not far wrong, for instead of having the boy whipped, Trimalchio ordered him to be set free, so that nobody could say that the great Trimalchio had been hurt by a mere slave.

[55] We gave this ample gesture our approval and remarked on the uncertainties of human existence. "Yes," said Trimalchio, "it would be a shame to let an occasion like this pass by without some enduring record of it." He then called for writing materials and after a brief but harrowing effort produced the following lines:

We think we're awful smart, we think we're awful wise,
but when we're least expecting, comes the big surprise.
Lady Luck's in heaven and we're her little toys,
so break out the wine and fill your glasses, boys!

From this beginning, the conversation went on to poetry, and for a considerable time somebody was maintaining that the best poet of all time was the Thracian poet, Mopsus. Then Trimalchio turned to Agamemnon and said, "Professor, what's the difference between Cicero and Publilius in your opinion? To my way of thinking, Cicero jogs along better but Publilius has him all beat when it

61

comes to the message. What, after all, could be more profound than this?

Extravagance and Waste have breach'd our walls,
and Mars' vast ramparts crumble down in ruin.
To please thy palate, Rome, that haughty bird,
the peacock, glisters in his cage to die;
the cock from Afric strand thy victim is;
upon thy plate the capon perisheth.
Lo, e'en the friendly stork, our peregrine,
blest bird of piety that stalks on stilts,
cold winter's refugee, who rattleth on
the tiles and struts the roof in sign of Spring,
now builds his final nest—upon the plate
of Greed!
   Ah, and why should distant Ind produce
the harvest of her pearl, that berried stone?
That matrons should, forsooth, in baubles dress
and raise their shameless legs upon the couch
of lust?
   Why, why should emeralds make
magnificence of green, and rubies glow
with coruscation of expensive fire,
unless sweet Chastity, among such stones,
might better blaze her innocence abroad?
O shame, that brides in gossamer should go,
and filmy gauze their nakedness should gloze!

[56] "But next to literature," he continued, "which profession do you think has the roughest time of it? To my mind, doctors and money-changers are the worst off. Doctors, because they have to guess what's going on in the tummies of poor mankind and when the fever comes. But doctors I despise: they're always sticking me on a diet of roast duck. Money-changers come next because they have to detect the phony copper beneath the silver. Now of dumb animals the ones who have things worst are oxen and sheep. Poor dumb oxen, because it's their work that puts the bread in our mouths, and sheep because the clothes on our backs we owe to them. And it's a dirty shame, I think, the way we eat their mutton and wear their wool when the poor dumb sheep pay the bill. But bees are really good; they're almost like gods, I say, because they vomit honey and pretend they got it from

Jupiter. Of course, they sting too, but that's because there's a bit of bitterness in all good things . . ."

He had started in easing the philosophers out of their jobs when servants brought around jars from which we all drew slips. Then the boy whose task it was read each of our slips aloud. Every one contained some conundrum or pun which entitled us to a humorous present. Thus when the slip SOUR SILVER SAUCES SOW was read, a leg of ham topped by a silver cruet filled with vinegar was carried in. HEADREST earned a neck of mutton, while HINDSIGHT AND LAMBASTING was matched by a bowl of lamb gravy with buckeyes floating around in it. HORSERADISH AND PRUNES won a riding whip and a pruning knife, and several wrinkled plums and a jar of Attic honey went to the slip reading PLUMAGE AND FLYTRAP. For GOOD FOOD FOR FOOT-WEAR? they produced a fillet of sole broiled on the sole of a sandal. SOMETHING FOR THE DOG, SOMETHING FOR THE FEET won a pair of rabbit-lined slippers, while MUSSELS AND SOME LETTERS IN AN ENVELOPE received a mouse tied between two eels and a pod of peas. We chuckled at these jokes, but there were hundreds of them and I have forgotten most of them by now.

[57] Ascyltus, however, was no longer able to swallow his snickers and he finally tossed back his head and roared and guffawed until he was almost in tears. At this one of Trimalchio's freedmen friends, the man just above me at the table, took offense and flared out in wild rage. "You cheap muttonhead," he snarled, "what are you cackling about? Entertainment isn't good enough for the likes of you, I suppose? You're richer, huh? And eat better too? I'll bet! So help me, if you were down here by me, I'd stop your damn bleating!

"Some nerve he's got, laughing at us. Stinking runaway, that's what he is. A burglar. A bum. Bah, he's not worth a good boot in the ass. By god, if I tangle with him, he won't know where he's headed! So help me, I don't often fly off the handle like this. Still, if the flesh is soft, I say, the worms will breed.

"Still cackling, are you? Who the hell are you to snicker? Where'd your daddy buy you? Think you're made out of gold, eh? So that's it, you're a Roman knight? That makes me a king's son. Then why was I a slave? Because I wanted to be. Because I'd rather be a Roman slave than a tax-paying savage. And as I live and breathe, I hope no man thinks I'm funny. I walk like a free man. I don't owe any man a thing. I've never been hauled into court. That's right: no man ever had to tell me to pay up. I've bought a few little plots of land and a nice bit of silver plate. I feed twenty stomachs, not counting the dog. I bought my wife's freedom so no man could put his dirty paws on her. I paid a good two hundred for my own freedom. Right now, I'm on the board for the emperor's worship, and I hope when I die I won't have to blush for anything. But you're so damn busy sneering at us, you don't look at your own behind. You see the lice on us but not the ticks on yourself. Nobody but you thinks we're funny. Look at your old professor there: he appreciates us. Bah, you're still sucking tit; you're limp leather, limper, no damn better. Oh you're rich, are you? Then cram down two lunches; bolt two suppers, sonny. As for me, I'd rather have my credit than all your cash. Who ever had to dun me twice? Forty years, boy and man, I spent as a slave, but no one could tell now whether I was slave or free. I was just a curly-headed kid when I came to this place. The town hall wasn't even built then. But I did everything I could do to please my master. He was a good man, a real gentleman, whose fingernail was worth more than your whole carcass. And there were some in that house who would have liked to see me stumble. But thanks to my master I gave them the slip. Those are real trials, those are real triumphs. But when you're born free everything's as easy as saying, 'Hurry on down.' Well, what are you gaping at now, like a goat in vetch?"

[58] At these last words, Giton, who was sitting at our feet, went rudely off into a great gale of whooping laughter which he had been trying to stifle for some time. Ascyltus' tormentor promptly trained his fire on the boy. "So you're snorting too, are you, you frizzle-headed scallion? You think it's time for capers, do you, carnival days and cold December? When did you pay your freedom tax, eh? Well, what are you smirking at, you little gallowsbird? Look, birdbait, I'll give it to you proper and the same for that master who won't keep you in line. May I never eat bread again, if I let you off for anyone except our host here; if it weren't for him, I'd fix you right now. We were all feeling good, nice happy party, and then those half-baked masters of yours let you cut out of line. Like master, like slave, I always say.

"Damnation, I'm so hopping mad, I can't stop. I'm no

sorehead either, but when I let go, I don't give a damn for
my own mother. Just you wait, I'll catch you out in the
street someday. You mouse, you little potato! And when
I do, if I don't knock your master into the cabbage patch,
my name's not Hermeros. You can holler for Jupiter on
Olympus as loud as you like, and it won't help you
one little bit. By god, I'll fix those frizzle-curls of yours,
and I'll fix your two-bit master too! You'll feel my teeth,
sonny boy. And you won't snicker then, or I don't know
who I am. No, not if your beard were made out of gold!
By god, I'll give you Athena's own anger, and that goes
for the blockhead who set you free! I never learned
geometry or criticism or hogwash of that kind, but I know
how to read words carved in stone and divide up to a
hundred, money, measure, or weights. Come on, I'll lay
you a little bet. I'll stake a piece of my silver set. You
may have learned some rhetoric in school, but let me
prove your daddy wasted his money educating you.
Ready? Then answer me this: 'I come long and I come
broad. What am I?' I'll give you a clue. One of us runs,
the other stays put. One grows bigger; the other stays
small. Well, that's you, skittering around, bustling and
gaping like a mouse in a jug. So either shut up or don't
bother your elders and betters who don't know you exist.
Or do you think I'm impressed by those phony gold rings
of yours? Swipe them from your girl? Sweet Mercury,
come down to the main square in town and try to take out
a loan. Then you'll see this plain iron ring of mine makes
plenty of credit. Hah, that finished you. You look like a
fox in the rain. By god, if I don't pull up my toga and
hound you all over town, may I fail in my business and
die broke! So help me! And isn't he something, that
professor who taught you your manners? Him a professor?
A bum, that's what he is. In my time, a teacher was
a teacher. Why, my old teacher used to say, 'Now, boys,
is everything in order? Then go straight home. No daw-
dling, no gawking on the way. And don't be sassy to your
elders.' But nowadays teachers are trash. Not worth a
damn. As for me, I'm grateful to my old teacher for
what he taught me . . ."

[59] Ascyltus was on the point of replying, but Trimalchio, charmed by his friend's eloquence, broke in first:
"Come on now. That's enough. No more hard feelings.
I want everyone feeling good. As for you, Hermeros, don't
be too hard on the boy. He's a little hotheaded, so show

him you're made of better stuff. It's the man who gives in in arguments like this who wins every time. Besides, when you were just a little bantam strutting around the yard, you were all cockadoodledoo and no damn sense. So let bygones be bygones. Come on, everybody, smile! The rhapsodes are going to perform for us now."

Immediately a troupe of rhapsodes burst into the room, all banging away on their shields with spears. Trimalchio hoisted himself up on his pillows and while the rhapsodes were gushing out their Greek poetry with the usual bombast, he sat there reading aloud in Latin. At the end there was a brief silence; then Trimalchio asked us if we knew the scene from Homer the rhapsodes had just recited. "Well," he said, "I'll tell you. You see, there were these two brothers, Ganymede and Diomedes. Now they had this sister called Helen, see. Well, Agamemnon eloped with her and Diana left a deer as a fill-in for Helen. Now this poet called Homer describes the battle between the Trojans and the people of a place called Paros, which is where Paris came from. Well, as you'd expect, Agamemnon won and gave his daughter Iphigeneia to Achilles in marriage. And that's why Ajax went mad, but here he comes in person to explain the plot himself."

At this the rhapsodes burst into cheers, the slaves went scurrying about and promptly appeared with a barbecued calf, with a cap on its head, reposing on a huge platter—it must have weighed two hundred pounds at the very least. Behind it came Trimalchio's so-called Ajax. He pulled out his sword and began slashing away at the calf, sawing up and down, first with the edge and then with the flat of his blade. Then with the point of the sword he neatly skewered the slices of veal he had cut and handed them around to the astounded guests.

[60] Our applause for this elaborate tour de force, however, was abruptly cut short. For all at once the coffered ceiling began to rumble and the whole room started to shake. I jumped up in terror, expecting that some acrobat was about to come swinging down through the roof. The other guests, equally frightened, lay there staring at the roof as though they were waiting for a herald from heaven. Suddenly the paneling slid apart and down through the fissure in the ceiling an immense circular hoop, probably knocked off some gigantic cask, began slowly to descend. Dangling from the hoop were chaplets of gold and little jars of perfume, all, we were informed, presents for us to

66

take home. I filled my pockets and then, when I looked back at the table, saw a tray garnished with little cakes; in the center stood a pastry statuette of Priapus with the usual phallus propping up an apron loaded with fruits and grapes of every variety. You can imagine how greedily we all grabbed, but then a fresh surprise sent us off again into fresh laughter. For at the slightest touch the cakes and fruit all squirted out jets of liquid saffron, splattering our faces with the smelly stuff. Naturally enough, the use of the sacred saffron made us conclude that this course must be part of some religious rite, so we all leaped to our feet and shouted in chorus, "LONG LIVE THE EMPEROR, FATHER OF OUR COUNTRY!" Even this act of homage, however, failed to prevent some of the guests from pilfering the fruit and stuffing their napkins full. And I, of course, was among the chief offenders, thinking nothing in this world too good to fill the pockets of my Giton.

Meanwhile three slaves dressed in snowy tunics had made their entrance. Two of them set out Trimalchio's household gods, small statues with the usual gold medallion of the owner on the chest. The third boy brought around a bowl of wine and solemnly intoned a prayer to the gods for blessings on the house and guests. The names of his household gods, Trimalchio told us, were Fat Profit, Good Luck, and Large Income. And because we saw all the other guests piously kissing Trimalchio's medallion, we felt embarrassed not to do likewise. [61] We then offered our congratulations to our host and wished him the best of health and soundness of mind.

Trimalchio now turned to his old friend Niceros. "You used to be better company, my friend," he said, "but now you're solemn and glum, and I don't know why. But if you'd like to make your host happy, why not tell us the story of your famous adventure?"

Niceros was delighted to have been singled out. "So help me," he said, "but may I never earn a thing, if I'm not ready to burst at your kind words. Well, here goes. Happiness here we come! Though I confess I'm a bit nervous our learned professors are going to laugh me down. Still, so what? I'll tell you my story and let them snicker. Better to tell a joke than be one, I say."

With these "winged words" our storyteller began. "When I was still a slave, we used to live in a narrow little street about where Gavilla's house stands now. There the gods decreed that I should fall in love with the wife

67

of the tavernkeeper Terentius. You remember Melissa, don't you? Came from Tarentum and a buxom little package, if ever I saw one. But, you know, I loved her more for her moral character than her body. Whatever I wanted, she gladly supplied, and we always went halves. I gave her everything I had, and she'd stow it all safely away. What's more, she never cheated.

"Well, one day, down at the villa, her husband died. Needless to say, I moved heaven and earth to get to her, for a friend in need is a friend indeed. [62] By a stroke of real luck my master had gone off to Capua to do some odds and ends of business. So I grabbed my chance and persuaded one of our guests to go with me as far as the fifth milestone. He was a soldier and strong as the devil. Well, we stumbled off at cockcrow with the moon shining down as though it were high noon. But where the road leads down between the graves, my man went off among the tombstones to do his business, while I sat by the road mumbling a song to keep my courage up and counting the graves. After a while I started looking around for him and suddenly I caught sight of him standing stark naked with all his clothes piled up on the side of the road. Well, you can imagine: I stood frozen, stiff as a corpse, my heart in my mouth. The next thing I knew he was pissing around his clothes and then, presto! he changed into a wolf. Don't think I'm making this up. I wouldn't kid you for anything. But like I was saying, he turned into a wolf, then started to howl and loped off for the woods. At first I couldn't remember where I was. Then I went to get his clothes and discovered they'd been changed into stones. By now, let me tell you, I was scared. But I pulled out my sword and slashed away at the shadows all the way to my girlfriend's house. I arrived as white as a ghost, almost at the last gasp, with the sweat pouring down my crotch and my eyes bugging out like a corpse. I don't know how I ever recovered. Melissa, of course, was surprised to see me at such an hour and said, 'If you'd only come a little earlier, you could have lent us a hand. A wolf got into the grounds and attacked the sheep. The place looked like a butchershop, blood all over. He got away in the end, but we had the last laugh. One of the slaves nicked him in the throat with a spear.'

"That finished me. I couldn't sleep a wink the rest of the night and as soon as it was light, I went tearing back home like a landlord chasing the tenants. When I reached the spot where my friend's clothing had been turned into stones, there was nothing to be seen but blood. But when I got home, I found the soldier stretched out in bed like a poleaxed bull and the doctor inspecting his neck. By now, of course, I knew he was a werewolf and you couldn't have made me eat a meal with him to save my own life. You're welcome to think what you like of my story, but may the gods strike me dead if I'm feeding you a lie."

[63] Far from doubting him, we were all dumb with astonishment. "I, for one," said Trimalchio, "wouldn't dream of doubting you. In fact, if you'll believe me, I had goosebumps all over. I know old Niceros and he's no liar. Nope, he's truth itself and never exaggerates. But now I'm going to tell you a horrible story of my own, as weird as an ass on the roof.

"When I was just a little slave with fancy curls—I've lived in the lap of luxury from my boyhood on, as coddled as they come—my master's pet slave happened to die one day. He was a jewel all right, a little pearl of perfection, clever as hell and good as good. Well, while his mother was tearing out her hair and the rest of us were helping out with the funeral, suddenly the witches started to howl. They sounded like a whole pack of hounds on the scent of a hare. Now at that time we had a slave from Cappadocia, a giant of a man, scared of nothing and strong as iron. That boy could have picked up a mad bull with one hand. Well, this fellow whips out his sword and rushes outside with his left arm wrapped in his cloak for a shield. The next thing we knew he had stabbed one of those wild women right through the guts—just about here, heaven preserve the spot! Then we heard groans and when we looked out, so help me, there wasn't a witch to be seen. Well, our big bruiser came stumbling in and collapsed on a bed. He was covered from head to toe with black and blue spots as though he'd been flogged, though we knew it was that evil hand that had touched him. We shut the door and went back to work. But when his mother went to give him a hug, she found there was nothing there but a bundle of straw. No heart, no guts, no anything. As I see it, the witches had made off with the body and left a straw dummy in its place. But it just goes to show you: there are witches and the ghouls go walking at night, turning the whole world upside down.

As for our big meathead, after the witches brought him back, he was never the same again, and died raving mad a few days later."

[64] We were, of course, dumfounded, and no less credulous than amazed. So we kissed the table and implored the spirits who walk by night to keep to themselves and leave us in peace when we went home from dinner that night.

I must admit that by this time I was beginning to see the lamps burning double and the whole room seemed to be whirling around. But Trimalchio was in splendid form and turned to another of his guests. "Come on, Plocamus," he joshed him, "won't you entertain us with a story? You used to be better company, you know. Remember those bits from the plays you used to recite and the songs you sang? Oh well, I suppose we're all getting along now and we're not what we used to be. So it goes, so it goes."

"My racing days ended," declared Plocamus, "the day I got the gout. But when I was younger, I almost got T.B. from singing so much. Remember? The dancing and the recitations and the good old times we had at the barbershop? Why, except for Apelles, I doubt the world has ever seen my equal." With that, he clapped his hand over his mouth and mumbled some hideous doggerel which he later boasted was Greek.

Not to be outdone, Trimalchio promptly launched into an imitation of a bugler. That over, he turned his attention to his pet slave, that cruddy-eyed little boy with hideously stained teeth whom he called Croesus. At the moment Croesus was busily engaged in wrapping up a disgustingly fat lapdog with a green shawl and at the same time trying to force half a loaf of bread down the poor dog's throat, though the dog was on the point of throwing up. This little tableau gave Trimalchio the brilliant idea of having Bowser, "the guardian of my hearth and home," as he expressed it, brought in. Immediately an immense mastiff on a leash was led into the room and ordered by a kick from the porter to lie down beside the table. Trimalchio tossed him several chunks of white bread. "Nobody in this whole house," he declared, "loves me as much as that mutt." Croesus, instantly jealous of this handsome praise of Bowser, dropped his lapdog to the floor and sicked him on to yap at the big dog. Bowser naturally responded by filling the room with ear-splitting barks and nearly tore Croesus' dog to pieces. The uproar continued until someone knocked the chandelier onto the table, smashing all the crystal goblets and splattering several of the guests with burning oil. Wishing to appear unruffled by the damage, Trimalchio kissed Croesus and told him to clamber up on his shoulders. This the boy promptly did, riding his master piggyback, beating him with the palms of his hands, and shrieking, "Horsey, horsey, guess how many fingers I'm holding up!" For a while the utter confusion and uproar silenced even Trimalchio. But at the first opportunity he ordered a great vat of wine to be mixed and divided among the slaves who were standing about ready to serve us. "If anyone refuses," he barked, "dump it on his head. The day's for work, the evening's for pleasure."

[65] Following this extravagant display of kindness came a course the very memory of which, if you will believe me, I still find sickening. For instead of the usual small bird or thrush, each one of us was served a plump chicken and several goose eggs sporting little pastry caps. Trimalchio insisted that we sample the eggs, saying that they were nothing but geese minus the bones. Meanwhile someone was hammering at the door and before long a carouser dressed in a splendid white robe and accompanied by a throng of slaves made his entrance. His face was dignified and stern, so stern in fact that I took him for the praetor, slammed my bare feet onto the cold floor and made ready to run for it. But Agamemnon laughed at my fright and said, "Relax, you idiot, it's only Habinnas. He's an official of the imperial cult and a mason by trade. They say he makes first-rate tombstones."

Somewhat reassured, I sat down again but continued to observe Habinnas' entrance with mounting amazement. He was already half-drunk and was propping himself up by holding on to his wife's shoulders with both hands. He was literally draped in garlands of flowers and a stream of perfumed oil was running down his forehead and into his eyes. When he reached the place reserved for the praetor, he sat down and called for wine and warm water. Trimalchio was delighted to see his friend in such spirits and called for bigger glasses before asking him how he had eaten.

"Only one thing was missing," Habinnas smiled, "and that was you. My heart was really here the whole time. But, by god, Scissa did it up brown. She put on one fine

71

spread for that poor slave's funeral, I'll say that for her. What's more, she set him free after his death. And what with the 5 per cent tax, I'll bet that gesture cost her a pretty penny. The slave himself was valued at about two thousand. Still, it was very nice, though it cut across my grain to have to pour out half my drinks as an offering to the poor boy's bones."

[66] "But what did they give you to eat?" Trimalchio pressed him.

"If I can remember, I'll tell you," said Habinnas. "But my memory's so bad these days, I sometimes can't even remember my own name. Let's see, first off we had some roast pork garnished with loops of sausage and flanked with more sausages and some giblets done to a turn. And there were pickled beets and some wholewheat bread made without bleach. I prefer it to white, you know. It's better for you and less constipating too. Then came a course of cold tart with a mixture of some wonderful Spanish wine and hot honey. I took a fat helping of the tart and scooped up the honey generously. Then there were chickpeas and lupins, no end of filberts, and an apple apiece. I took two apples and I've got one wrapped up in my napkin here. If I forgot to bring a little present to my pet slave, I'd be in hot water. And oh yes, my wife reminds me: the main course was a roast of bearmeat. Scintilla was silly enough to try some and almost chucked up her supper. But it reminds me of roast boar, so I put down about a pound of it. Besides, I'd like to know, if bears eat men, why shouldn't men eat bears? To wind up, we had some soft cheese steeped in fresh wine, a snail apiece, some tripe hash, liver in pastry boats and eggs topped with more pastry and turnips and mustard and beans boiled in the pod and—but enough's enough. Oh yes, and they passed around a dish of olives pickled in caraway, and some of the guests had the nerve to walk off with three fistfuls. But we sent the ham back untasted. [67] See here, Gaius, why isn't Fortunata eating?"

"You know how she is," said Trimalchio. "Until she's put the silver away and divided the leftovers among the servants, she won't touch even a drop of water."

"Well, if she doesn't come and eat right now," said Habinnas, "I'm leaving."

With that he started to rise and probably would have left if Trimalchio had not signaled and the whole corps of slaves shouted four or five times in chorus: "FOR-

72

TUNATA!" She promptly appeared, her dress bound up so high by a pale green sash that beneath her cherry-colored tunic I could glimpse her massive ankle-rings of twisted gold and a pair of golden slippers. She wiped her fingers on the handkerchief she wore around her neck and sat down on the couch beside Habinnas' wife, Scintilla. Scintilla clapped her hands, Fortunata kissed her and burst out, "Why, darling, it's been just ages since I've seen you!"

In this way the two women chattered on for some time. The next thing I knew Fortunata was undoing the bracelets on her grotesquely fat arms and showing them off for Scintilla to admire. Then she undid her anklets and finally her hair net, which she kept insisting was woven of pure gold. Trimalchio, who was observing this byplay with interest, ordered all her jewelry brought to him. "Gentlemen," he said, "I want you to see the chains and fetters our women load themselves with; this is how we poor bastards are bankrupted. By god, she must be wearing six and a half pounds of solid gold. Still, I must admit I've got a bracelet that weighs a good ten pounds on its own. That was the value of two or three thousandths of my profits for the year, the same amount I give to Mercury as the patron-god of business." To prove his boast, he ordered a pair of scales brought in and the weights passed around for us to test. For her part, Scintilla was not to be outdone and took off the large locket which she wore around her neck and called her "lucky piece." Out of it she drew a pair of golden earrings and handed them over for Fortunata's inspection. "They're a present from my husband," she said. "Thanks to his generosity, no woman on earth has a finer pair."

"Generosity, my ass," snorted Habinnas. "You'd pester the life out of me to get a couple of glass beans. If I had a daughter, so help me, I'd have her ears chopped off. If it weren't for the women, things would be as cheap as dirt. But money—they waste it like water. Swallow it cold and good and piss it hot and useless."

By this time both the women were high and sat there giggling and exchanging little hugs and kisses, Fortunata boasting about her abilities as a housekeeper and Scintilla complaining of her husband's favorites and his indifference to her. At one point during this tender scene Habinnas rose stealthily to his feet, tiptoed over behind their couch and, grabbing Fortunata by the knees, toppled her over backwards onto the couch. As she fell her tunic slipped up above her knees. Fortunata gave a piercing shriek, threw herself into Scintilla's arms and tried to hide her blushes in her handkerchief.

[68] Once the confusion had died down, Trimalchio ordered the dessert brought on. The servant immediately removed not merely the dirty dishes but the tables themselves and replaced them with fresh ones. The floor was sprinkled with saffron sawdust and powdered mica, something I had never seen used for this purpose before. "Behold your dessert, gentlemen, these fresh tables," said Trimalchio. "I've made a clean sweep of everything, and that's all you get. That's what you deserve; that's your dessert. Haw, haw. But if there's still anything in the kitchen worth eating, boys, bring it on." Meanwhile an Alexandrian slave was passing us hot water for our wine and at the same time doing an imitation of a nightingale, but Trimalchio kept muttering, "Change that stinking tune." Then the slave seated at Habinnas' feet and clearly acting on his master's orders started to chant a passage from Vergil, the one beginning:

Meanwhile Aeneas' fleet still rode the heavy swell . . .

Altogether it was the most atrocious sound that ever fell on my ears. Not only was his pronunciation barbarous, a kind of sing-song rising and falling of the pitch, but he also jumbled in verses from some obscene farce, so that for the first time in my life Vergil actually jarred on me. At the end, however, Habinnas clapped enthusiastically and said: "You wouldn't believe it, but he's never had any formal training. I sent him off to learn from the hawkers at the fairs, and he can't be beat at imitating muledrivers and barkers. And he's real smart, does everything: makes shoes, cooks, bakes . . . In fact, he'd be perfect if he didn't have two bad points: he's been circumcised and he snores. He's cross-eyed too, but I don't mind that. Venus has a bit of a squint, they say. And I bought him for next to nothing . . ."

[69] "You haven't mentioned all the little bugger's tricks," broke in Scintilla angrily. "He's a little pimp and a fairy, that's what he is, and someday I'll see he's branded for it."

Trimalchio guffawed at this. "Come on, Scintilla, don't be jealous. We know what the score is with you too. And why not, I'd like to know. Cross my heart and hope to

74

die, if I didn't have a few tussles in the sheets with my old master's wife too. In fact, the old man got suspicious, so much so that he shipped me off to a farm in the country. But stop wagging, tongue, and I'll give you some bread to munch."

At this point that damned slave of Habinnas, obviously under the impression that we had been praising him, pulled a clay lamp with a spout out of his tunic and for a full half hour sat there mimicking a bugler while Habinnas hummed and fiddled his lower lip up and down in a kind of jew's harp accompaniment. Then, to crown all this, the slave stepped out before us all and first parodied with two straws the flutists at the plays and next, waving a whip and twisting himself in his cloak, did an imitation of a muledriver. Habinnas called him over finally, gave him a kiss and a glass of wine and said, "Nice work, Massa. I'll see that you get a pair of shoes for this."

This deadly entertainment would never have ended if the servants had not brought on another course, consisting of pastry thrushes with raisin and nut stuffing, followed by quinces with thorns stuck in them to resemble sea urchins. We could have put up with these dishes, if the last and most sickening course of all had not killed our appetites completely. When it was first brought in, we took it for a fat goose surrounded by fish and little birds of all kinds. But Trimalchio declared, "My friends, everything you see on that platter has been made from one and the same substance." I, of course, not the man to be deceived by appearances, had to turn and whisper to Agamemnon, "I'd be very surprised if everything there hadn't been made out of plain mud or clay. At the Carnival in Rome, I've seen whole meals made from stuff like that."

[70] I was still whispering when Trimalchio said, "As surely as I hope to get richer—but not fatter, please god— my cook baked all that junk out of roast pork. In fact, I doubt if there's a more valuable chef in the whole world. Just say the word, and he'll whip you up a fish out of sowbelly, pigeons out of bacon, doves from ham and chicken from pigs' knuckles. That's why I've named him Daedalus, and it suits him to a T. And because he's an inventor and a genius, I've brought him back some fine cutlery from Rome." He then ordered the knives brought in and passed around for us to admire and inspect. He also gave us permission to test the blades on the stubble of our cheeks.

Suddenly two slaves came rushing in looking as though they'd had an argument while drawing water at the well; at least they were carrying large jars on their backs and were obviously furious with each other. Trimalchio offered to act as arbiter of their argument but they refused to abide by his decision and began to pummel each other with their sticks. We were appalled by this drunken insolence but nonetheless kept our eyes glued to the fight. Suddenly we noticed that oysters and mussels were sloshing over from the jugs and a slave caught them as they fell and handed them around in a dish. Unwilling to be outstripped in extravagance, the clever chef matched the oysters by bringing around hot buttered snails on a silver grill and singing all the time in a hideously dismal, quavering voice.

What happened next was an extravagance so fantastic that I am almost embarrassed to mention it. However, young slaves with long flowing curls came around to each of us in turn, wreathed our legs and ankles with garlands of flowers and anointed our feet with perfume from a silver bowl. Then a generous amount of this same perfume was poured into the oil lamps and even into the wine bowl.

By now Fortunata was almost desperate to dance and Scintilla was clapping her hands even more frequently than she opened her mouth. Suddenly Trimalchio had an idea. "You there, Philargyrus," he called out to a slave, "I know you're a fan of the Greens in the races, but come and sit with us anyway. You too, Cario, and tell your wife to do the same." Well, you can imagine what happened. The dining room was by now so packed with slaves that in the rush for seats the guests were almost shoved bodily from the couches. For my part, I had to endure seeing the cook—the one who had made the goose out of pork and who reeked of pickles and hot sauce—installed just above me on the couch. Worst of all, not content with a place at the table, he had to do an imitation of the tragic actor Ephesus and then had the brass to bet his master that the Greens would win the next race in the Circus.

[71] But Trimalchio was charmed by the challenge. "My friends," he brayed, "slaves are human too. They drink the same mother's milk that we do, though an evil fate grinds them down. But I swear that it won't be long —if nothing happens to me—before they all taste the

76

good water of freedom. For I plan to free them all in my will. To Philargyrus here I leave a farm and his woman. Cario inherits a block of flats and the tax on his freedom and his bed and bedding. To my dear Fortunata I leave everything I have, and I commend her to the kindness of my friends. But I'm telling you the contents of my will so my whole household will love me as much when I'm still alive as after I'm dead."

Once the slaves heard this, of course, they burst out with cheers and effusive thanks. But Trimalchio suddenly began to take the whole farce quite seriously and ordered his will brought out and read aloud from beginning to end while the slaves sat there groaning and moaning. At the close of the reading, he turned to Habinnas. "Well, old friend, will you make me my tomb exactly as I order it? First, of course, I want a statue of myself. But carve my dog at my feet, and give me garlands of flowers, jars of perfume and every fight in Petraites' career. Then, thanks to your good offices, I'll live on long after I'm gone. In front, I want my tomb one hundred feet long, but two hundred feet deep. Around it I want an orchard with every known variety of fruit tree. You'd better throw in a vineyard too. For it's wrong, I think, that a man should concern himself with the house where he lives his life but give no thought to the home he'll have forever. But above all I want you to carve this notice:

THIS MONUMENT DOES NOT PASS INTO
THE POSSESSION OF MY HEIRS.

In any case I'll see to it in my will that my grave is protected from damage after my death. I'll appoint one of my ex-slaves to act as custodian to chase off the people who might come and crap on my tomb. Also, I want you to carve me several ships with all sail crowded and a picture of myself sitting on the judge's bench in official dress with five gold rings on my fingers and handing out a sack of coins to the people. For it's a fact, and you're my witness, that I gave a free meal to the whole town and a cash handout to everyone. Also make me a dining room, a frieze maybe, but however you like, and show the whole town celebrating at my expense. On my right I want a statue of Fortunata with a dove in her hand. And oh yes, be sure to have her pet dog tied to her girdle. And don't forget my pet slave. Also I'd like huge jars of wine, well stoppered so the wine won't slosh out. Then sculpt me a broken vase with a little boy sobbing out his heart over it. And in the middle stick a sundial so that anyone who wants the time of day will have to read my name. And how will this do for the epitaph?

HERE LIES GAIUS POMPEIUS TRIMALCHIO
MAECENATIANUS,
VOTED IN ABSENTIA AN OFFICIAL OF THE
IMPERIAL CULT.
HE COULD HAVE BEEN REGISTERED
IN ANY CATEGORY OF THE CIVIL SERVICE AT ROME
BUT CHOSE OTHERWISE.
PIOUS AND COURAGEOUS,
A LOYAL FRIEND,
HE DIED A MILLONAIRE,
THOUGH HE STARTED LIFE WITH NOTHING.
LET IT BE SAID TO HIS ETERNAL CREDIT
THAT HE NEVER LISTENED TO PHILOSOPHERS.
PEACE TO HIM.
FAREWELL.

[72] At the end he burst into tears. Then Fortunata started wailing, Habinnas began to cry, and every slave in the room burst out sobbing as though Trimalchio were dying then and there. The whole room throbbed and pulsed to the sound of mourning. I was almost in tears myself, when Trimalchio suddenly cried, "We all have to die, so let's live while we're waiting! Come on, everybody, smile, be happy. We'll all go down to the bath for a dip. The water's hot as an oven."

"Hurrah!" shouted Habinnas. "We'll make one day do the work of two!" With that he leaped up in his bare feet and ran after Trimalchio who was clapping his hands with approval and excitement.

I turned to Ascyltus. "Well, what do you think? As for me, the mere sight of a bath would finish me off."

"Pretend to go along," he whispered back, "and when they head for the baths, we'll make off in the confusion."

Agreed on our strategy, we followed Giton's lead through the portico to the main entrance. There, however, we were given a deafening welcome by the chained watchdog, and his furious barking and growling so terrified Ascyltus that he tumbled backwards into the fishpond. The mere painting of that same watchdog had nearly been my ruin earlier, and the real thing frightened me so

78

horribly that, between my fear and my drunkenness, I managed to fall into the pool myself while trying to haul Ascyltus out. Fortunately for us the porter soon appeared, which somewhat calmed the dog. Finally the porter succeeded in dragging us both, wet and shivering, out of the pool to terra firma. Meanwhile Giton had prudently made friends with the dog by tossing him all the tidbits we'd carefully saved from supper, and bribed by these offerings, the dog had finally stopped barking. Utterly soaking and shaking all over, we asked the porter to open the gate and let us out. "You're badly mistaken, gentlemen," he replied, "if you think you can leave by the same way you came. No guest in this house ever goes out by the same door again. There's one way in and another way out."

[73] So what were we poor devils to do now, trapped in this strange labyrinth of a place? As it was, we would have given anything in the world to be standing in a hot bath. At last, however, we succeeded in persuading the porter to lead us to the baths. There we stripped off our soaking clothes and went in, leaving Giton at the entrance so he could dry our clothes over the bath furnace.

The bath itself was narrow and shaped like a coldwater cistern, and we found Trimalchio standing in the middle of the pool. But even here there was no escape from his revolting bragging. As for himself, he was saying, he preferred to bathe in private, away from the crowd. In this very spot, moreover, there once used to be a bakery which he had bought out, etc., etc. Finally when simple exhaustion forced him to sit down, he became fascinated by the weird acoustics of the vaulted room and began in a drunken bass to murder some of Menecrates' songs. At least I was told by those who pretended to understand his gibberish that they belonged to Menecrates' repertoire. Meanwhile some of the other guests were cavorting around the edge of the pool and screeching out popular songs. Others, holding their hands behind their backs, were trying to pick up rings from the floor with their teeth, and still others, kneeling down on the ground, were attempting to arch themselves backward until they touched their toes. Leaving the drunkards to their games, we went on ahead and sampled the hot bath which had been drawn for Trimalchio.

In no time at all the water had cleared the wine fumes from our heads, and we were taken into a second dining room where Fortunata had laid out some of her prize possessions. There was a number of curious lamps, but I particularly remember several figurines of fishermen in bronze and some tables of solid silver covered with gilded goblets into which fresh wine was being strained before our eyes. "My friends," said Trimalchio, apropos of nothing, "my pet slave is having his first shave today. He's a good boy and a model of thrift. So let's celebrate. We'll drink until dawn!"

[74] Pat to these last words, a cock ominously crowed somewhere. Alarmed by the coincidence, Trimalchio superstitiously ordered the servants to pour some wine under the table and even to sprinkle the lamps with wine. Then he slipped his ring from his left hand to his right and said, "Buglers don't bugle for kicks, and that cockcrow means there's a fire nearby or somebody's died. Don't let it be bad luck for us, please heaven. Whoever fetches me that calamity-crowing rooster first, gets a fat reward." In half a minute, somebody had brought in the rooster from somewhere, and Trimalchio promptly ordered it cooked. The chef, Daedalus, that culinary genius who had whisked up birds and fish from the leg of pork, beheaded the bird and tossed it into a pot. And while the cook drew off the boiling broth, Fortunata ground up the pepper in a little wooden mill.

We were sampling this unexpected snack, when Trimalchio suddenly remembered that the servants had not yet eaten. "What?" he roared, "you haven't eaten yet? Then off with you. Go eat and send in another shift to take your places." So a fresh shift of slaves soon appeared at the door, all shouting, "Greetings, Gaius!" while the first shift went out with a cry of "Goodbye, Gaius!"

At this moment an incident occurred on which our little party almost foundered. Among the incoming slaves there was a remarkably pretty boy. Trimalchio literally launched himself upon him and, to Fortunata's extreme annoyance, began to cover him with rather prolonged kisses. Finally, Fortunata asserted her rights and began to abuse him. "You turd!" she shrieked, "you hunk of filth." At last she used the supreme insult: "Dog!" At this Trimalchio exploded with rage, reached for a wine cup and slammed it into her face. Fortunata let out a piercing scream and covered her face with trembling hands as though she'd just lost an eye. Scintilla, stunned and shocked, tried to comfort her sobbing friend in her arms, while a slave solicitously applied a glass of cold water to her livid cheek. Fortunata herself hunched over the glass heaving and sobbing.

But Trimalchio was still shaking with fury. "Doesn't that slut remember what she used to be? By god, I took her off the sale platform and made her an honest woman. But she blows herself up like a bullfrog. She's forgotten how lucky she is. She won't remember the whore she used to be. People in shacks shouldn't dream of palaces, I say. By god, if I don't tame that strutting Cassandra, my name isn't Trimalchio! And to think, sap that I was, that I could have married an heiress worth half a million. And that's no lie. Old Agatho, who sells perfume to the lady next door, slipped me the word: 'Don't let your line die out, old boy,' he said. But not me. Oh no, I was a good little boy, nothing fickle about me. And now I've gone and slammed the axe into my shins good and proper.— But someday, slut, you'll come scratching at my grave to get me back! And just so you understand what you've done, I'll remove your statue from my tomb. That's an order, Habinnas. No sir, I don't want any more domestic squabbles in my grave. And what's more, just to show her I can dish it out too, I won't have her kissing me on my deathbed."

[75] After this last thunderbolt, Habinnas begged him to calm himself and forgive her. "None of us is perfect," he said, "we're men, not gods." Scintilla burst into tears, called him her dear dear Gaius and implored him by everything holy to forgive Fortunata. Finally, even Trimalchio began to blubber. "Habinnas," he whined, "as you hope to make a fortune, tell me the truth; if I've done anything wrong, spit right in my face. So I admit I kissed the boy, not because of his looks, but because he's a good boy, a thrifty boy, a boy of real character. He can divide up to ten, he reads at sight, he's saved his freedom price from his daily allowance and bought himself an armchair and two ladles out of his own pocket. Now doesn't a boy like that deserve his master's affection? But Fortunata says no.—Is that your idea, you high-stepping bitch? Take my advice, vulture, and keep your own nose clean. Don't make me show my teeth, sweetheart, or you'll feel my anger. You know me. Once I make up my mind, I'm as stubborn as a spike in wood.

"But the hell with her. Friends, make yourselves comfortable. Once I used to be like you, but I rose to the top by my ability. Guts are what make the man; the rest is garbage. I buy well, I sell well. Others have different notions. But I'm like to bust with good luck.—You slut, are you still blubbering? By god, I'll give you something to blubber about.

"But like I was saying, friends, it's through my business sense that I shot up. Why, when I came here from Asia, I stood no taller than that candlestick there. In fact, I used to measure myself by it every day; what's more, I used to rub my mouth with lamp oil to make my beard sprout faster. Didn't do a bit of good, though. For fourteen years I was my master's pet. But what's the shame in doing what you're told to do? But all the same, if you know what I mean, I managed to do my mistress a favor or two. But mum's the word: I'm none of your ordinary blow-hards.

[76] "Well, then heaven gave me a push and I became master in the house. I was my master's brains. So he made me joint heir with the emperor to everything he had, and I came out of it with a senator's fortune. But we never have enough, and I wanted to try my hand at business. To cut it short, I had five ships built. Then I stocked them with wine—worth its weight in gold at the time—and shipped them off to Rome. I might as well have told them to go sink themselves since that's what they did. Yup, all five of them wrecked. No kidding. In one day old Neptune swallowed down a cool million. Was I licked? Hell, no. That loss just whetted my appetite as though nothing had happened at all. So I built some more ships, bigger and better and a damn sight luckier. No one could say I didn't have guts. But big ships make a man feel big himself. I shipped a cargo of wine, bacon, beans, perfume and slaves. And then Fortunata came through nicely in the nick of time: sold her gold and the clothes off her back and put a hundred gold coins in the palm of my hand. That was the yeast of my wealth. Besides, when the gods want something done, it gets done in a jiffy. On that one voyage alone, I cleared about five hundred thousand. Right away I bought up all my old master's property. I built a house, I went into slave-trading and cattle-buying. Everything I touched just grew and grew like a honeycomb. Once I was worth more than all the people in my home town put together, I picked up my winnings and pulled out. I retired from trade and started lending money to ex-slaves. To tell the truth, I was tempted to quit for keeps, but on the advice of an astrologer who'd just come to town, I decided to keep my hand in. He was a Greek,

fellow by the name of Serapa, and clever enough to set up as consultant to the gods. Well, he told me things I'd clean forgotten and laid it right on the line from A to Z. Why, that man could have peeked into my tummy and told me everything except what I'd eaten the day before. You'd have thought he'd lived with me all his life.

[77] "Remember what he said, Habinnas? You were there, I think, when he told my fortune. 'You have bought yourself a mistress and a tyrant,' he said, 'out of your own profits. You are unlucky in your friends. No one is as grateful to you as he should be. You own vast estates. You nourish a viper in your bosom.' There's no reason why I shouldn't tell you, but according to him, I have thirty years, four months, and two days left to live. And soon, he said, I am going to receive an inheritance. Now if I could just add Apulia to the lands I own, I could die content.

"Meanwhile, with Mercury's help, I built this house. As you know, it used to be a shack; now it's a shrine. It has four dining rooms, twenty bedrooms, two marble porticoes, an upstairs dining room, the master bedroom where I sleep, the nest of that viper there, a fine porter's lodge, and guestrooms enough for all my guests. In fact, when Scaurus came down here from Rome, he wouldn't put up anywhere else, though his father has lots of friends down on the shore who would have been glad to have him. And there are lots of other things I'll show you in a bit. But take my word for it: money makes the man. No money and you're nobody. But big money, big man. That's how it was with yours truly: from mouse to millionaire.

"In the meantime, Stichus," he called to a slave, "go and fetch out the clothes I'm going to be buried in. And while you're at it, bring along some perfume and a sample of that wine I'm having poured on my bones."

[78] Stichus hurried off and promptly returned with a white grave-garment and a very splendid robe with a broad purple stripe. Trimalchio told us to inspect them and see if we approved of the material. Then he added with a smile, "See to it, Stichus, that no mice or moths get into them, or I'll have you burned alive. Yes sir, I'm going to be buried in such splendor that everybody in town will go out and pray for me." He then unstoppered a jar of fabulously expensive spikenard and had us all

anointed with it. "I hope," he chuckled, "I like this perfume as much after I'm dead as I do now." Finally he ordered the slaves to pour the wine into the bowl and said, "Imagine that you're all present at my funeral feast."

The whole business had by now become absolutely revolting. Trimalchio was obviously completely drunk, but suddenly he had a hankering for funeral music too and ordered a brass band sent into the dining room. Then he propped himself on piles of cushions and stretched out full length along the couch. "Pretend I'm dead," he said, "say something nice about me." The band blared a dead march, but one of the slaves belonging to Habinnas—who was, incidentally, one of the most respectable people present —blew so loudly that he woke up the entire neighborhood. Immediately the firemen assigned to that quarter of town, thinking that Trimalchio's house was on fire, smashed down the door and rushed in with buckets and axes to do their job. Utter confusion followed, of course, and we took advantage of the heaven-sent opportunity, gave Agamemnon the slip, and rushed out of there as though the place were really in flames.

VI

GITON, ASCYLTUS, AND I AGAIN

[79] We had no torch to light us on our way as we wandered, and the lateness of the hour—it was now the dead of night—precluded all hope of meeting someone with a light. Worse still, we were drunk and so unfamiliar with the area that even in broad daylight we would have lost our way. So for nearly an hour we stumbled about, dragging our bleeding feet over the shards and splinters of broken crockery scattered along the streets, and it was only Giton's remarkable act of foresight which saved us in the end. Terrified of getting lost even in daylight, the boy had shrewdly blazed every column and pilaster along our route with chalk, and now, even through the pitch blackness, the blazings shone brightly enough to keep us on our path. At last we reached the inn, only to find that our ordeal was not yet over. For the old landlady had spent the night getting drunk with her boarders and I

doubt she would have stirred even if you set the bed on fire. Indeed, we would have been doomed to spending the night on the doorstep if one of Trimalchio's agents had not happened to come by with a convoy of ten wagons. For a short time he pounded and hammered at the door; then, getting no answer, he smashed it down and we entered through the breach.

> O gods in heaven, what a night we kept,
> how soft the bed! Together warmed, we slept
> so twined in love, so crossed upon a kiss,
> it seemed his soul was mine and mine was his.
> Goodbye, I thought, to every grief of man.
> Farewell, all care!
> —That night my doom began.

Alas, I boasted of my happiness too soon. For the instant my drunken hands relaxed their grip on Giton, Ascyltus, that wizard of my destruction, ravished the boy away in the darkness to his own bed and took his pleasure of another man's love. Whether Giton felt nothing at all, or merely pretended not to notice, I do not know; but all night long, oblivious of every moral law, every human right, he lay with Ascyltus in adulterous embrace. Waking, I went groping with my hand for the boy's body in the bed and found, O gods, my treasure stolen! For one instant—if the word of a lover can be believed—I was tempted to run myself through with my sword and join, as the poets say,

> that sleep I slept to the endless sleep of death.

But in the end prudence prevailed. I slapped Giton awake, and fixing Ascyltus with a look of terrible fury, I cried, "Since, in your perversity, you have broken your promise and trampled upon our friendship, pack your belongings and leave. Go stain some other bed with your adulteries."

He made no objection, and we divided our spoils with painstaking fairness. Then he said: "Very well. Now we split the boy."

[80] I took this as merely some feeble parting joke, but the next thing I knew he had wrenched out his sword with fratricidal fury. "No longer, miser," he cried, "shall you hunch over your treasure in lonely lust. Either give me my share, or I'll cut off my piece with my sword in revenge."

85

I pulled out my sword, threw my cloak about my arm and prepared to give battle. Leaping between us as we raved, poor Giton took us by the knees in turn, and with the tears streaming down his face implored us not to let that humble tavern witness a new Thebaid, nor to soil with each other's blood the sanctity of a glorious friendship. "If you must have murder," he cried, "behold, I offer you my throat, bared to your blow; plunge your swords home; kill me, for it was on my account that you broke your word as friends."

Touched by this pitiful entreaty, we put our swords away. For his part, Ascyltus promptly proposed a solution to our problem. "Let the boy," he said, "follow the one he prefers. Let him have a free choice of his own lover." Convinced that a relationship as old as Giton's and mine was like a bond of blood, unbreakable, I accepted without fear. In fact, I fairly jumped at the proposal and the decision was referred to the judge without delay. With no hesitation, without even the pretense of hesitation, the boy rose and chose—Ascyltus! Thunderstruck by this bolt from the blue, I dropped my sword and collapsed on the bed. Had I not begrudged my enemy a total triumph, I would have done away with myself then and there. Ascyltus, flushed with success, swaggered out with his winnings, leaving me, once the dearest of his friends, the companion of his every joy and sorrow, alone with my anguish and despair, in a strange land, dejected.

> Friendship lasts while there's profit in the name.
> The dice are fickle; fortune spins about.
> But oh, my smiling friends of better days,
> where was your love, when my luck ran out?

> The comic actors strut the stage, bow and grin.
> The cast: old Moneybags, Father and Son.
> The farce ends, the smiles come off, revealing
> the true face below, the bestial, leering one.

[*81*] My suicidal frenzy soon vanished. But fearing that Agamemnon's assistant, Menelaus, might come up and find me in my room alone and so compound my miseries, I packed my possessions and went with my grief to a lonely lodging house along the shore. There, for three days I shut myself up alone, tasting over and over again all my wrench-

ing loneliness and humiliation. Again and again I beat my
breast; my heaving lungs were weak from sobbing and my
sighs and groans rose so frequently and so deeply that I
could barely give voice to my grief. Over and over again
I cried aloud:

"O gods, why could not the earth have swallowed me
up, or this sea that rages so wildly even against the innocent? Was it for this that I fled from justice, that
I deserted the ring and murdered my host? Is this the
reward of all my courage and my crimes—to be abandoned,
an outcast, a beggar, in a cheap inn in a Greek town?
And who is the author of my loneliness? A young man
polluted with every perversion and vice; a man who by his
own admission deserves to be banished; who paid for
his freedom with his debauchery and his debauchery with
his freedom; whose body is bought as one buys a ticket;
who was treated like a woman even by those who knew
him to be a man! And what of his partner in crime? A
little boy who gave up his trousers for skirts; whose mother
persuaded him never to be a man; who played the part
of a girl in a prison for slaves; who broke his word,
destroyed a friendship sanctified by time and usage to go
romping in another bed, and then—O unspeakable shame!
—sold his all, like a whore, for one night's work! And
now the lovers lie all night tangled in each other's arms,
and when their lust has run its course, perhaps they mock
me, jeering at my loneliness. By god, but they shall pay
me for it! Either I am no free man, or they shall pay me
for this crime with their own lives!"

[82] With that, I belted on my sword and sat down to a
good meal as a precaution against losing my battle through
simple weakness. Then I dashed down into the street and
began to race like a madman up and down through the
arcades and porticoes. My face was taut with fury, images
of blood and slaughter kept pounding through my head,
and my hand clutched convulsively at the hilt of my
sword. Suddenly some soldier—though deserter or plain
thief was probably what he was—caught sight of me. "You
there, soldier," he shouted, "what's your regiment? Who's
your commanding officer?" With splendid presence of
mind, I promptly supplied him with a fictitious regiment
and imaginary officers. "Since when," he asked me, "do
soldiers in your army do their marching in white shoes?"
At this my confusion and trembling gave the show away
and he ordered me to surrender my sword to him and to

87

look sharper next time. In this way, cheated of both my sword and my revenge, I made my way back to my room. Gradually, however, my temper began to cool and in a short time I was feeling quite grateful to him for his high-handedness in taking away my sword.

❦

Knee-deep in water, the ripe fruit dangling overhead,
　　poor Tantalus stands, devoured by his need.
So the miser too, I think, must look, licking
　　with dry tongue, unsatisfied, the taste of greed.

❦

There is little point in expecting much of your own projects, when Fate has projects of her own.

VII

I MEET EUMOLPUS

[*83*] In this way I entered a gallery filled with a superb collection of paintings of remarkable range and variety. There were several by Zeuxis, still untouched by the injury of time, and two or three sketches by Protogenes, so vivid and true to life that I touched them with almost a shudder of admiration. There was also a piece by Apelles, the one the Greeks call the "One-legged Goddess," before which I knelt with a feeling of almost religious veneration. The human figures were all executed with such striking natural-ness and exquisite delicacy that it seemed as though the artist had painted their souls as well. In one of them the eagle was ravishing the shepherd of Ida away to heaven; another showed Hylas, splendid in his innocence, reject-ing the advances of the passionate Naiad. Further on, I saw Apollo cursing his hands for the murder of Hyacinth and wreathing his unstrung lyre with the blossoms of the newborn flower. But surrounded by these images of painted lovers, I cried out in lonely anguish, "So even the gods in heaven are touched by love! Jupiter himself found in the skies no goddess worthy of his passion, but came down to earth to sin; yet he at least never harmed or

injured another man. The Nymph who ravished Hylas
would have mastered her passion had she known that
Hercules would come back to reclaim his own. Apollo
made his Hyacinth live once more in the form of a flower.
And all the myths alike tell of passion satisfied without
a rival, while I have taken as my companion a traitor, a
man more cruel than Lycurgus himself."

But while I stood there telling my sorrows to the empty
air, an old man with flowing white hair entered the
gallery. From his seedy clothes and his haunted, tortured
face with its indefinable aura of greatness, I instantly
recognized him as being one of that class of writers whom
rich men despise and hate.

"I am a poet, sir," he said, introducing himself, "and
one, I like to think, of no ordinary talent, at least if prizes
and crowns of laurel are any indication of genius. Though,
needless to say, I recognize the regrettable part played
by influence and connections these days in rewarding the
unworthy."

"Then why are you so shabbily dressed?" I asked him.

"For that very reason," he replied. "Selfless devotion
to the arts has never yet made any man rich:

> Say merchant: you're talking of money.
> Say soldier, and valor is sold.
> Good money's the gigolo's meaning.
> The toady's lies are gilded with gold.
>
> But poets are poor by profession:
> alone, in their rags, in the cold,
> they stand at the grave of the arts
> and lower the Ages of Gold.

[84] No, there's no doubt about it. Any man these days
who takes a firm stand against corruption and tries to
walk the straight and narrow path promptly finds himself
hated by all those who differ from him, since no one can
afford to like what differs from himself. Those, moreover,
whose only passion in life is the making of money are
unwilling that any other profession should be more highly
regarded than their own. Therefore they persecute the
lovers of literature in every way possible in order to demonstrate their inferiority to businessmen and the makers
of money . . ."

"I don't know why, but Genius has always had Poverty as his sister."

❧

"I only wish," I said, "that the enemy who has forced me to become a celibate had the goodness to relent. But he is a veteran of vice, cleverer than the pimps themselves."

❧

[85] "When I was in Asia," Eumolpus began, "on work connected with the administration of finance there, I was billeted in a private house in Pergamum. My stay there was a delightful one. Not only were my accommodations both comfortable and civilized, but my host's son was a boy of extraordinary beauty. Under the circumstances, my strategy, as you may have guessed, was to become the boy's lover without in any way arousing the father's suspicions. So whenever the conversation at dinner happened to touch on pederasty, I affected to be so scandalized and protested so vigorously that my modesty was offended even by the mere mention of such things, that everyone, and especially the boy's mother, took me for some sort of philosophical saint. In no time at all, on the pretext of keeping possible seducers from setting foot in the house, I was soon chaperoning the boy on his way to the gymnasium, supervising his studies, and acting as his adviser and moral tutor.

❧

"One day, as it happened, we were taking our rest in the dining room, since a public holiday had cut short our studies and the fatigue that comes of too much merry-making had left us too tired even to climb upstairs to bed. Towards midnight I suddenly noticed that the boy was not sleeping. With a trembling voice I made my prayer to Venus: 'O goddess,' I whispered, 'if I can kiss this sleeping boy without his noticing it, tomorrow I will present him with a pair of doves.' Tempted by the price I put on my pleasure, the little impostor started to snore away. For my part, I crept close to him and stole several kisses. Pleased with this auspicious beginning, I rose early the next morning, brought back a pair of doves to the waiting boy, and so fulfilled my vow.

[86] "The following night the same opportunity presented itself, but this time I made a slight change in the form of my vow. 'O goddess,' I whispered, 'if I can caress this boy's body with a free hand, tomorrow I will bring him a pair of the finest fighting-cocks in the world. But he must not feel anything at all.' At this the boy himself quickly snuggled closer, half afraid, I think, that I might fall asleep before I touched him. I swiftly relieved him of his fears and with roving hands took my pleasure of his whole body, all but the supreme bliss. The following morning, to his delight, I brought him back the gift I had promised.

"Once again on the third night, I seized my chance. By this time the boy barely pretended to be asleep, and I rose and whispered in his ear: 'O immortal gods, if I may take from this sleeping boy the perfect pleasure of my dreams, I will bring him tomorrow a splendid Macedonian stallion. But on one condition only: he must not feel a thing.' Never did the boy sleep more soundly. Filling my hands with his milk-white skin, I bound my lips to his, and with one supreme effort, fulfilled my every dream. The next morning he sat eagerly waiting for me in his room. As you can perhaps imagine, it is one thing to buy doves and fighting-cocks, but quite another to buy a stallion. Besides, I was apprehensive that the sheer size of such a gift might make my generosity suspect. So I strolled about for a few hours and then came back, giving the boy nothing more than a kiss. Bewildered, he looked about everywhere, then threw his arms around my neck and said, 'Please, sir, where's the stallion?'

❧

[87] "This breach of my word, of course, shut the door against me, but it was not long before I had my way with him again. In fact, several days later, another festival gave me my opportunity once more. As soon as I heard his father snoring away, I begged the boy to make it up with me, or rather, to let me make love to him; in short, I used all those arguments which only a frustrated lover knows how to use. He was still angry, however, and to all my pleas he said nothing but, 'Go back to sleep or I'll tell my father.' But there is no refusal so final that

a determined lover cannot somehow get around it. So, quite ignoring his refrain about waking his father, I slipped into bed beside him, and after a brief and none too convincing resistance on his part, I had my way with him. Apparently this highhanded treatment did not in the least displease him. True, he reproached me for breaking my word and told me all he had suffered from the jeers of his friends to whom he had boasted of my generosity, but then he said: 'Just to show you I'm not like you, you can do it again if you want.' So we made it up, and after enjoying myself a second time at his own invitation, I fell off into a deep sleep. But the boy, with all the passive ardor of his age, was still dissatisfied even with my double proof of affection, and in a short while he prodded me awake, whispering, 'Don't you want to do it again?' The offer was by no means unwelcome and I accepted with pleasure. Finally, after a great deal of panting and sweating, I managed to oblige him and immediately dropped off to sleep, completely exhausted. In less than an hour he was pinching me again: 'Why don't we do it some more,' he asked. I was furious at being constantly reawakened and angrily turned his own words against him. 'Go back to sleep,' I cried, 'or I'll tell your father.'"

❦

[88] Somewhat comforted by this story, I began questioning my mentor about the dates of the paintings and those whose subjects escaped me. From this I went on to inquire from him how he accounted for the decadence of our own times and how it had happened that the fine arts had withered and painting had vanished almost without a trace. "It was the love of money," he replied, "that began our catastrophic decline. In earlier ages, merit and achievement were honored for themselves, the arts flowered, and there was the keenest kind of competition among men to discover any secret of Nature which might benefit posterity. Thus Democritus, for instance, extracted the essence of every known herb and then devoted the rest of his life to researches into the properties of minerals and plants. Eudoxus grew old sitting on his mountain top, painfully tracking down and recording the motions of the planets and stars, while Chrysippus, on three different occasions, dosed himself with hellebore to purge and invigorate his inventive powers. And if you

turn to the plastic arts, you find examples of the same selfless dedication. Thus Lysippus, for instance, became so utterly absorbed in the formal problems of a statue that he forgot to eat and starved to death, while Myron, whose genius it was to render the very souls of animals and men in vivid bronze and stone, left no natural heir.

"As for our own times, why, we are so besotted with drink, so steeped in debauchery, that we lack the strength even to study the great achievements of the past. One and all, we traduce the dead and slander our great tradition. We are professionals of corruption; vice is the subject we teach and learn. What, I ask you, has become of logic and dialectic? Where is astronomy now? What has become of that great and lovely highway of philosophy, once so thronged with students and amateurs? Who nowadays, tell me, goes to a temple and prays the gods to grant him the great gift of eloquence? Who asks to slake his thirst at the primal fount of philosophy? Why, even prayers for health and soundness of mind are out of fashion nowadays. Money is our only prayer. Before they even reach the temple, they're praying for cash. 'Let me bury my rich relative,' asks one; 'Let me dig up a treasure,' says another; the next one wants to come by thirty millions without even taking a risk. The Senators themselves, once the teachers of morality and religion, now vow a thousand pounds of gold to decorate the Capitoline, gilding even Jupiter himself with cash so that no one need be ashamed of his greed. So is it any wonder, young man, that painting is decadent, when men and gods alike all think an ingot of gold more beautiful than anything those poor crazy Greeks, Apelles and Phidias, ever made?

[*89*] "But I see that that painting of the Fall of Troy has caught your attention. Let me give you my own poetic commentary on the work:

THE FALL OF TROY

For ten long harvests now, by apprehension torn,
the Trojans had been besieged; old faith in Calchas fell
as time ran out, and the balance plunged, pulled down
by doubt.
        Then lo, Apollo spoke, and Ida's wooded flanks
were felled, the forest seaward dragged, and the tall trees
chopped and shaped to make a horse of war, a giant hulk,
within whose mass a cavelike hole was hollowed out.

93

Here in this caverned void, the chafing host was hid,
ten long and weary years of soldier bravery confined,
ambushed in their gift to god.

O Ilium, O my country!
At last it seemed the thousand ships had spread their sail
and fled. At last, O gods, we thought our land was free!
And this our dearest hope the votive horse confirmed,
and Sinon's lie, that mind for ruin made, that treachery
so potent for the doom of Troy.

One huge, excited throng,
we went, crowding about the horse, crying for joy,
for joy, like terror, has her tears. Our tears were joy—
which fear as quickly dried.

For the priest of Neptune,
Laocoön, hs white hair streaming loose, cried terror to the
crowd
and hurled his spear. It struck the giant belly of the horse,
but the Fates had slowed his hand; the spear glanced off,
rebounding,
and gave a credence to the Greek deceit. Once more the
priest
nerved his trembling arm, then raised his axe and struck.
Beneath the heavy blow, the body creaked and throbbed;
the soldiers locked inside groaned aloud, and the wooden
mass
hummed with an alien terror. Alas, it went unheard,
and the captive Greeks rode on, rode on to capture Troy
by fraud unparalleled.

And other portents too;
for where the sheer ridge of Tenedos usurps the sea,
the water writhed and rose, and the long swell, reverberant,
shattered the calm, as sometimes in the dead of night,
the beat of stroking oars shatters the hush upon the sea,
and the ships race on, and the marbled water, sundered
by the cleaving prow, turns froth and furrows white
beneath the slicing keel.

We turned to stare, and saw
twin serpents, a twine of writhing coils, drive on
and the water thrown against the rocks as by two ships
the waves are battered back. Their tails drummed the
water;
blazing like their eyes their great crests crowded the sea;
lightnings ruddied the waves, and beneath their breath of
flame,
the waters, seething, hissed.

94

                              Our hearts stopped dead.
The priest's two boys, two little pledges of a father's love,
stood, their hair with sacred fillets bound, upon the shore,
when suddenly the snakes enclosed them both in twisting
    loops
like flame. Each flung his hand in terror overhead;
each for the other; each moved to shield his brother,
both boys altered by their love, and when death came,
even then, each brother trembled only for the other.
Helpless, before our eyes, their father ran to help—
and piled his life on theirs. For gorged with double death,
they fell upon the priest and bore him to the ground.
    There,
between the altars, thrashing the earth in death, he lay,
the priest, a victim to the gods. And so doomed Troy
profaned her little life with death, and lost her gods.
    But now the rising moon drove on with larger light,
leading her long cortege of stars across the night.
Steeped in wine and dark, the sleeping Trojans lay,
as the Greeks undid the doors and streamed in manhood
    forth
from the cave. Each leader now made trial of his strength,
as when a mettled horse, loosed from his yoke at last,
tosses its head and mane before it bolts away.
So now, they drew their swords and set their shields in
    place
and rushed to war. One kills the Trojans where they lie,
joining that sleep they slept to the endless sleep of death.
Another lights his torch from the dying flame of the altars
and invokes the Trojan gods against the men of Troy . . ."

[90] At this moment, several of the people who were
strolling about the gallery greeted Eumolpus' epic effusion
with a volley of stones. Eumolpus, clearly no stranger to
these tributes to his talent, wrapped his head in his robes
and dashed from the temple. Fearing they might accuse
me of being a poet too, I raced after him and caught him
at the shore. "Look here," I said, "can't you rid yourself
of this loathsome disease? I've been with you for less than
two hours, but in all this time you've talked more like a
Homer than a man. No wonder people pelt you with
stones. In fact, I'm going to fill my pockets with stones
right now, and every time you start spouting, I'll bloody
your head for you."
    At this threat his face fell. "Young man," he said sadly,

"this is not the first time that this has happened to me. In fact, every time I recite in the theater, the audience gives me a similar reception. However, to make sure that there's no cause for differences between us, I'll promise to abstain for the rest of the day."

"Well, if you can manage to forego your madness for that long," I said, "then come and have dinner with me."

❦

I gave the porter of my lodging house instructions for our meager supper . . .

VIII

OLD LOVES AND NEW RIVALS

[*91*] There I caught sight of Giton, towels and scrapers in his hands, standing beside the wall, utterly desolate and forlorn. It was clear that he served Ascyltus with reluctance. But scarcely able to believe my eyes . . .

❦

Then he turned toward me, and his face glowed with sudden happiness. "Encolpius," he cried, "have pity on me. Take me away from this bloody brigand and then punish your poor repentant judge as cruelly as you like. I am so miserable now that I could die happy in the mere knowledge that it was you who wished me dead."

But afraid that someone might overhear us and foil my plans, I told him to hush and stop weeping. Then leaving Eumolpus alone in the baths—where he was spouting one of his poems—I took Giton by the hand, dragged him out through a filthy, black hole and rushed him to my room as quickly as I could. Once there, I slammed the door and threw myself on the boy, hugging him with all my strength and kissing away the tears that stained his poor cheeks. For the longest time, neither of us could speak a word, and the poor boy lay there, his lovely chest choking and heaving with sobs.

"I am so incredibly weak," I said at last, "that even though you abandoned me, I still love you. But how strange it seems that where this heart of mine was once a gaping wound, now there is not even the trace of a scar. But what excuse can you plead for giving your love to a passing stranger? How have I deserved such treatment?"

Once he sensed that, despite everything, I still loved him, his face cleared and he brightened up . . .

❦

"I laid my case before no other judge but you," I cried. "But still, I don't complain, and I'll promise to forget the past if you, for your part, will prove the sincerity of your repentance by behaving well in the future." All this, of course, I accompanied with a great flood of sighs and tears.

"Encolpius," he replied, wiping his eyes on his cloak, "I ask you, I appeal to your own memory: was it I that left you, or you that betrayed me? I admit, I confess it freely, that when I saw two armed men standing before me, I ran to the side of the stronger."

How prudently, I thought, the dear boy had acted! Again and again I kissed him to show that I forgave him, and with a huge hug declared that our friendship was born anew on a firmer footing than before.

[92] It was now dark, however, and the woman had seen to my orders for supper, when Eumolpus came pounding at the door.

"How many of you are there?" I asked, and peered out at him through a chink to see if Ascyltus had come with him. When I was quite satisfied that he was alone, I promptly opened the door.

He threw himself down on the bed. Then, noticing Giton busy at setting the table, he sat up and wagged his head. "Well, well," he laughed, "I *like* your Ganymede. Things are at last looking up today."

This lover's interest in Giton displeased me intensely, and I began to wonder whether I had taken on a second Ascyltus. Eumolpus, however, persisted. When the boy brought him a drink, he said, "You know, I like you better than the whole bathful."

He drained off the glass at a single gulp. "I don't know," he said, "when I've had a worse day of it. First of all, I was nearly flogged to death in the baths when I tried to recite a few lines of verse. You would have thought that bath was a theater the way they tossed me out. Well, I started to wander about, poking into every corner and shouting loudly for Encolpius. On the other side of the room stood a young man, stark naked—it seems he'd just lost his clothes—and bellowing away just as loudly for someone called Giton. But you know what happened? The little boys started to jeer at me and imitated my shouts as though I were completely mad, while a huge crowd gathered around the other fellow, all of them clapping their hands and gaping with admiration. As well they might, for that man had a pecker of such extraordinary length that you would have thought the man was appended to the pecker rather than the pecker to the man. What a Hercules! Why, I'll bet that fellow could start today and still be going strong tomorrow. I don't need to tell you that he soon found someone to give him a hand. Some Roman knight—notorious, I was told, for his strange tastes —threw a cloak over him as he prowled about and then led him off, doubtless anxious to savor his find in privacy. As for me, I doubt I could even have recovered my own clothes from the attendant if I hadn't found someone to vouch for me. But it shows you how much more it means in this world to have a great tool than a grand talent."

During this account, my face changed expression a dozen times. I wrinkled with pleasure at Ascyltus' troubles and scowled angrily when told of his good luck. However, I prudently held my tongue, pretending that all this had happened to total strangers, and then gave orders for supper to be served.

❧

[93] "We look with contempt on simple, available pleasures," Eumolpus observed, "and our foolish hearts, in love with trouble, hanker after the strange and the rare:

> For importing a pheasant enhances its savor:
> the rarer the bird, the finer the flavor.
> But the blazoned duck and the snow-white goose
> seem banal, seem vulgar, they're unfit for use.
> And what can compare with an African dish?
> If the fisherman drowns, that makes the fish
> exquisite, divine! But mullet's a bore.
> And the wife surrenders to mistress or whore.
> And the roses of Rome bow down to the spice,
> And our Taste is tagged with a ticket of price."

"Eumolpus," I broke in, "what about your promise that you would give up poetry for the rest of the day? The very least you could do is spare us. God knows, we never pelted you with stones. What's more, if a single one of those drunkards downstairs so much as sniffs the presence of a poet in the house, he'll rouse the neighborhood, and your damned doggerel will be the ruin of us all."

But Giton, always sensitive to the feelings of others, reproved me. It was rude of me, he said, to insult my elders. Worse, I had failed in my duty as host by spoiling with my impoliteness a dinner which had been offered in the first place out of simple kindness of heart. All this and more, each rebuke tempered by that sweetness and concern for others which harmonized so wonderfully with his physical beauty.

[94] "Happy the mother who gave birth to such a boy as you," Eumolpus exclaimed in admiration. "Be good, my son, and prosper. Ah, how rare a sight it is, this conjunction of goodness with beauty. And lest you think your kind words have been wasted, let me tell you that you have won yourself a lover. Yes, I shall laud you to the skies in my verse. I will teach you and protect you and follow behind you wherever you go. Yes, even against your will. Have no fear. Encolpius won't be offended: he loves another."

It was fortunate for Eumolpus that that thieving soldier had robbed me of my sword or I should have vented on him all my pent-up fury against Ascyltus. Giton, immediately sensing my state of mind, discreetly left the room on the pretext of fetching some water. His absence calmed me somewhat, and when I felt I had mastered my feelings, I said: "Eumolpus, I would rather that you spouted poetry than nurse such hopes as these. I am by nature an angry and a jealous man; you are a lecher. So you can see how poorly matched our natures are. Believe, if you wish, that you're dealing with a madman, but make one small concession to my madness and GET OUT!" Eumolpus, utterly bewildered by this attack, without even stopping to ask why, rushed out, first slamming and then locking the door behind him. Taking the key with him, he dashed off in pursuit of Giton, leaving me, to my astonishment, a prisoner in my own room.

Finding myself locked in, I made up my mind to hang myself then and there. Upending the heavy bed against the wall, I tied the knot and was just inserting my neck in the noose when the door was unlocked and Eumolpus walked in, followed by Giton. It was as though from the edge of the grave I had suddenly been restored to life. Giton was almost beside himself with grief. With a wild scream, he rushed to me and with both hands pinned me back against the bed. "No, Encolpius," he shrieked, "I won't let you! I won't let you die without me. I tried to kill myself earlier when I was still with Ascyltus. I looked everywhere for a sword. If I hadn't found you, I would have thrown myself over a cliff. But just to show you how easy it is to die when you want to, watch the scene you prepared for me."

With that, he snatched a razor from Eumolpus' servant, drew it once, twice, across his throat and slumped in a heap at our feet. I gave a shout of horror, fell down beside him and tried with the same razor to do away with myself. Suddenly I saw that there was not the slightest sign of a cut on Giton's throat and, stranger still, I seemed to feel no pain. Then I realized that the razor had no cutting edge, that it was, in fact, merely a practice-razor which had been purposely blunted in order to give apprentice barbers a feeling of confidence. This was why the servant had shown no alarm when the razor was ripped from the sheath and Eumolpus had not intervened in our little play of death.

[95] In the midst of this lovers' farce, the innkeeper arrived with the rest of our modest meal, and to his consternation, found us lying there, covered with filth, on the floor. "What's going on here?" he bellowed. "Are you drunk, or runaway slaves, or both? What's that bed doing propped up against the wall? What's this coil of rope for? Aha, so that's your little game, is it? You were going to slide down the rope in the dark and skip out on your rent. By god, you won't get away with those tricks here. You're not dealing with some poor old widow. No, this house belongs to Marcus Mannicius himself."

"What's that?" shouted Eumolpus, "are you trying to threaten us?" and caught him a savage blow across the face with the heel of his hand. At this, the innkeeper, half drunk from carousing with his guests, let himself go. Snatching up a clay jug, he slammed it against Eumolpus' forehead and then scampered out of the room. Eumolpus, infuriated with pain, armed himself with a great wooden candlestick, gave chase and soon avenged his bleeding head with a whole barrage of blows. Before long the entire household appeared, and a large crowd of drunken boarders as well. For my part, seizing my chance to even the score with Eumolpus, I quickly turned the key and locked him out. This revenge on my depraved rival not only pleased me but, what was more, guaranteed my enjoyment of my room and my sleep in privacy once more.

Meanwhile Eumolpus was being assailed on both sides by cooks and tenants alike. One of them kept jabbing at his eyes with a skewer loaded with steaming meat; another, snatching a fork from a bureau, stood en garde like a gladiator. But his most persistent and dangerous opponent was an old bleary-eyed hag dressed in a hideously filthy nightgown and unmatching slippers, who had led up a huge hound on a leash and was now sicking the beast against Eumolpus. But armed with his doughty candlestick, he managed to beat off his attackers.

[96] By peeking through the gaping hole left in the door when the handle was torn away, we managed to follow the whole course of the battle. I, of course, was perfectly delighted to see Eumolpus get a thrashing, while Giton, tender-hearted as ever, thought we should unlock the door and rush out to Eumolpus' defense. But I was still burning with resentment and, unable to control myself, I smashed the poor boy across the head with a sweep of my clenched knuckles. Bursting into tears, he collapsed on the bed, while I applied first one eye and then the other to the hole in the door, feasting greedily on Eumolpus' plight and mocking his screams for help. Suddenly the caretaker, Bargates, roused from his dinner, appeared on the scene in a litter—he was helpless with gout—carried by two bearers. In a furious flood of atrocious Latin, he launched out into a long tirade against drunkards and runaway slaves. Suddenly, however, he recognized Eumolpus.

"What! Is that you there, most elegant of poets?" he cried. "Damn it, clear out of here, you blasted slaves! What? They dared lift a hand against you, dear man?"

❀

"My mistress," said Bargates, "is giving me the cold treatment. And I'd be obliged if you'd do me the favor

101

of cursing her out in your verse and bringing her back to her senses."

🔻

[97] While Eumolpus and Bargates were whispering together, a public crier followed by a policeman and a fairly large crowd entered the building. Brandishing a torch which gave out far more smoke than light, he read aloud the following proclamation:

HEAR YE!
RECENTLY LOST IN THE PUBLIC BATHS:
A BOY, APPROXIMATELY SIXTEEN,
CURLY-HAIRED, ATTRACTIVE, EFFEMINATE.
ANSWERS TO THE NAME OF GITON.
A REWARD OF ONE THOUSAND PIECES OFFERED
FOR INFORMATION LEADING TO HIS RECOVERY.

Near the crier stood Ascyltus himself in a splendid rainbow-colored robe, and holding the reward on a platter in evidence of his good faith.

I instantly ordered Giton to scramble under the bed and hook his hands and feet into the webbing which supported the mattress, just as Odysseus once escaped the searching fingers of the Cyclops by clinging to the ram's belly. The boy obeyed at once; in the twinkling of an eye he had inserted his hands in the webbing with a dexterity which would have won him even Odysseus' admiration. Finally, to remove any remaining room for suspicion, I stuffed some clothing under the limp and sagging mattress so the bed would look as though it had been occupied by a man of my build, sleeping by himself.

Ascyltus, meanwhile, had searched all the other rooms and came at last to mine. There, finding the door securely bolted, his hopes began to rise. The police agent inserted the blade of his axe into the joints and twisted until the bolts sprang and gave way. Throwing myself at Ascyltus' feet, I implored him in the name of our old friendship and the many hardships we had suffered together, at least to let me see Giton before I died. Then I added for effect: "You needn't deny that you've come here to kill me, Ascyltus. Why else would you have brought an axe? Here: I bare my throat to your blow: strike, kill me. That is why you came. This search is just a screen."

102

Ascyltus denied that he bore me any grudge at all; the only thing he wanted, he said, was the return of his runaway slave. Certainly he desired no man's death, least of all the death of a suppliant. Further, far from wishing to kill me, now that our deadly argument was over, he felt for me nothing but the warmest affection.

[98] The policeman, however, was not to be put off by this exchange of kind words. Brusquely snatching a cane from the innkeeper, he jabbed away at the cracks in the walls and then started prodding beneath the bed. At each jab, Giton neatly ducked away; then holding his breath in terror he snuggled his face tightly against the bug-infested mattress.

❦

A few seconds after Ascyltus left, Eumolpus pushed aside the broken door and entered the room, his face wild with fury. "Well," he said, "that reward of a thousand pieces is mine. By god, I'm going to stop that crier on his way out and tell him you're holding Giton here. That will be my revenge, and you deserve it too."

I clasped his knees and begged him to have pity, but he was adamant. "Eumolpus," I said, "I admit you have every reason in the world to be angry and claim that reward, but first you must tell them where the boy has gone. You see, he ran away in the crowd, I can't imagine where. So do whatever you like, Eumolpus; you can even turn him over to Ascyltus, if you must. But, I beg you, in the name of heaven, bring the boy back!"

I had nearly persuaded him when Giton, unable to hold his breath any longer, sneezed three times in rapid succession, so violently that the whole bed trembled. Eumolpus whirled around and cried, "God bless you, Giton." Then, lifting the mattress, he uncovered that poor little Ulysses, so pitiful that even a starving Cyclops might have been moved to mercy.

"Well," he said, turning on me, "what do you have to say for yourself now, you liar? If the gods in heaven hadn't knocked a sign out of that poor, suspended boy, I'd be running around now from tavern to tavern like a bloody fool."

❦

Giton, however, was far more versed in the art of cajolery than I. Steeping several spiderwebs in oil, with great gentleness he stanched the bleeding cut on Eumolpus' forehead. Then, removing his own tunic, he made Eumolpus take off his tattered robe and exchange with him. Finally, seeing the poet begin to relent, he covered him with a warm poultice of kisses and hugged him tightly. "Dear father," he pleaded, "our fate is in your hands. If you love your Giton at all, help him, save him. Oh, how I wish the cruel fire would consume me or the winter sea swallow me down! For all Encolpius' crimes, I must bear the blame. I was the cause of them all. If only I were dead, you two might once again be friends . . ."

❦

[99] "For my part," Eumolpus declared, "at all times and in all places, I have lived as though the present day were my last and would never return again."

❦

With the tears streaming down my face, I begged Eumolpus to make his peace with me too. After all, I reminded him, it was simply not in the power of a lover to master his transports of jealousy. For my part, I solemnly promised neither to say nor do anything in the future which could possibly give him offense. Only let him, as a poet, that most humane of all humane vocations, cure himself of this scabrous anger, yes, efface even the scars of it from his mind. "Reflect," I cried, warming to the occasion, "how, on the rough barren uplands, the winter snows lie late and long. But where the land, tamed by human love, glisters beneath the plow, the frost falls light and vanishes away in the twinkling of an eye. So too with the anger in our hearts; it strikes deep where the spirit is harsh and gross, but glances lightly away from a civilized mind."

"True," said Eumolpus. "How true you may know by this kiss with which I now banish my anger. Now pick up your luggage, and may good fortune go with us. Follow me, or lead on yourself, if you prefer."

He was still in mid-sentence when there came a rap at the door and a sailor with a scraggly beard appeared on the threshold. "The way you dally, Eumolpus," he said, "you'd think we had time to waste." We rose immediately. Eumolpus woke his sleeping slave and ordered him to go on ahead with the luggage. Giton and I packed a duffel bag with all our worldly possessions; I made a prayer to the stars for a safe voyage, and we went aboard the boat.

IX

LICHAS AND TRYPHAENA

That night, in the quiet corner of the deck we had staked out for ourselves, I lay tossing sleeplessly and debating with my fears.

[*100*] "Encolpius, admit it," I argued with myself, "Eumolpus finds the boy attractive, and you are irked. Can this be right? Look about you, man. Why, aren't the good things of this world made for our common enjoyment, every lovely thing free for the taking? The sun shines down upon us all; the moon with her train of countless stars leads all animals alike to their common pasture. What is lovelier than water? Yet it flows for us all. Is love therefore exempt from the universal law, a bliss to be stolen and hid, and not our common reward? No, no, better to have nothing at all, unless the world envies you what you have. Besides, what do you have to fear from one rival, and an old one at that? Even if he should try to take an unfair advantage, his horrible wheezing would give him away."

All these reflections, of course, were intended to put my mind at rest, but somehow I remained stubbornly unconvinced. In the end, I buried my head in my cloak and tried to force myself asleep. But suddenly, as though Fate herself were bent on crushing what little confidence I had left, I heard a loud groan from the deck and then a man's voice angrily cry out, "By god, he won't get away with it!" My heart skipped a beat: somewhere I had heard that voice before. Then a woman's voice, shrill with indignation, exclaimed, "Oh, if I could only get my hands on Giton, what a welcome I'd give that little runaway!" Utterly unexpected, the sound of those two voices came as such a shock that Giton and I—but especially I—went white with terror. I felt as though I were being whirled

105

round and round in some awful nightmare. Finally I found my voice and, my hands shaking with fright, started tugging at Eumolpus' robes. "In god's name," I whispered, "who's the captain of this ship? Who are the passengers?" Grumpy at being wakened from sleep, he growled back, "Is this why you made us pick out a quiet spot on deck, so you could keep us awake all night with your damned questions? For all the good it will do you, the captain is Lichas from Tarentum and he's taking Tryphaena to exile in Tarentum."

[101] Those two names fell on my ears like two claps of thunder. I shuddered with terror, bared my throat and cried out, "Now, O Fortune, thou hast destroyed me quite!" Giton collapsed and lay sprawled out across my lap in a dead faint. Then the sweat came pouring out through our pores and we slowly came back to life. I threw myself at Eumolpus' feet and clasped his knees. "Mercy," I cried, "have mercy on two doomed men. I implore you, Eumolpus, in the name of our common citizenship in the Republic of Letters, despatch us with your own hand. Our hour has struck. Kill us, I beseech you, for death itself would be sweeter than the fate that awaits us."

Quite overwhelmed by this tragic appeal, Eumolpus swore by every god in heaven that he had no idea what I was talking about. Moreover, he was utterly innocent of any evil design upon us and had brought us on board the boat in absolute good faith; in fact, if we needed proof, he had reserved his passage a long time before. "In any case," he snorted, "what is this sinister plot? Who is this horrible Hannibal you imagine we've got on board? Lichas of Tarentum is an extremely respectable man. Not only is he captain of this ship but also its owner. Moreover, he's a large landowner and the head of a trading house; at the present moment, he's shipping a cargo on consignment. This is the ferocious Cyclops and pirate chief to whom we owe our passage. Besides Lichas, there's Tryphaena, the loveliest woman in the world, who spends her life roaming about in search of pleasure."

"But it's just these two that we're running away from," Giton broke in, and with a torrent of words, he quickly outlined to the startled Eumolpus the causes of our feud and the dangers which threatened us. Obviously completely at a loss, Eumolpus asked each of us to state his

106

opinion. "Imagine," he said, "that this ship is the Cyclops' cave in which we're trapped. The problem before us is to break out. Unless, of course, we prefer to win our freedom by purposely wrecking the ship."

"No," Giton replied. "Persuade the helmsman instead to put the ship into some harbor. Tip him well, of course, and tell him your little friend is so seasick he's likely to die. A worried look and a few tears will do for a front. The pilot will begin to feel sorry for you, and so do what you want."

"Impossible," Eumolpus answered. "In the first place, it's no easy matter to get a big ship like this one into harbor; second, it's extremely unlikely that you could be that seasick so soon. Besides, what if Lichas out of simple kindness should take it into his head to pay a call on the sick man? A pretty mess that would be, leading the captain right to the stowaways. Anyway, even if we could persuade the pilot to change course and Lichas didn't make the rounds of the cabins, how in the world could we get off the ship without being seen? Do we cover up, or make a run for it as we are? If we cover up, everyone will want to give a hand to the poor, ailing passengers. If we go bareheaded, we might as well just give ourselves up."

[102] "No," I said, "what we need now is boldness and daring. Listen: we'll slide down the rope to the lifeboat, cut the cable and leave the rest to luck. I don't ask Eumolpus, of course, to share our dangers. Since he's not involved, I don't see any reason why he should have to run our risks. All I ask is that Fortune give us a little help."

"Not a bad plan," Eumolpus observed, "if there were the slightest chance of making it work. But everybody would see us leaving. Even if they didn't see us, the pilot who sits there on duty all night, charting his course by the stars, is certain to spot us. You might elude him, I suppose, if you made your escape from another part of the ship, but as it is, you want to escape from the poop beside the pilot's wheel where the boat rope is tied. Besides, Encolpius, I'm surprised that it hasn't struck you that one of the crew is stationed in the skiff night and day, and you can't get rid of him unless you're prepared to kill him or throw him overboard. Whether that's possible or not is something that only your own courage can answer. Finally, so far as my coming with you is concerned, I am prepared to run any risk which offers a sporting chance of escape; but to throw our lives away for nothing is something I doubt you can want, even in your present situation. See now what you think of this plan. I'll roll you both up in my bedding, leaving the ends just enough open so that you can breathe and get food, and stow you away as part of my personal luggage. Then I'll give it out that two of my slaves, terrified of a beating, took the easy way out and threw themselves overboard during the night. Then, the instant we land, I'll have you disembarked with the rest of my baggage and there won't be the slightest suspicion."

"What the hell do you think we are?" I cried. "A couple of logs to be baled up in your baggage? We've got bodies, man. Our insides aren't made of stone; we have to sneeze and snore. Maybe Menelaus made this trick work, but that was in a poem; what makes you think we could get away with it here? Anyway, even supposing we were able to stand being rolled up like that for a day, what happens if we get becalmed or held up by rough weather? Even clothing gets creased and mussed from being packed; rolled-up papers develop a permanent curl, don't they? Then what in god's name will happen to us? We're made of flesh; we're young; we can't take that kind of treatment. No sir, if you think our poor bodies are going to stand being wrapped in dirty rags and roped up like a couple of statues, you're sadly mistaken."

❦

"No, Eumolpus," I said, "it just won't do. We'll have to think of something else. See, for instance, what you think of this. As a literary man, Eumolpus is certain to have some ink with him. Very well, we'll smear ourselves with ink from head to toe until we're as black as two Ethiopian slaves. For his part, Eumolpus will acquire two slaves, both overjoyed at having escaped punishment and eager to serve him, while our sudden transformation will completely fool our enemies."

"Oh, just splendid," Giton broke in sarcastically. "And while you're at it, why not circumcise us too, so we look like Jews, and pierce our ears like Arabs, and plaster our faces with chalk like Gauls? As though a mere change of color could alter a man's whole appearance, and you didn't need perfection in every detail to sustain a good lie. Besides, what makes you think the dye would last? Won't even a single drop of water spot it? Wouldn't our clothes stick to it? God knows, they're sticky enough with sweat without adding ink. Anyway, even supposing the dye was fast, how can we get that fat-lipped Ethiopian look? Do we frizzle our hair with curlers? And plough up our foreheads with crisscross scars? Can we walk around bowlegged and sag in at the ankles? How do we give our beards an African cut? No, dye merely stains the body; it doesn't change it. As I see it, there's only one way out; let's cover our eyes with our robes and jump overboard."

[103] "God and man forbid," Eumolpus exclaimed, "that you should make such a miserable conclusion of your lives! No, here's what I suggest. My slave, as you will have recognized from his razor, is a barber. Very well, we'll have him shave you both right now, everything, your hair and eyebrows too. Then I'll carefully letter your foreheads so you look like a couple of branded slaves. The brandmarks will not only divert suspicion but will help to conceal your faces under the shadow of punishment."

We immediately adopted this plan. Tiptoeing softly to the other side of the deck, we offered our heads and eyebrows to the barber's razor, while Eumolpus, with generous strokes, traced out on our foreheads in large letters the well-known inscription for runaway slaves. By bad luck, however, we were seen being shorn by one of the passengers who happened to be leaning over the rail, relieving his seasickness. Angrily cursing the shearing, so ominously reminiscent of the last offering of shipwrecked sailors, he slumped back on his hammock. Pretending we hadn't heard his puking curses, we went on with our melancholy work, and then spent the rest of the night tossing restlessly in uneasy sleep.

X

DISCOVERED

[104] "I thought I saw Priapus in a dream last night," said Lichas, "and he said to me: 'I have led Encolpius, the object of your search, on board your ship.'"

"You'd think," replied Tryphaena with a shudder, "that
109

we'd been sleeping together. I had a dream too in which the statue of Neptune I saw in the gallery at Baiae seemed to say to me: 'You will find Giton on board Lichas' ship.'"

Eumolpus hastily broke in. "Exactly. And this shows you why we consider Epicurus almost superhuman. As you may remember, he very wittily disposes of such coincidences as mere silly superstitions."

Lichas, nonetheless, was troubled by Tryphaena's dream and ordered libations poured to avert the bad omen. "I take it," he added, "that no one will object if I order the ship to be searched. After all, we don't want to seem to scoff at the workings of divine Providence."

At this point a certain Hesus, the passenger who had witnessed our furtive work the night before, suddenly recognized us. "Those are the ones," he shouted, "those are the men I saw being shaved last night in the moonlight! Gods in heaven, what a stupid thing to do! At least I've heard it said that nobody on board a ship is allowed to cut his hair or pare his nails except in a terrible storm."

[105] Lichas was scandalized. "Where's the man who dared cut his hair on board my ship in the dead of night?" he bellowed. "Bring the culprits here this instant. By god, I want to know who's going to lose his head in order to get this ship purified again!"

"I gave the orders to shave them," said Eumolpus. "And you can be quite sure that, as a passenger on this ship myself, I had no intention of doing anything that might cause trouble. No, I ordered them shorn because their hair was so horribly shaggy and I didn't want the ship looking like a prison. What's more, they've both been branded and I was particularly anxious that the marks should be legible, not hidden away under tufts of scraggly hair. You wouldn't believe it, but last night I found these two having a party with their girlfriend on the money they'd stolen from me, and I had to drag them away in an absolute stink of wine and cheap perfume. In short, they stank of the remains of my inheritance."

❧

In order to appease the patron goddess of the ship, it was decided that each of us would be given forty strokes with the lash. The order was executed immediately. Sailors armed with knotted ropes threw themselves upon us, determined to placate their goddess with our blood. For my part, I bore three strokes with almost Spartan endurance; but at the first blow Giton screamed so shrilly that Tryphaena recognized his voice. Not only Tryphaena; all the maidservants came rushing up at the sound of that well-known voice. Giton's extraordinary beauty, however, had already disarmed the sailors; far more eloquently than any words they pleaded his case to his tormentors. But now the maids came screaming and shrieking: "It's Giton, it's Giton! Help, ma'am, they're beating Giton! Stop beating him, you brutes!"

Tryphaena's heart, however, had already told her who it was and she fairly flew to the boy. Lichas, an old acquaintance of mine, indeed once an intimate friend, ran up as though he'd heard me shout and, quite ignoring my face and hands, stared fixedly at me. Then, exploring me with an expert hand, he said, "Hello, Encolpius." So it can hardly be a matter for much surprise that Ulysses' old nurse, even after an absence of twenty years, should have recognized her master's scar, when this clever man instantly put his finger on the one physical peculiarity that gave me away, even though my face and clothing were completely disguised. Tryphaena, thoroughly convinced that the marks painted on our foreheads had been made by the branding iron, burst into tears and began to commiserate with us, asking what prison had interrupted our wanderings and what inhuman hands had inflicted this ghastly punishment upon us. "Of course," she added, "it was only to be expected that runaway slaves who had returned her every kindness with hatred should have to suffer for it in the end . . ."

[106] At this Lichas completely lost his temper. "You simple-minded fool," he shouted, "do you really believe those letters were burnt in with a hot iron? By god, I only wish they had been: that would be some satisfaction at least. As it is, we're being taken in by cheap actors' tricks. That inscription is nothing but a sham."

Tryphaena, however, had not yet lost all her old appetite for Giton, and was therefore inclined to mercy. But Lichas, still smarting from the memory of his wife's seduction and the insults he had received in the Porch of Hercules, was harsh and vindictive. "Tryphaena," he said, his face twisted with fury, "even you, I think, will agree that the gods exercise some control over human affairs. These two criminals have been led by the gods on board our ship without knowing whose it was, and the gods themselves have advised us of their actions through two strikingly similar dreams. I ask you then: how can we presume to pardon them when the gods themselves have led them to punishment? Personally, I am not a vindictive man, but I fear that if I pardon them I may live to regret it."

Swayed by this superstitious reasoning, Tryphaena veered around and said she had no objection to punishing us. In fact, the revenge was quite justified and, for her part, she approved it. After all, she had been as badly wronged as Lichas: hadn't her honor been publicly impugned?

❦

[107] Eumolpus managed our defense. "The accused," he said, "have invited me, as a man of known probity, to act as mediator here in effecting a reconciliation between both parties, once good friends but now estranged. Let me ask you, first of all, Lichas, whether you believe that these young men fell into your clutches by mere chance and not intention? But surely the first concern of every passenger is to make inquiries about the captain to whom he entrusts his welfare during the voyage. In any case the claims of honor have surely been more than satisfied already. I appeal to your mercy; relent and allow these two young men, free citizens both, to proceed on their journey unharmed. Even the harshest and most vindictive of masters checks his anger when the runaway returns repentant. It is Roman to show mercy to a fallen foe. What more can honor exact? What more could you possibly wish? There, prostrate at your feet, lie two free and respectable young men, and what is more, men who were once bound to you by the closest of ties. Had they robbed you or betrayed your trust, surely the punishment they have already suffered would suffice to atone for their crime. Look at those unhappy heads, those faces once so bright with the light of freedom defiled with the self-imposed marks of slavery, by their own decree proscribed from civil society."

"You're confusing the issue," Lichas interrupted him. "Let me deal with your arguments point for point. In the first place, if they've come here of their own accord, why have they shaved off their hair? A man disguises himself because he wants to make mischief, not because he wants to make amends. Again, if you, as their official spokesman, wanted to get them pardoned, why have you done everything in your power to keep them out of sight? No, Eumolpus, the evidence couldn't be more conclusive: they fell into our hands quite by accident, and all these arguments of yours have been concocted to protect them from our anger. As for your attempt to embarrass us by calling them 'free' and 'respectable,' take care lest your effrontery cost your clients their case out of hand. Besides, what in god's name do you expect an injured man to do when his enemies run right into his hands? Ah, but these men were once our friends, you say; all the more reason then for dealing harshly with them. The man who injures a total stranger is guilty of a crime, but there's no word to describe the man who wantonly injures his friends."

Lichas was being outrageously unfair, and Eumolpus cut him off by saying, "I am quite aware that the most damning evidence yet adduced against my clients is the fact that they shaved off their hair. From this you conclude that it was mere chance that led them on board your ship, not a sincere desire to make amends. Now I want you to hear the plain truth of the matter, quite as simply as it happened. Before we sailed, my clients had both intended to rid themselves of that ugly tangle of useless hair; meanwhile, however, a fresh breeze had sprung up, and your sudden decision to sail forced them to postpone their project until later. And, being completely ignorant of sailor's superstitions and nautical custom, they never imagined it could make the slightest difference where they cut their hair."

"But what in god's name," replied Lichas, "does shaving yourself bald have to do with asking for forgiveness? Or do they think that baldness is pathetic in itself? But I see that it's a waste of time to try and get the truth here at secondhand.—All right, birdbait, what do you have to say for yourself? What salamander singed off your eyebrows? What god did you dedicate your curls to? Answer, scum!"

[*108*] But I was too petrified with terror to speak; besides, the evidence was only too conclusive, and what could I say? So I stood there, mutilated and miserable, my head as bald as brass, with no eyebrows at all, utterly unable to speak a word. The next thing I knew someone was sloshing at me with a soaking sponge; the ink trickled down my

113

face and the letters painted on my forehead ran together in a huge black blob. Lichas was staring at me, less in anger than loathing. Then Eumolpus intervened, protesting vigorously that he could not allow two free men, in violation of every law of god and man, to be willfully disfigured; when, despite his protests, our persecutors persisted, Eumolpus beat them back with his fists. His slave, of course, stood staunchly by him and several passengers even offered to assist him, so feebly, however, that their help amounted to little more than moral support for our side.

Not the man to whine for pity, I promptly leapt into action myself. Rushing up to Tryphaena, I shook my fist in her face, shrieking that she was a filthy whore, that nobody on board that boat more richly deserved a flogging than she, and that I would use every resource at my disposal to keep her from hurting Giton. At this Lichas went livid with rage and accused me of attacking her in order to divert attention from my own lost cause. Tryphaena herself was wild with indignation and, in less than a second, the whole ship divided into two hostile camps. On our side Eumolpus' slave armed himself with a razor and passed out the remaining razors among us, while Tryphaena's cohorts, spurred on by the hysterical screaming of her maids, prepared to attack us with their bare hands. Only the pilot remained aloof, cursing the whole fracas as the lunatic work of a mob of perverts and threatening to abandon his post unless we stopped immediately. Even this dire threat, however, failed to quench our martial ardor. And so we fought, both sides heavily crippled by casualties—none of them fatal, however—as the wounded, drenched in their own blood, limped stricken from the field. But still the battle raged implacably on.

Suddenly, however, our gallant Giton turned the edge of his razor against his own manhood, threatening at one fell blow to lop away that root of all our troubles. Tryphaena, overcome with horror, cast all pretense aside and rushed forward to prevent the consummation of such a catastrophe. For my part, following Giton's example, I several times lifted my razor to my own throat, no more intending, of course, to kill myself than Giton intended to castrate himself. Giton meanwhile, bolstered by his knowledge that the razor was the same one with which he had earlier tried to slit his throat, was carrying off his tragic role with magnificent self-assurance. But there

114

we stood, both sides drawn up in full battle array, poised for the slaughter. And almost certainly our little fracas must have ended in general disaster, had not the pilot at the last minute persuaded the reluctant Tryphaena to play the part of peacemaker. So the customary ritual phrases were pronounced, and Tryphaena, waving an olive branch torn from the ship's figurehead, advanced slowly toward us, chanting as she came:

What folly, what fury, transposes peace with war?
What excuse for war have we? No prince of Troy
here bears his ravished Spartan bride away;
no frenzied Medea at her brother's body hacks.
Only love disprized; unrequited love,
our only casus belli. Why then this war
when the raging sea makes war against us all?
When the sea itself is death, why, why, should we
compound our doom and stain the swirling waters red?

[109] Her lines were delivered with such effective pathos that a lull settled over the ship and our hands slowly relaxed around their weapons, opening with peace. Taking advantage of the momentary lull, our general Eumolpus delivered a brief tirade against Lichas and then drew up for signature the following articles of peace:

I.

I, Tryphaena, do hereby solemnly contract and agree to renounce all projects of vengeance against the person of Giton, binding myself to seek no redress for any injuries I may have suffered prior to the making of this agreement, and freely waiving all claims for damage attending thereto. I further pledge myself to exact nothing from the boy against his will, to wit, neither kisses, nor hugs, nor plenary cohabitation; or, if I do so exact, I agree to pay a fine of one hundred pieces for each such infraction thereof.

II.

I, Lichas, do hereby solemnly agree and contract neither to insult Encolpius by word or look nor to inquire where he sleeps at night; or, should I so inquire, to forfeit the sum of two hundred pieces in satisfaction of any and all injuries attendant upon such inquiries.

On these terms and conditions the peace was signed and we laid down our arms. But to ensure that no vestige of old rancor or resentment should trouble our new-made peace, it was decided to efface the past entirely by means of a general embrace all around. And so, to universal applause, we formally laid our hatred to rest and, appropriating some refreshments prepared originally for the battle, we ratified our agreement with festivity. The whole ship rang with our songs, and then when a sudden calm held us in our course, we tried our luck at spearing the fish as they burst, leaping, from the water, while others reeled in their thrashing prey on baited hooks. And when a flock of seabirds settled on the rigging, a sailor skillfully caught them with limed twigs. Snared, the poor creatures fell helplessly into our outstretched hands and their down was caught by the rising breeze and their feathers were whirled away and lost in the windblown spray.

XI

THE PLEASURES OF PEACE

Our efforts at peace seemed to be succeeding. In no time at all, Lichas and I were well on the way to a genuine reconciliation, and Tryphaena was already amorously dumping the dregs of her drink over Giton's head. Eumolpus, meanwhile, his tongue loosened by the wine, was pouring forth a great stream of satire against bald men and branded slaves. Having finally exhausted his chilly wit on this subject, he reverted to verse and improvised the following little elegy on hair:

> Your body's glory's fled, your hair is dead;
>   your leaf has perished with the year's.
> On naked brows the shadeless sun beats down:
>   Sahara starts above your ears.
>
> O gods above, how cruelly you deceive us:
>   the first of all your gifts, the first to leave us.

This effort was immediately followed by a special apostrophe to Giton:

> Unhappy boy, your curls once shone
> more brightly than Apollo's own,
> and Artemis, though wondrous fair,
>   combed duller hair.
>
> Now, bald as brass, thy bulbous brain,
> like mushroom cap in pelting rain,
> prinks up, and all thy quondam curls
>   are mocked by girls.
>
> But so we die; so death comes on,
> as, even now, thy life has gone,
> and every curl that graced thy head,
>   dear lad, lies dead.

[*110*] I suspect he was on the point of following this doggerel with something even sillier, but before he could open his mouth, Tryphaena's maid snatched Giton away below deck and disguised that poor bald head with one of her mistress' wigs. Then taking a pair of eyebrows from a tiny case, she deftly fitted them to the vanished hairline, quite restoring the boy to his pristine beauty. Recognizing her true Giton at last, Tryphaena burst into tears of joy and kissed him for the first time with unmistakable warmth. For my part, although overjoyed to see the boy blossom forth in all his old beauty, I felt, by contrast, so horribly disfigured and so hideously ugly—even Lichas couldn't bear to look at me—that I covered my face in shame. But the same little maid proved my savior too, and leading me off, covered me with a head of hair quite as splendid as Giton's. In fact, if anything, I acquired rather more than I had lost, for the wig was blonde, and my head fairly shone with a tangled, golden glory . . .

❦

Meanwhile Eumolpus, our spokesman in the hour of danger and the author of our present reconciliation, anxious that our gaiety should not be broken, began, in a sudden moment of silence, to gibe at the fickleness of women, the wonderful ease with which they became infatuated, their readiness to abandon their children for their lovers, and so forth. In fact, he declared, no woman was so chaste or faithful that she couldn't be seduced;

117

sooner or later she would fall head over heels in love with some passing stranger. Nor, he added, was he thinking so much of the old tragedies and the classics of love betrayed as of something that had happened in our own time; in fact, if we were willing to hear, he would be delighted to tell the story. All eyes and ears were promptly turned to our narrator, and he began:

[*111*] "Once upon a time there was a certain married woman in the city of Ephesus whose fidelity to her husband was so famous that the women from all the neighboring towns and villages used to troop into Ephesus merely to stare at this prodigy. It happened, however, that her husband one day died. Finding the normal custom of following the cortege with hair unbound and beating her breast in public quite inadequate to express her grief, the lady insisted on following the corpse right into the tomb, an underground vault of the Greek type, and there set herself to guard the body, weeping and wailing night and day. Although in her extremes of grief she was clearly courting death from starvation, her parents were utterly unable to persuade her to leave, and even the magistrates, after one last supreme attempt, were rebuffed and driven away. In short, all Ephesus had gone into mourning for this extraordinary woman, all the more since the lady was now passing her fifth consecutive day without once tasting food. Beside the failing woman sat her devoted maid, sharing her mistress' grief and relighting the lamp whenever it flickered out. The whole city could speak, in fact, of nothing else: here at last, all classes alike agreed, was the one true example of conjugal fidelity and love.

"In the meantime, however, the governor of the province gave orders that several thieves should be crucified in a spot close by the vault where the lady was mourning her dead husband's corpse. So, on the following night, the soldier who had been assigned to keep watch on the crosses so that nobody could remove the thieves' bodies for burial suddenly noticed a light blazing among the tombs and heard the sounds of groaning. And prompted by a natural human curiosity to know who or what was making those sounds, he descended into the vault.

"But at the sight of a strikingly beautiful woman, he stopped short in terror, thinking he must be seeing some ghostly apparition out of hell. Then, observing the corpse and seeing the tears on the lady's face and the scratches her fingernails had gashed in her cheeks, he realized what

118

it was: a widow, in inconsolable grief. Promptly fetching his little supper back down to the tomb, he implored the lady not to persist in her sorrow or break her heart with useless mourning. All men alike, he reminded her, have the same end; the same resting place awaits us all. He used, in short, all those platitudes we use to comfort the suffering and bring them back to life. His consolations, being unwelcome, only exasperated the widow more; more violently than ever she beat her breast, and tearing out her hair by the roots, scattered it over the dead man's body. Undismayed, the soldier repeated his arguments and pressed her to take some food, until the little maid, quite overcome by the smell of the wine, succumbed and stretched out her hand to her tempter. Then, restored by the food and wine, she began herself to assail her mistress' obstinate refusal.

" 'How will it help you,' she asked the lady, 'if you faint from hunger? Why should you bury yourself alive, and go down to death before the Fates have called you? What does Vergil say?—

Do you suppose the shades and ashes of the dead
are by such sorrow touched?

No, begin your life afresh. Shake off these woman's scruples; enjoy the light while you can. Look at that corpse of your poor husband: doesn't it tell you more eloquently than any words that you should live?'

"None of us, of course, really dislikes being told that we must eat, that life is to be lived. And the lady was no exception. Weakened by her long days of fasting, her resistance crumbled at last, and she ate the food the soldier offered her as hungrily as the little maid had eaten earlier.

[*112*] "Well, you know what temptations are normally aroused in a man on a full stomach. So the soldier, mustering all those blandishments by means of which he had persuaded the lady to live, now laid determined siege to her virtue. And chaste though she was, the lady found him singularly attractive and his arguments persuasive. As for the maid, she did all she could to help the soldier's cause, repeating like a refrain the appropriate line of Vergil:

If love is pleasing, lady, yield yourself to love.

To make the matter short, the lady's body soon gave up the struggle; she yielded and our happy warrior enjoyed

119

a total triumph on both counts. That very night their marriage was consummated, and they slept together the second and the third night too, carefully shutting the door of the tomb so that any passing friend or stranger would have thought the lady of famous chastity had at last expired over her dead husband's body.

"As you can perhaps imagine, our soldier was a very happy man, utterly delighted with his lady's ample beauty and that special charm that a secret love confers. Every night, as soon as the sun had set, he bought what few provisions his slender pay permitted and smuggled them down to the tomb. One night, however, the parents of one of the crucified thieves, noticing that the watch was being badly kept, took advantage of our hero's absence to remove their son's body and bury it. The next morning, of course, the soldier was horror-struck to discover one of the bodies missing from its cross, and ran to tell his mistress of the horrible punishment which awaited him for neglecting his duty. In the circumstances, he told her, he would not wait to be tried and sentenced, but would punish himself then and there with his own sword. All he asked of her was that she make room for another corpse and allow the same gloomy tomb to enclose husband and lover together.

"Our lady's heart, however, was no less tender than pure. 'God forbid,' she cried, 'that I should have to see at one and the same time the dead bodies of the only two men I have ever loved. No, better far, I say, to hang the dead than kill the living.' With these words, she gave orders that her husband's body should be taken from its bier and strung up on the empty cross. The soldier followed this good advice, and the next morning the whole city wondered by what miracle the dead man had climbed up on the cross."

[113] The sailors greeted this story with great guffaws, while Tryphaena blushed to her ears and tried to hide her head in embarrassment against Giton's shoulder. Lichas alone was not amused. "By god," he burst out, shaking his head angrily, "if that governor had done his duty, he would have had the husband returned to his tomb and the wife strung up on the cross!" He was remembering, I suppose, what had happened with Hedyle and how his ship had been pillaged by that mob of lecherous passengers. But the terms of our treaty forbade him to hold a grudge,

120

and the general atmosphere of good feeling outlawed any show of resentment.

In the meantime, however, Tryphaena was lolling in Giton's lap, smothering his chest with kisses and amorously snuggling the curls of his wig back in place. Uneasy and depressed, increasingly impatient myself of our peace treaty and its clauses, I sat there, utterly incapable of drinking or eating, glaring furiously at the two of them. Every kiss, every caress that that lecherous slut could invent, cut me to the quick. I hardly knew whether I was angrier with the boy for stealing my mistress than with the mistress for seducing the boy. More painful than the memory of my past captivity, the sight of the two of them offended my eyes unbearably. Worse yet, Tryphaena spoke to me with undisguised coldness, not at all as one speaks to a chosen lover and intimate friend, while Giton pointedly refused to drink my health, neglecting even to include me in the general conversation, the very least he could have done. It may have been, I suppose, that he was afraid of opening a fresh wound in the initial stages of our reconciliation. But for whatever reason, I felt utterly rejected; my chest heaved with sobs and I almost died from trying to cover my groans of despair with my sighs.

❧

Lichas tried to gain admission to our pleasures, no longer affecting the arrogance of a master, but begging us, as his friend, to do him a favor.

❧

"Encolpius, if you had any blood in you at all," Tryphaena's maid cried out, "you'd treat her like the whore she is. If you're a real man, you'll stay away from that filthy slut."

❧

Above all, I was haunted by the fear that Eumolpus might have witnessed the whole scene and would take his revenge in a storm of sarcastic verse . . .

❧

Eumolpus made a solemn promise . . .

❧

XII

SHIPWRECKED

[*114*] But while we were talking aimlessly of this and that, the sea suddenly grew rough and great thunderheads towered up on every quarter, utterly blacking out the light of day. Shaking with terror, the sailors scrambled to their posts and hastily furled the sails against the gathering storm. But the raging winds cracked down on the ship from every side at once, battering us so wildly that the pilot completely lost his sense of direction. At one moment we seemed to be driving straight for Sicily; at the next, we were caught by the North Wind, that squalling tyrant of the Italian coast, and pitched about completely at its mercy. But even more ominous than the winds was the sudden darkness, a blackness so intense that the pilot, standing on the stern, could no longer see the prow.

Then, at the very peak of our danger, Lichas, wild with fright, stretched out his hands to me. "For god's sake, Encolpius," he shrieked, "help us! Save us from danger! Give back the robe and sistrum you stole from the goddess of the ship. In the name of heaven, I implore you, pity us! Show us that compassion you have always shown to others!"

He was still pleading when the wind suddenly snatched him up and dropped him into the sea; an instant later he reappeared, only to be whirled about by a gust and sucked under by the seething waves. As for Tryphaena, her maids forcibly carried her away and set her in the skiff with the greater part of her baggage, saving her from almost certain death.

I, meanwhile, was clinging to Giton with all my strength, sobbing with terror and tragic despair. "O gods in heaven," I cried in bitterness of heart, "is this your justice, that two lovers should be united only at the moment of death? Alas, not even that: for the Fates are cruel, and soon the seas will overturn the ship and the wild waves sunder even two lovers' last embrace. Oh Giton, if you truly love your Encolpius, kiss him while you can and let us ravish together our last happiness from the hungry Fates!"

Quickly stripping off his clothes, Giton snuggled under-

122

neath my tunic and lifted his face to be kissed. Then, to keep the jealous sea from breaking our embrace, he bound his belt about us both and buckled it tight. "One last solace at least remains, Encolpius," he cried. "Whatever may happen now, at least we shall lie united in love upon the heaving swell a while, and if perchance some kinder current than the rest should cast us on the shore, some passerby, by simple human kindness moved, may build us both a single grave. Lacking that, there still remains one mercy which the angry sea has never yet refused: the same careless sands, I mean, may then enclose us both."

Resigned, I let myself be bound in that final bond and stood there patiently awaiting a death by now divorced of all its terror. Meanwhile, loyal to the grim fiat of the Fates, the storm ripped away the last remnants of the ship. Masts, tiller, ropes and oars, all were battered away, leaving behind only a rough and shapeless hulk to drift slowly on the surface of the aimless sea.

❦

Fishermen in skiffs came darting out in hopes of salvage, but when they found living men on board, ready and willing to defend their property, they hastily changed their minds and offered us help instead.

❦

[115] Suddenly we heard a strange sound, rather like the snarl of a wild animal trying to escape, coming from the direction of the pilot's cabin. Tracking the sound to its source, we discovered Eumolpus sitting on the floor and furiously scribbling verses on a huge sheet of parchment. Astounded that he had found time for composing poetry in the very teeth of death, we nonetheless, despite his angry protests, dragged him out and begged him to come to his senses. But he was fuming with rage at having been interrupted. "Dammit," he bellowed, "let me finish this stanza. The last lines limp." I took the lunatic by the shoulder and somehow, thanks to Giton's help, managed to haul the bellowing bard ashore.

❦

Our task at last completed, we made our way dejectedly to a fisherman's hut where we somehow scraped up a supper from the water-soaked provisions we had salvaged from the ship and spent an altogether miserable night.

The next morning while we were trying to decide in what direction we ought to strike out, I suddenly saw a human body slowly rocking shorewards in the gentle surf. Breaking off in mid-sentence, I felt the tears tugging at my eyes and with a heavy heart I began to reflect on the fatal treachery of the sea.

"Think of it," I exclaimed sadly. "Somewhere in this world some wife perhaps sits waiting for that man, never doubting his return. Or somewhere a son to whom this storm at sea has no meaning yet. Or a father perhaps; but surely, surely there was someone whom he kissed goodbye when he sailed away to death. But drowned! To think our every human hope must someday come to this, this corpse of great ambitions, this poor drowned body of our dreams! O gods, and was this once a man, this thing that floats now merely?"

Up to now I thought I was mourning a stranger, some man I never knew, but at that moment the surf dropped the body on the beach, face up, its every feature distinct, and I recognized the face of Lichas. The very man, Lichas himself, once so formidable, so terrible and relentless in his hatred of me, now tossed up by the sea almost at my feet! Fighting my tears no longer, I wept openly, unashamedly, and beat my breast in a frenzy of grief.

"Where are they now," I cried, "all your anger and your greatness? But two little hours ago you boasted of your pride of power and your manhood's strength and yet, what are you now? Food for the fish, for every crawling creature in the sea. Of all that mighty ship you once commanded, not one poor saving spar is left you in your utter shipwreck. And yet we scheme and hope, stuffing our foolish hearts with dreams, scrimping and saving, hoarding the wealth we win by wrong, planning our lives as though we had a thousand years to live! Why, why? One little day ago this man too looked over his accounts and reckoned up his worth; he too had fixed the day on which he thought his ship would dock. And now, O gods, how far he lies from his destination! Why, doom is everywhere, at any time. And other things betray, not just the sea alone. Look how the soldier's weapons fail him. You see the consummation of your every hope, and what happens? The great house you built falls in, crumbles, buries you in the rubble of your dreams. The man who

124

had no time to lose falls from his chariot and loses his time forever. The glutton chokes to death; the miser starves of his own stinginess. Why, if you calculate our chances in this life, what do they cry but death? Shipwreck is everywhere. But I hear someone object: those who drown at sea die unburied. Lord, lord, as though it mattered how this deathbound flesh should die! Fire or water or the wear and tear of time, what does it matter? Death or death: the end is always the same. But objections again: wild beasts may mutilate the body. And so? Is the fire that someday cremates your corpse more friendly? Gentle fire, the cruelest death to which an angry master can sentence his slave? Why, what madness all this frantic pother is, these great efforts to annihilate our bodies completely, so they won't be mutilated after death!"

❧

And so Lichas' body was burned on a bonfire gathered and laid by the hands of those he hated. Eumolpus, meanwhile, composed the epitaph. Fixing his gaze on the distant horizon as though searching for inspiration . . .

❧

XIII

THE ROAD TO CROTON
❧

[116] So we buried Lichas as well as we could and set out in the direction we had decided upon. Not long afterward, we arrived, drenched with sweat, at the peak of a mountain, and from here we could see, no great distance away, a large town perched on the crest of a high hill. Since we were traveling completely blindly, we had no idea where we were, but we learned from a peasant that the town was Croton, one of the oldest cities of Italy, and once the foremost. Our curiosity aroused, we questioned him for details of the people who inhabited that famous place; how in particular, we wanted to know, did they earn their livelihood now that the long wars had destroyed their old prosperity.

"Strangers," said our informant, "if you are merchants, let me advise you to change your plans and look for some

125

other way of earning your living there. If, however, you belong to that class of cultured men-of-the-world who can sustain with ease a lifetime of lying, the road you are walking runs right to riches. In that town literature and the arts go utterly unhonored; eloquence there has no prestige; and those who live the good and simple life find no admirers. Any man you meet in that town you may be certain belongs to one of two classes: the makers of wills and those who pursue the makers of wills. You will find no fathers there, for those with natural heirs of their own are regarded as pariahs. A father is someone who is never invited to dinner, never entertained, who, in short, is compelled to spend his life, outcast and excluded, among the poor and obscure. Those, however, who remain bachelors in perpetuity and have no close relatives are held in the highest honor and esteem: they and they alone are men of honor and courage, brave as lions, paragons without spot or flaw. In short, sirs, you are going to a place which is like a countryside ravaged by the plague, a place in which you will see only two things: the bodies of those who are eaten, and the carrion crows who eat them."

❧

[117] More astute than the rest of us, Eumolpus considered this new situation very carefully, declaring that such a method of getting rich did not at all displease him. At first I took this as mere whimsey, some passing poetic fantasy, but he was quite serious. "I only wish," he said, "we could afford better scenery and props for the little comedy I have in mind. More expensive clothing, for instance, would help; and if we could manage to travel more comfortably, we could sustain our little illusion somewhat better. No, gentlemen, if the choice were mine, I'd set to work right now and in no time at all I'd make every one of you a rich man."

For my part, I promised faithfully to do anything he should ask of me so long as there was no objection to my wearing the same clothes I had worn during the robbery of Lycurgus' villa or to making use of our plunder. "As for any sums required for our immediate needs," I added, "surely the Mother of gods and men will supply us with all her usual generosity."

❧

"Very well, then," said Eumolpus, "let's write the plot of our little play right now. Now if no one objects, I'll take the part of the master."

This suggestion seemed harmless enough, and no one dared to object. But in order to keep the secret from ever being divulged, we all took a solemn oath to obey Eumolpus in everything, to endure burning, imprisonment, flogging or even death by the sword. In short, like gladiators, we dedicated ourselves utterly, body and soul, to the service of our master. Then, when the oath of service had been administered, we gathered around our master and saluted him and learned from his lips the plot of our play.

Eumolpus, it seemed, had recently lost his only son, a boy of great eloquence and a promising future. Prostrated by grief and unable to bear the daily sight of his son's friends and dependents or even to look at the grave, the poor old man had tried to forget his sorrow by leaving his native land. Then, as though he had not suffered enough already, he had been shipwrecked, and his losses in the wreck had exceeded twenty millions. It was not, however, the loss that grieved him but the fact that, having no servants, he could no longer recognize his own importance in the world. In Africa, moreover, he possessed in land and capital investments a sum equivalent to thirty millions; and as for slaves, he had such an army of them scattered over the farms of Numidia that he could, had he wished, have sacked Carthage.

As the finishing touches, we suggested that Eumolpus should cough constantly, complain now and then of diarrhea, and loudly proclaim that all food set before him was revolting stuff. The only subjects of his conversation must be gold and silver, the atrocious returns on his farms, and the intractable sterility of the soil. Every day without fail, moreover, he must scrutinize his accounts and his will must be totally revised every thirty days. Finally, as the crowning detail, he must invariably call us by the wrong names whenever he asked for something, so that it would look as though he couldn't remember which servants were with him and which were still in Africa.

So, having concerted our plan of action, we prayed the gods to grant us success in our venture, and set off on our journey. But Giton stumbled under the weight of his unaccustomed load, while the porter we had hired, a worthless shirker by the name of Corax, kept setting his

load down, cursing our rush and threatening to throw our
luggage away or run off with it. "What do you think
I am," he grumbled, "a beast of burden, a boat for carrying rocks? I hired out as a man, dammit, not a horse.
What's more, I'm as free as you are, though my father left
me a poor man." Not content with grumbling and cursing,
he kept lifting his leg and laying down a barrage of smelly
farts, while Giton roared with laughter at his impudence
and matched his every noise, fart for fart . . .

❧

XIV

EUMOLPUS ON THE WRITING
OF POETRY

[118] "In my opinion," Eumolpus declared, "many
young people nowadays who write verse do so in the
insane delusion that poetry is an easy art. Why, no
sooner have most of them mastered the bare rudiments
of a meter and wrestled some flimsy idea into stanza form
than they think they're standing on the very peak of
Helicon. Take those budding lawyers of ours, for example.
You must have seen them, I think, rushing away from
the courtroom to soothe their jangled nerves by turning
out a poem or two, as though the Muses ran a rest haven
for tired lawyers and poetry were mere child's play as
compared with grinding out one of those epigram-studded
orations of theirs. Serious poets, of course, despise this
dilettante approach to their art; from hard experience
they know that the imagination is utterly incapable of
conceiving, let alone producing, a real poem unless the
poet's mind has been literally saturated in the poetry of
the past. Cliché and cheap language, for instance, must
be ruthlessly resisted. No great poetry has ever been
founded on colloquial language, language that has been,
so to speak, debased and corrupted by popular usage. Its
motto is that of Horace:

I loathe the vulgar crowd, and shun it.

Again, no reference or allusion, no idea not strictly relevant
to the inner logic of the poem can be admitted; the texture
of great poetry is intrinsic; its beauty is formal and internal.
Witness in this connection the work of Homer and the

lyric poets; or of our own Roman Vergil, or that painstaking formal rightness that gives the poetry of Horace
its peculiar felicity. As for the others, they either missed
the true road, or seeing how stern a road it was, timidly
turned away.

"Any poet, for instance, who undertakes an epic on our
own civil wars must inevitably collapse under the sheer
mass and weight of his subject unless he has trained himself to write, as it were, with the whole literature of the
past in his bones, a whole tradition at his finger tips.
In any case, epic is not a matter of writing chronicles
in verse: historians can do that sort of thing far more
effectively. No, true epic requires freedom from strict
historical fact. The poet must be given that freedom he
needs to develop his poem according to its own inner
logic, to construct, if he wishes, sudden wrenching reversals
of human fortune, to arrange for divine interventions, and
so on; free, in short, to construct that whole, fabulous,
complex, allusive fabric that great epic at all times de-
mands. Only through such freedom can the poet attain
his proper goal: a poem moving with all the passion and
power of prophetic speech, language, as it were, gone
wild with divinity; not some dry humdrum scrannel narrative hemmed in by a niggling piety toward attested fact.
Something, if you like, along the lines of the following
little effort of my own; though you must bear in mind
that it still lacks the finishing touches:

[*119*] THE CIVIL WAR

Lord and master of the world, our Roman stood supreme,
on land, on sea, and where the daystar dawned and
plunged;
but unappeased. Everywhere his cargoed keels
swirled the marble water white; but if, beyond, unknown,
some landfall lay, some shore touched to amber by the
blaze of gold,
Rome called it foe, Rome dealt it fate. Through war to
wealth
we hacked our way.
            Boredom and greed.
                        Old pleasures palled,
decayed. Attrition of dirty hands, pawing, soiling.
And the savor eroded, the bloom of goodness rubbed away.
Vulgarity by plenty spawned.

129

                                      Now rarity seemed all,
plunder of boredom born.

                        At Corinth, soldiers of Rome,
gaping, connoisseurs of bronze, collectors of antiques.
And the gashed earth bleeding:

                                    the red rocks ripped away,
the marbles, the rare, the rose, the porphyries pryed up,
peers of ocean's purple.

                        And the plunder:
                                    Numidia a waste;
desert through Cashmere, the splendid fleeces shorn away;
Arabia ravished, the spices scattered.

                                    Rome rampant
on a victim world.

                        New shapes of slaughter everywhere,
Peace a pool of blood.

                        With gold the hunters' snares are set:
driving through Africa, on and on; the hunters at Ham-
    mon,
and the beaters thrashing the thickets where the flailing
    tiger screams.
Hunters, hawkers of death. And the market for murder at
    Rome:
fangs in demand. At sea sheer hunger prowls the ships;
on silken feet the sullen tiger pads his gilded cage,
crouches at Rome, and leaps! And the man, gored and
    dying,
while the crowd goes wild.

                        I see the shame, unspeakable:
the shame of Rome, the shape of doom to come.

                                    The boys,
epheboi,
            and the Persian steel, the slashing blade
descending, and manhood, budding, shorn away, eunuchs,
shorn of love to stay for lust the apple years,
the ripe but running time, while Nature seeks her own
and cannot find.

                        Finds instead:
                                    perversion everywhere—
the mincing gait, effeminate, the girl-men, their hair
curried to silk, and the clothes, so many and so strange,
to mew our manhood up.

                        Or find the story in a table told:
a plank of citronwood, this limed and blonded board
                            130

chopped from Africa, this whorled and golden-knotted
    grain
whose every lovely blemish makes its gold comparisons
seem vile, snaring the senses, reflecting in its sheen
that slick, expensive glow, a society of slaves,
parvenus in purple and the raffish, rabble guests,
drowned in drink: a barren and ignoble board,
for which the Roman legions sack the world with steel,
caterers of greed.
            Gluttons of genius, the belly inventive,
scouring Sicilian waters for the parrot-fish, the scare;
and the wrasse borne swimming to the table, still alive;
the oysters from Lucrino torn, the fabulous, the rare,
jogging jaded hunger with the fillip of expense.
And Phasis of pheasants plundered, and the dull shore
    dumb,
and the leaves, dumb of song where the slow wind soughs.
                        At Rome
rottenness, power garbled with gold.
                          Quirites of cash,
Romans bought by the sellers of sops, and the golden rain,
staining the ballots yellow.
                  The people, the Senate corrupt.
Senatus Romanus,
           turned auctioneer, bidder for a fee,
consulta for cash. And freedom lies withered in nerveless
    hands
while the elders grabble for gold.
                  Greatness ripened to rot,
ipsaque maiestas,
          old majesty gone in the teeth;
the dignitas slimed over, Romanitas decayed:
foetor the color of gold.
                And Rome in Cato rejected;
honor cast out with Cato. But sadder than Cato that man
who conquered Cato, who wrenched his rod of office away.
Here Rome's ruin was; here in Cato, Rome's decay;
not Cato's sole defeat, but Rome in Cato symbolized,
mos maiorum in one man, Rome in him rejected:
self-betrayed, self-sold, self-prey and quarry made.
Whence no avenger rose.
             And usury, a rot:
the people drowning in a double sea, by debt pulled down,
by usury,
      a filth.

131

                    With usura hath no man a house;
no man's body but by debt is bound, in mortmain hard
of usura,
              the rot within, the impostumé in the guts,
foetor-infestation that flameth the blood to fever,
that bays the body down.
                       Usura, a ruin,
whence springeth war, whence revolution breaketh;
whence desperation taketh arms, and profligate and pauper
make cause together. Beggary hath daring.
O Rome,
                in such a sewer sunk, in such a sleep,
what surgery could cure, what skill could waken into life,
but war, the rage of war, the passion of the steel?
And war arose:
               [120] three generals did Fortuna raise;
three by Enyo died, each chief by goddess War
struck down in death, each mounded, buried under arms.
In Parthia hath Crassus perished; lieth Pompey dead
by Libyan shore; and last of three, the blood of Caesar
staineth red ungrateful Rome. Each in death divided;
as though the earth could not have borne such greatness in
      a grave,
they are ashes, they are scattered. Such is glory,
such its wages.
               Between Dicharchis' fields and Parthenope
cleaves a place, a chasm blasted out, in earth incised,
where underground Cocytus slides and Stygian air
as through a funnel spills, freighted with the sulphur
      fumes
of hell:
         Solfatara called,
                        where greenery is gone,
no meadow yields its harvest, where the turf springs not,
nor groweth glad nor green, nor thickets loudly ring
with springtime song of birds, descanting of their loves
in rivalry of voice. But Chaos holds this place,
and brooding rocks of pumice black, and cypresses,
tall tumuli of shade, mounding all the darkness
with a barrowed gloom.
                      Here it was that Father Dis
raised from hell his awful head, his halo shot
with funeral fires, flecked with charnel ashes white,
and cried to wingèd Fortune where she flew:

                                        "O Fortune,
of gods and man disposer,
                                despiser of the stable world,
you who changeth all,
                                power who will not stay,
who will not keep,
                        O relinquisher, O forsaker,
                                                        say,
do you not feel the weight of Rome, this dying mass
that grinds you down beyond endurance now?
                                                Look:
degenerates inherit Rome, despise their ancient strength,
supporting barely what great hands have raised.
                                                See:
their greed goes everywhere, their sumptuary greed,
gold in ruin ripened. And the houses intricate of gold;
their homes invade the skies, their moles expel the seas.
Ocean in their meadows burgeons, and all condition
turns awry, as man, rebellious, mocks his fate
contra naturam, invaders of sky and sea.
                                        And now
my earth invaded; Rome assaults the buried dead,
and earth before their crazed foundations opens wide,
and hollowed mountains groan with caves and caverns cry,
and while my ravaged marbles garb their mortal pride,
the ghosts and shades of hell assert their hope of heaven,
and the dead demand the light.
                                Therefore, Fortune, arise,
gird your brows for war, and hound these Romans on!
Whelm my kingdom with the legionary dead of Rome
and give me blood!
                Blood!
                                Since Sulla's sword drank deep
and earth, convulsed in labor, brought to light that crop
of ruddy wheat, that tasseled gory yield of war,
no human blood has touched my lips, no rain of blood
has washed the hungry body of Tisiphone!"
                                [121] So he spoke,
and stretched to take her hand in his, and as he reached,
earth, dehiscent, gaped and cracked.
                                Spoke Fortune then:
"O Father,
                you for whom Cocytus flows intestinal
through hell,

133

if I may speak the future unreproved,
thy wish shall come to pass. My anger chafes as hot;
my fury flareth too. All, all my gifts
to beetling Rome I now revoke, rescind my love with hate.
I who piled these buildings high shall pull them low,
incinerating Rome, glutting my awful hunger
on the blood of men.

Lo,
　　　　　　I see the field of Philippi
with double slaughter strewn, Thessaly ablaze
with funeral fires and Iberia interred in blood.
Clangor of war woundeth the ear. And now, O Nile,
I see thy freighted waters burst their desert bounds,
lapping at Libya; and Apollo's arms at Actium,
and the peoples afraid, the soldiery in terror.

　　　　　　　　　　　　O Father,
open the jaws of earth and summon down these dead,
these stricken multitudes, more murdered men
than Charon's little craft could ferry over hell:
ghosts requiring fleets.

　　　　　　　　O pale Tisiphone,
fulfill thyself in ruin, rend the body of this world,
and let this earth, a mangled wreckage, spindle down
beneath the waters of the Styx."

　　　　　　　　　　　[122] Scarcely had she spoken
when the clouds splintered, and shafts of lightning cleft
　　　the sky,
then vanished, and the Father of the dead sank slowly
　　　down,
subsiding into hell, and wrapped the mantling earth
about him as he sank, in terror of his brother's fire.
Then signs were seen, murder made manifest in omens
declaring doom.

　　　　　　　　His golden features flecked with blood,
the blazoned Titan sun withdrew, hiding his eye
against pollution from the civil wars below.
And Cynthia, the rising moon, now swollen to the full,
snuffed out her light and held no candle to the crime.
The mountains broke and avalanches thundered down,
cascading cliffs. And slow the unfamiliar rivers ran
between their ancient banks, a feeble, trickling flow,
arid, dying. Clangor of armor in the air;
bewilderment of bronze, as bugles shrilled the heavens,
arousing Mars. And Etna spoke, erupting rocks;
flambeaux of mountain-ruin arched the midnight sky,

134

rumbling with light. Among the tombs the dead arose,
and ghosts went gibbering with menacings and cries,
diro stridore,
> while at night, entraining stars,
the awful comet climbed, a finger of fire, streaking on,
pointing to fire, and Jupiter, a rain of blood,
drizzled on the world.
> Ephemeral, these omens flared,
then stopped, and Caesar threw procrastination off,
exchanging arms of Gaul for the steel of civil war,
and drove for his revenge.
> High upon the windy Alps,
where once a god of Greece in servitude had gone,
where the slopes in easy grade descend, accessible,
there lies an altared place, sacred to Hercules.
Here with solid sheeted ice the winter seals the peaks;
a mounded bulk so white against the silvered sky,
the crags and candid air seem one, continuous
with snow. Here the dulcet summer does not touch;
here there blows no gentle breath of spring, but glacier
has it all, so buttressed up in rigid ice,
so riveted with snow, it seems the muscled rocks
could hold the weighted world.
> Hither Caesar came,
exultant legions at his back. Here he camped,
surveying from this vantage-ground where Italy below
her lovely tapestries unrolled. And raising his hands
to the stars, he cried:
> "O Jupiter, omnipotent,
and thou, O land of Saturn, that rejoiceth in my deeds,
with my triumphal arches crowned,
> bear me witness:
not of my own will do I call the god of war;
unwillingly, I swear, I raise my hands to strike.
But by my hurts compelled to war—
> I, Caesar,
exiled from my country while I reddened Rhine with
blood,
while I shut the Alpine gates against the driving Gauls
and saved our Capitol from storm.
> Of what am I accused?
Victory.
> Because I rode in triumph sixty times,
because I cut the Germans down, I am an outcast now,
hounded from my home.

135

And who sees treason in my victories?
Who watches while I fight?

Cowards, mercenary men,
bribed by gold, the slavish stepsons of my mother
Rome.

But not so easily, not without revenge,
shall cowards bind my arms.

On to victory!
March on, my men, and plead our common cause with
steel.
One common crime arraigns us all; one single sentence
dooms us each. And so, to all my thanks are owed:
I do not win alone.

But now, since punishment
rewards my victory, since conquest stands accused
of treason, let Fortune be our judge.

Let war begin,
and show your mettle once again.

My plea is done:
armed, among so many men, I cannot lose."
So he spoke, when suddenly Apollo's bird,
the mantic raven, sliced the air with beating wings,
omina laeta,

with augury that all was well;
and from the left, the old, adjoining, sacred grove,
strange voices cried approval out, and tongues of flame
flashed up. And Phoebus swelled with unaccustomed light,
glistering with aureoles of fire.

[123] Encouraged, Caesar
gave the word to march, unfurled the flags of war,
and, striding on ahead, paced his daring's way,
unparalleled.

At first that hard and glacial ground
resisted not; severe and silent lay the snows;
the cold was kind. But when the squadrons cracked
the misted ice, and skittish horses shouldered through
the chains of cold that locked the streams, and the snows
thawed,
then suddenly, through mountain gorges plunging down,
the torrents burst in spate—

but then, as though commanded,
stopped short, their courses caught, cascadings tamed
to ice, immobile, all that rippling, liquid thing
turned hatchet-hard. If treacherous before, now worse:
slippery, it mocked the feet, no purchase gave.

Horses, men and arms in regimental ruin
fell. And then, compounding chaos, came the rains,
as the clouds, beneath the flailing of the glacial winds
ondriving, loosed their loads, and the unimpeded gusts,
like hurricanes, cracked down. And whirlwinds were;
and from the ruptured skies the hail descended, swollen,
battering the world. And rain in cloudburst fell,
inundating all, and wave on wave of sudden ice,
till all the world lay overwhelmed in white defeat
of snow. White the rivers ran; the stars were gray.
A white, defeated world.
                                    But Caesar was not stopped.
His spear his staff, he crushed the bristling ground beneath
his feet,
                    as when great Hercules comes striding down
from Caucasus returning, strides and does not stop,
or as when fierce Jupiter in strength and rage came
springing from Olympus to hurl the armed giants down
in massive doom.
                              But now while Caesar strode in wrath
upon the Alps, Rumor whirled with terror swift
to Rome, and soared and perched upon the Palatine.
There struck the statues of the gods with brazen news,
and Roman thunder boomed:
                                              the fleets of Caesar throng
                                                        the sea;
through Alpine passes, pouring down, the horsemen come,
a stain of German blood,
                                        sanguine Germano,
the blood of Rome, germanely red.
                                                        Arms and murder,
arma, cruor, caedes,
                              incendiary war.
Images of total war, whence confusion cometh,
whence panic in the heart, minds in counsel divided:
what the better course? Some prefer to flee
by land; others choose the sea, as though wild water were
safer, surer than the earth of Rome. One thinks of
                                                                  fight,
and so fulfills the Fates. In fear, the measure of flight:
how far they flee, so great their fear. And the people,
populus Romanus,
                              a sight of shame,
                                                        pricked by fear,
abandoning their citied Rome. Are glad to flee.

Look: their homes deserted at a whisper of alarm,
and fear, fear:
                    Romans in terror, clutching their children,
and the household gods,
                         Penates Laresque,
hidden in clothes, the women weeping, and the men in
                         tears,
calling farewell to their homes and cursing with their
     cries—
as though a curse could kill—their distant enemies.
Clasping of wives, and young men shouldering their
                         fathers,
bent down in weakness by the unaccustomed weight,
youth burdened with age. Each takes the thing he loves,
while fools drag all away, bear the booty of their homes
to war:
                    and all is now as when the sudden wind
rageth on the sea, lashing the waters to fury,
and the spar helps not the sailor, nor wheel, nor rope
from rigging torn, but one man builds a flimsy raft
of timbered pine in planks; one heads for quiet coves
where surf breaks not; another runs, anywhere running,
entrusting life to luck. But why lament these little things?
Pompey the Great,
                    Magnus,
                         he who trembled Pontus
                         once,
who walked upon those fabled shores where far Hydaspes
coils its sluggish way,
                    he, the pirate-scourge,
upon whose triumphings great Jupiter went pale
with wounded pride and spite,
                         to whom the raging Pontus,
the Bosporus, bowed down—
                         Pompey, frightened, ran,
twin consuls in his train, and let his titles lapse
and pride of empire fall, and Fortune saw at last
great Pompey's back,
                    saw Magnus running.
                              [*124*] Doom,
contagion of doom, as man's disasters sweep the skies,
and fear in heaven swells the mortal rout.
                              Lo,
dejectedly they leave, the milder, gentler gods,
abandoning the world, with loathing turn away

138

in exile from the stricken earth where frantic armies
dye the night with doom.
                              First goeth Peace,
she of the white arms, the white arms bruised with war—
Peace, hiding her conquered head beneath her helm,
descending to the downward world of Dis, implacable.
And with her gentle Faith; goeth Justice too,
Iustitia with streaming hair, and the lady of order,
goddess Concord too, in tears, with mantle torn.
So these gentle gods went down.
                              But as they went,
the gates of Dis in darkness yawned, spitting up
the horded gods of hell.
                              Came the Fury first,
Erinys, fiend of horror; issueth Bellona;
Megaera moveth forth, with whirling torches leapeth;
cometh Treachery, Destruction cometh on;
stalketh Death, that leached, that pallid presence. And
    there
among them moveth Madness, deity amok,
bursting bonds as when a warhorse shatters loose
and the reins are snapped; so she, Madness, breaketh forth,
her gory head flung high, with helmet bound by blood,
and livid, under blood, a face so slashed with scars
it seemed a living wound—breaketh, clasping shield,
battered, slashed by blade, moveth, with blazing torches,
to wrap the world in flame.
                              Earth felt these gods,
the weight of deity awry and the world unbalanced.
And the stars shook, reeling, and sought their former poise.
And the fundaments of heaven slid, toppling in ruin,
as the greater gods broke forth.
                              Issued Venus,
champion of Caesar; came Pallas too, with Romulus,
brandishing his spear, while Phoebus with his sister,
and Mercury, the son of Maia, came to Pompey's side;
and with them Pompey's peer in wandering and war,
Hercules, hero of Tiryns.
                              Shrilled the trumpets then,
and Discord with disheveled hair raised her awful head
to the dark skies,
                    Discord,
                              her face a scurf of blood,
eyes with livid bruises wet, with broken fangs
a mail of rust and filth, and her lolling tongue spilled

its dribbled poison down. Snakes twined her face;
her tattered clothes were torn above her writhing breasts,
and in her shaking hands she shook a flaming torch.
Came on,
    leaving Tartarus below where dark Cocytus
coils its way,
     striding the high peaks, the Apennines,
and here from vantage-ground looked down on earth
 below,
the lands, the shores, the armies streaming on and on
across the globe.
    And cried aloud:
        "O peoples of this
        earth,
to arms!
  To arms!
     Rise in your fury, O nations,
and seal with flaring torches all this citied world!
Here no refuge is:
     none, not woman, not child,
nor helpless age, shall safety find.
      This earth itself
shall quake, its shattered houses in rebellion fall.
Thou, Marcellus, hold the law!
      Inflame the mob,
O Curio!
  Let war brook no rebuke, O Lentulus!
And you, O Caesar, why such hesitation now?
Batter down the gates, rend the very walls away,
whirl their wealth away!
     Do you abandon Rome,
O Pompey?
   Then go, make your stand by Epidamnus'
   shore,
and dye the shores of Thessaly with blood of Rome."
So Discord spoke, and what she said was done on earth.

XV

LIFE AT CROTON

Eumolpus poured out his epic with a great, bursting
torrent of eloquence, and at last we entered Croton. That
night we ate and slept at a dirty little inn, but early the

next morning we set out to find quarters a little more in keeping with the grandeur of our pretensions. On the way, however, we ran into a crowd of legacy-hunters who promptly asked us who we were and where we came from. As prearranged, we answered with such a flood of information that they were quickly satisfied on both counts and accepted our story without further question. Immediately a great struggle broke out among them to see which could shower Eumolpus with the most money . . .

❧

All of them did their best to curry favor with Eumolpus by heaping him with presents . . .

❧

[125] And so we lived for some time at Croton . . . Eumolpus, drunk with his success, had so far forgotten the past that he began to boast to his intimates that no one in Croton dared to cross him and that, for any crimes we might commit, he could easily get us off through the influence of his new friends. For my part, thanks to the excellent food and the other gifts which Fortune showered on us in prodigious profusion, I had begun to put on weight again and had almost convinced myself that luck was no longer my enemy. Still, I couldn't help reflecting now and then on our present life and how it had come about. "What would happen," I used to wonder, "if one of these legacy-chasers had the wit to send off to Africa for information and then exposed us? Or suppose Eumolpus' hired servant got bored with his present luck and dropped a hint to his friends, or gave the whole show away out of spite? No mistake about it: we'd have to run for it, right back to our old life of poverty. Why, we'd have to start begging again. And, gods in heaven, an outlaw's life is a miserable business. Always waiting to be punished . . ."

❧

XVI

CIRCE

[*126*] "Your good looks have made you so conceited,"
said Chrysis, scolding me, "that instead of giving your
love away, you offer yourself for sale like some common
whore. If not, why do you comb your hair with such
fastidious care and plaster your face with cosmetics? How
else do you explain that affected, drooping languor in your
eyes and the way you walk, those tiny mincing steps you
take? That's what I think you are, a plain whore. I may
not know anything about omens and astrology and such,
but I can tell a man's character from his face and I guess
his thoughts from the way he walks. So, if you'd prefer
to sell us what we want, you have found a buyer. If, on
the other hand, you would rather do the gallant thing and
bestow your beauty freely, we shall be deeply indebted.
As for your admission that you are merely a humble slave,
that only makes my mistress want you more. Some women,
as you probably know, are only aroused by a lower-class
lover; only when they catch sight of some slave or footman
in a short tunic do their passions kindle. Some of them
even develop a hankering for gladiators or mule drivers
smothered in dust or one of those cheap actors who expose
themselves on the stage. My mistress belongs to this class
of women. She dodges the rich men in the orchestra,
skips fourteen rows back and looks for her lovers among
the riffraff in the gallery."

Needless to say, my vanity was enormously tickled by
this flattering proposition. "It wouldn't be you, by any
chance," I asked her, "who want me so much, would it?"

"Don't flatter yourself," replied the girl, bursting out
laughing at the clumsiness of my question. "I have never
slept with a slave yet, and god forbid that I should start
by climbing into bed with a convicted criminal. No, I
leave it to the married women to kiss the scars of a
flogging. I may be only a slave, young man, but my taste
runs more to knights." I hardly need to add that I was
impressed by their contrary inclinations, the maid with the

142

tastes of a lady of birth and breeding, the lady with the appetites of a chambermaid.

For some time we chatted on, joking and teasing and flirting. Finally I suggested that the girl should bring her mistress into the grove of plane trees nearby. She immediately agreed and, hitching up her tunic, slipped away into the swag of laurels which grew along the path. In a few minutes she returned, leading her mistress from her hiding place and seating her at my side.

What shall I say of that lady? In beauty she was more perfect than any masterpiece, incomparably more lovely than any artist's dream. Her hair, in long natural waves, rippled down over her shoulders; her brow was exquisitely small and her eyebrows, arching softly from the edges of her temples, rose almost joining just above her eyes. And her eyes! They shone like the stars on a moonless night. Her nose was gently tilted and she had such a mouth as Praxiteles must have dreamed for his Diana. Her chin, her neck, her hands and tiny feet, a sheen of white beneath their delicate straps of gold, must have eclipsed the marble of Paros. And suddenly, for the first time, my old love for Doris vanished away into thin air . . .

❧

What has happened, Jove, that your thunders are not heard,
  that deity is dumb, a silent tale in heaven?
Now, now were the time to let your bull's head lower,
  to clothe your body in the candor of the swan.
Here is the true Danae. Dare only touch her flesh
  and yours shall be by such a heat so drawn . . .

❧

[127] In her happiness she smiled so sweetly that it seemed as though I saw the risen moon, Cynthia in her splendor, break through the scudding clouds. She spoke shyly and sweetly, a grace in every word, every gesture. "Young man," she said, "if you do not despise a woman of birth, a woman who this year for the first time has tasted love, let me be your sister. I know, you have a brother too, but why should this prevent your taking me as your sister? As such I offer you my love. Deign only to accept my kiss."

"On the contrary," I replied, "it is I who beg you, who

143

implore you by your beauty, not to scorn me, to receive a poor stranger among your worshipers. Only let me adore you, and I shall be your loyal devotee. And do not think I kneel before your altar now with empty hands. In token of my love, lady, I freely offer you my brother, my Giton."

"What!" she exclaimed, "you offer me your brother, without whom you cannot live, who holds your life suspended on his lips, whom you love as I now wish you might love me?"

She spoke with such a grace, her words fell so sweetly on my ears that I seemed for an instant to be hearing the songs of the Sirens floating on the gentle air. I sat there in ecstasy and suddenly a shaft of light, a light more splendid than the sun's, burst upon my eyes. Dazzled, I asked my goddess her name.

"Didn't my maid tell you," she said, "that my name is Circe? No, I am not that famous Circe who was daughter of the sun, nor has my mother ever made the wheeling sun stop still until her love was done. But, if the Fates bring us two together now, I shall know that heaven has intervened. Yes: I can feel it now, that strange insensible power of some god acting on us both, drawing us together. Circe must love Polyaenos for a reason: always from the meeting of those names a great fire is born. So take me if you want me. Have no fear: no eye is watching now. Your brother is far away."

And folding me in her arms, those arms softer than the wings of a bird, she drew me gently to the ground where a thousand flowers bloomed:

Such flowers as once on Ida's peak the fruitful earth
in gladness spilled, when Jupiter with Juno lay
in lawful love, and all his heart was touched to flame:
bursting roses blew, and violets, and rush,
and from the fields, like snow, the sudden lilies laughed.
Such earth, it seemed, as summons Venus to the grass:
the light spilled brighter, bursting on our hidden love . . .

❧

There, ambushed in the grass, we lay, wrapped in each other's arms, exchanging kisses by the thousands, on the road to sterner play . . .

❧

144

[128] "Tell me the truth," she cried, "do my kisses offend you? Is my breath bad? Do my armpits smell? If it's none of these things, is it because you're afraid of Giton?"

At this I went purple with shame, completely losing even what little strength I had left. I felt as though my whole body had suddenly wilted away. "For god's sake," I begged her, "take pity on my misery. Don't mock me. I must be under a spell. Someone must have cursed me . . ."

❧

"Am I so ugly, Chrysis?" she asked. "Am I dirty or untidy? Is there some blemish on my beauty? Tell me the truth: don't deceive your mistress. I must be guilty of something, but what have I done?"

Receiving no answer from the maid, she snatched a mirror from her hands. Then, one after another, she made all of those lovely faces, those seductive looks, that normally make a lover go wild with delight. Finally she leaped up, shook the earth from her grass-stained cloak and hurried away in the direction of the temple of Venus, while I lay there in utter misery, trembling all over like one of the damned in hell, wondering if I were now cut off forever from my only hope of joy:

As when a dream in the dead sleep of night deceives
our wandering eyes, and we see beneath the digger's spade
earth spill her hidden treasures out, and greedy hands
go grabbling after gold, and then the sudden sweat,
and the twisting knife of fear that other men may know,
may find some golden clue and claim our cache as theirs.
And then the dream recedes, the conscious mind is
        mocked;
reality swirls back, and the cheated heart goes wild
for what it lost, moving, groping with all its strength
among the shadows of the past, like a ghost, obsessed . . .

❧

[129] "Thank you, Encolpius," said Giton, "for a love as pure as Socrates'. Never did Alcibiades sleep more chastely in his master's bed than I in yours."

❧

"Believe me, little brother," I replied, "I no longer recognize myself at all. That part of my body with which I once was an Achilles is dead and buried."

❧

Terrified, I suppose, that if he were caught alone with me, it would give rise to gossip, the boy tore himself from my arms and rushed away to a room in the inner part of the house.

❧

XVII

A SECOND ATTEMPT

Chrysis entered my room and handed me a letter from her mistress. The message read as follows:

My dear Polyaenos:
  If I were a lecherous woman, I might justifiably complain that your conduct towards me had been offensive in the extreme, or that you had deliberately deceived me. On the contrary, I find myself grateful for your somewhat drooping interest. Hollow pleasures perhaps, but only rarely have I experienced such a sweet protraction of the prelude to performance.
  In any case, I am anxious to hear how you are and whether or not you were able to walk home on your own. At least I have heard doctors say that impotent men are incapable of even standing up straight. So, my dear, you must take good care of yourself, or your paralysis will be total. Never before, I confess, have I seen a young man in such infirm health or so close to death. One might almost say you were dead already. Clearly, if the chill spreads to your hands and knees as well, you had best call in the undertakers.
  What's to be done? Despite your shameful treatment of me, your present condition is far too precarious for me to withhold any possibility of a cure. But the solution lies with Giton. In my opinion, you will recover your manhood only if you avoid sleeping with

your little friend for at least three days.

As for myself, I feel confident that I shall have no trouble in finding a more ardent lover. Neither my mirror nor my reputation lie.

Keep well—if you can,
Circe

Chrysis waited until I had finished reading this ironic little message of reproach before breaking in. "Accidents like yours are not uncommon," she said, "particularly in these parts where there are witches who can pull the moon right down from the sky. But generally their spells don't last very long, and we'll look into it. In the meantime, however, write a sweet little note back to my mistress. Be frank about your failure and ask her to forgive you. I might as well tell you that she hasn't been herself since the day you humiliated her."

Overjoyed to comply with the little maid's request, I sat down and wrote off the following reply:

[130] Dearest Circe:

I confess, dear lady, that I have sinned. After all, I am a man, and a young man at that. But never until now have I committed a mortal sin.

I am a criminal and I admit it. Any punishment you choose to inflict, lady, I richly deserve. Thus I confess that I betrayed a friend; I killed a man; I committed sacrilege. For each of these crimes you have only to prescribe the punishment. If your sentence is death, I shall bring you my sword in person. If you order me flogged, I shall strip off my clothes and run to you naked. But before you pass sentence, remember this: it was less myself than my instrument that failed. As your soldier, lady, I stand ready to die in the breach, but I am a soldier now without a spear. Who despoiled me so, I do not know. Perhaps my hopes outran my heat; excess of passion perhaps cut off my pleasure prematurely. I cannot explain what happened. You tell me, however, to beware of total paralysis. As though that sickness could be worse which deprives me of my power to possess you. Lady, my whole apology comes to this: I will give you satisfaction if you will permit me to make amends . . .

147

Sending Chrysis off with this pledge of improved performance, I turned my whole attention to my offending body. Renouncing a hot bath as probably harmful, I contented myself with a quick massage. Then I sat down to a supper of the strongest and most fortifying foods I could think of: raw onions followed by snails' heads without sauce and a few swallows of weak wine. Finally, I took a short stroll and then went to bed without Giton. For I was so anxious to make amends to Circe that the mere thought of even brushing thighs with Giton terrified me.

[131] Early the next morning I rose feeling refreshed in body and mind, and walked down to the grove of plane trees where our previous meeting had taken place. Nervously recalling that ill-omened assignation, I tried to calm myself by strolling up and down through the grove while waiting for my guide, Chrysis. No sooner had I sat down to rest from my walk—in the very spot where yesterday's accident had taken place—than Chrysis appeared, followed by a little old woman. After we had exchanged the usual greetings, Chrysis said, "Well, fastidious lover, have you come to your senses today?"

Meanwhile the old woman pulled a rainbow-colored scarf from her dress and proceeded to swathe my neck with it. She then mixed some dust and spittle into a little ball with her third finger and made a mark on my forehead. Despite all my resistance . . .

❦

At the conclusion of her incantations, she commanded me to spit three times. Next she handed me some pebbles, each of which had been individually charmed and wrapped in purple cloth, and told me to drop them down my crotch. Then she reached in with her hand to see what response, if any, she had awakened. And lo, pat to her spells, that ghostly part of me obeyed, inching and lurching into enormous life until it quite filled her hand. "Ooh, Chrysis," she gasped delightedly, "just look at the hare I've started for the hunters."

❦

There the twining trees had cast their summer shade:
cypresses and planes, the berried laurel rustling in the breeze,

148

and the great shorn pines, their crowns a-quiver.
And there, among the trees, a racing brook ran down,
lapping with a chirr of pebbled water all the grove.
It seemed a place for love; whereof in witness sang
the woodland nightingale, the swallow from the town,
through violets and grass, all calling as they flew . . .

❦

There she lay, languidly stretched out upon the grass.
Her neck, white as marble, rested on a golden cushion
and she was lazily fanning herself with a spray of flowering
myrtle. Suddenly catching sight of me, she reddened,
blushing, I suppose, to remember her deep humiliation of
the previous day. Then, dismissing her women, she
motioned to me to sit down beside her, but screened her
face with her branch of myrtle to conceal her embarrassment. At last, somewhat emboldened by the barrier of
flowers, she said, "Well, my paralytic lover? Have you
come here a whole man today?"

"Don't ask me," I answered, "try me." With that, I
threw myself into her arms and, immune at last from any
evil spells, took my pleasure of her kisses till I could kiss
no more . . .

❦

[132] The beauty of his body summoned me to love.
Our lips, bruised by an endless rain of kisses, murmured
our delight, while our hands, tangled with each other,
wove and unwove every way of love, every caress. Then,
binding our bodies together in one supreme embrace, our
breathing so confounded on a kiss that we seemed a
single soul . . .

❦

XVIII

I TAKE MYSELF IN HAND

❦

Stung by this public rebuff and frantic for revenge, she
ran off shrieking for her grooms and ordered them to flog
me. Even this savage punishment, however, failed to ap-

pease her fury, and she sent for her spinning-women, the very dregs of her household, and told them to spit at me. Hiding my face in my hands and completely dumb with shame—god knows, I deserved to be punished—I was flogged, spat at, and then thrown bodily out the door. Proselenos was thrown out with me, Chrysis was flogged, and the whole household went around grumbling, asking each other in whispers who had upset their mistress so . . .

❧

For my part, somewhat consoled by the presence of companions in my misery, I did my best to conceal the stripes of my flogging, knowing perfectly well that those wounds would please Eumolpus as much as they would distress Giton. But there was only one means of salvaging the pitiful remnants of my lost honor, and that was to feign sickness. So I climbed into bed, picked up a razor and unleashed my full fury against the sole author of my disgrace. Taking him firmly by the hand:

> Three times with razor raised I tried to lop;
> three times my trembling fingers let it drop,
> while he, as limp as cabbage when it's boiled,
>   with prickish fright my purpose foiled.
>
> For, cold as ice, he shrank, too scared to watch,
> and screwed his crinkled length against my crotch,
> so cramped along my gut, so furled and small,
>   I could not see to cut at all.
>
> Baffled, I mused: how bring the blade to bear?
> How lop that thing so wee it seemed not there
> at all? But wait, I thought: if steel won't kill,
>   perhaps my verbal engines will.

With that, hunching myself on my elbow, I lashed the laggard with my tongue. "What do you have to say for yourself," I cried, "you shame of gods and man? Obscenity, unspeakable sullen pendant, is this what I deserved? To be snatched from the doors of heaven and spindled down to hell? To have this scandal of decrepit, limp old age fixed upon my youth, my green and swelling years? By your mercy, I implore you, declare me cured, or give me my

certificate of death." But utterly unmoved by my bitter
reproaches:

He turned his head away and gazed upon the ground,
unstirred, unmoved, as on a windless day
of summer heat, the languid willow leaves lie still,
and wilted poppies on their slender stems hang down . . .

But suddenly the whole overwhelming shame of this
obscene palaver with myself swept over me. The blood
rushed to my head, and I blushed all over to think how
far I had forgotten my self-respect by stooping to argue
with that part of me which no serious man thinks worthy
of his thoughts. For some time I lay there, ruefully rubbing my forehead. Then the absurdity of my shame struck
me. After all, I thought, why not? What's so unnatural or
wrong about working off one's feelings with a little plain-
spoken abuse? Don't we curse our guts, our teeth, our
heads, when they give us trouble? Didn't Ulysses himself
have a parley with his heart? Why, the way those heroes
in the tragic plays strut around cursing their eyes, you'd
think their eyes had ears. Gouty people damn their toes;
arthritics curse their joints; the crud-eyed blast their eyes
and even toe-stubbers take out their feelings on their feet.

Then why in heaven's name
must every nagging prude
of Cato's ilk cry shame,
denounce my work as lewd,
damning with a look
my guileless, simple art,
this simple, modern book?
To prudes I now assert
my purity of speech;
such candor in my pen
as will not stoop to teach.
I write of living men,
the things they say and do,
of every human act
admitted to be true.
Then where's the shame in that,
if loving men enjoy
the pleasures of the night
whereby each girl and boy
experience delight?

151

> Let prudes in need of proof
> heed what Epicurus said,
> old master of the truth,
> who held that all are led
> by their senses to the goal,
> life-perfecting Pleasure,
> Pleasure is the goal of all,
> omnis vitaeque perfector.

❧

Nothing is falser than people's preconceptions and ready-made opinions; nothing is sillier than their sham morality . . .

❧

XIX

OENOTHEA

[133] Finished with my profession of faith, I promptly sent for Giton. "On your word of honor," I asked him, "answer me the truth: that night when Ascyltus stole you from my bed, did he force you to sleep with him? Or was he content to pass the night decently by himself?"

Solemnly touching his hands to his eyes, the boy swore by everything holy that Ascyltus had not so much as touched him . . .

❧

Kneeling down on the threshold, I made my prayer to my tormentor, Priapus:

Comrade of Bacchus and the nymphs, you whom lovely Dione
set as god upon our woodlands in their glory;
O lord of Lesbos, god of Thasos' holy green,
whom Lydia, the seven-streamed, adores beside Hypaepa;
O mentor of Bacchus, come!
                              Hear me, dryad-lover,
welcome this humble prayer.

                    Innocent of harm,
pure in heart, with pious hands, I come to you:
a poor man, in impotence and need, by weakness worn.
I sinned, O lord, yet sinned in part: not all of me
offended. Weakness was my crime, the thing I did not,
could not, do; and being such, was less than crime.
I implore you, lord, purge my tortured soul of guilt;
forgive my petty crime.
                    And when once more I see
good fortune laugh, then you shall have the gifts
your deity deserves.
                    To your shrine shall go
the ram, the father of the flocks, in hornèd glory;
to you the squealing sow shall lead her suckling young.
And this year's wine shall froth in bowls for you,
and round about your shrine three times shall dance
the randy, drunken lads in praise, O god, of you.

❀

While I was praying, I kept an anxious eye cocked to
see if that poor dead part of me would raise its fallen head.
But suddenly Proselenos, her dress black with ashes and
her hair half ripped out, came rushing into the temple.
Snatching me by the hand, she led me through the
entranceway and outside . . .

❀

[134] "What screech-owl," she shrieked at me, "has eaten
your manhood away? Did you step on some dung in the
dark? What corpse did you kick by the crossroad at night?
Eh? Why, you can't even redeem yourself with the boy.
Look at you: soft, flabby, limp, huffing and puffing like
an old hack on a hill. Ugh. All that work and sweat for
nothing. And as though it weren't enough that you should
have sinned, you have to go and get me in trouble with
the gods too!"

❀

She led me unresisting into the priestess' cell. Then,
pushing me back on the bed, she snatched a stick from
the back of the door while I lay without a word of protest,
meekly waiting for my beating. Luckily for me, however,

the stick broke at the first stroke and so lessened the force of the blow; otherwise she would probably have broken both my head and my arm. But this thought so terrified me that I gave a great groan, burst into tears, and covering my face with my hands, buried my head in the pillow. Proselenos, equally upset, collapsed on the bed in tears and began with a shaking voice to complain of the bitterness of being old. This lament, however, was interrupted by the sudden arrival of Oenothea.

"Well," she exclaimed, "what are you two doing in my room? You look as though you were sitting beside a freshly dug grave. What, crying on a holiday? Why, even mourners should be laughing on a day like this."

❧

"Oenothea," said Proselenos, "this poor miserable creature was born under an unlucky star. Right now there's not a girl or boy in the whole world who'd take his goods at any price. Yes, you've never seen such a wretched thing. Why, he's limp as wet leather; there's nothing there at all. Just to show you, what would you think of a man who could get out of bed with Circe without having been satisfied?"

At this, Oenothea came and sat down between us on the bed. "Young man," she said, wagging her head gravely, "I am the only person in the world who can cure your disease. I mean that. All I require is that you agree to spend one night here in bed with me, and if I don't make you stand up stiffer than a bull's horn, my name's not Oenothea. Listen:

All visibles obey my words. All this flowered world,
at my command, must wilt, the saps run sluggish in the
    stems;
they spring again as I give leave. These barren cliffs,
at my bare word, must rivers spill, each crag a Nile.
For me the sea falls still, the spanking waters hush;
the winds of winter gentle at the passing of my feet.
As I please, the rivers flow. Dragons and tigers,
like puppies, wag their tails and follow where I go,
tamely at my feet.
                    But these are trifles, bagatelles.
Why, by my spells, the lovely circled moon is drawn,
enchanted down, and flaring Phoebus, terrified,

154

drives his raging horses backwards down the sky
and makes a dusk of dawn.
                              Such are words: a power.
So once the ruddy fury of a charging bull was quenched
by a virgin's speech. Such was Circe's magic once,
of all Ulysses' crew, she made a piggery of men.
So Proteus is the image of his wish. And so, I too
have skills to spell the trees of Ida to the sea
and draw the rivers to the peaks, uphill where they began."

[135] I shuddered with genuine terror when I heard
these fabulous promises and began to study the old woman
with undisguised respect . . .
    "Very well, young man," she said, "you must do exactly
as I tell you." With that she carefully washed her hands,
and leaning over the bed, kissed me once, twice . . .

❦

In the center of the altar she set a rickety table
which she heaped with glowing coals. She then reached
down a winecup, badly cracked with age, patched it with
hot pitch and replaced the nail which had come away
from the blackened wall when she took the winecup down.
Next, she put on a square apron, placed a large clay pot
on the hearth, and with a long fork took down from the
cupboard an old sack in which she kept her stock of beans
—along with an old, battered head of pork, badly nicked
and sliced all over. She undid the bag, poured a pile of
beans on the table and ordered me to shell them as quickly
as possible. I did as I was told, slowly and laboriously
separating each bean from the dirty pods with my fingers.
Scolding me for a slowpoke, she snatched up the beans and
ripped the husks away with her teeth, spitting them out
on the floor like so many dried-up flies.

❦

I was amazed at the inventiveness of her poverty and
the skill, the loving frugal care displayed in every detail
of that humble house:

No ivories of India, inworked with gold, shone here;
no trampled marbles underfoot mocked the giving earth
for what she gave. Instead, a simple willow bed,

a pallet of straw; pots and pans of common clay,
freshly turned by the potter's unpretentious skill.
And bowls of water, bright with beaded sweat. Baskets
of woven reed. A pitcher purpled with the god of wine.
The walls were wattled straw, spatter-daubed with clay;
long rows of rustic nails, and there beside the door
a broom of living rush hung down. Overhead,
suspended from the blackened beams in drying loops,
the simple harvest stores: sorb-apples, ripe,
wreaths of fragrant herbs and sprigs of savory
in raisin-clusters twined.

                        In such a house as this,
near Athens once, I think, Theseus found his welcome,
found a hostess there, hospitable as heaven,
Hecale by name, the Muse of Battus' son—
Callimachus, who sang for generations yet to come
and made the name of Hecale with welcome, one.

❧

[136] First she took down a tiny scrap of meat. Then,
picking up the head of pork—which couldn't have been
a day younger than she was—she tried to reach it back
up to the hook with her fork. But suddenly the rotten
stool on which she was standing crumbled and collapsed,
and she tumbled down into the fireplace, smashing the
neck of the pot as she fell. The water slopped out,
quenching the fire which had just begun to blaze, but not
before she touched her elbow to a burning stick and,
lashing out in fright, spattered soot and ashes all over
her face. When I recovered from my own alarm, I helped
her to her feet, though not, I confess, without a laugh.
Anxious not to delay the sacrifice, she scurried off
to a neighbor's house to borrow some coals to relight the
fire, while I went to the door to see her off. But suddenly
three sacred geese, who came there daily, I suppose, to
demand their noonday meal from the old woman, surrounded me, cackling furiously while I stood there shaking.
One of them ripped my tunic; the second untied the laces
of my sandals and tugged them off, while the third,
obviously the ringleader of the brutes, sank his jagged
beak into my leg. It was no laughing matter. Snatching up
the leg of a table, I began to batter the ugly, aggressive
brute. Too angry to be content with merely beating him

156

away, however, I kept on hammering at him until my
honor was avenged and the goose lay dead at my feet:

So once, they say, the strength of Hercules prevailed,
and the wild, Stymphalian birds fled honking off to heaven.
So too, on fetid wings, the filthy Harpies flew,
while Phineus sat below, disconsolate and sad,
and saw his lovely dinner dunged. So now as then,
the frightened air with unaccustomed clamor shook,
and the skies, bewildered, throbbed with beating wings . . .

❧

By now the two surviving geese had gobbled down the
beans which had scattered all over the floor; then, obviously
demoralized by the loss of their leader, they strutted away
to the temple. Delighted with my taste of victory and my
spoils, I went back in, tossed the dead goose behind the
bed and carefully douched the shallow cut on my leg with
vinegar. But fearing that there might be a row over the
lost beans, I decided to make off while I still could. So
I gathered up my things and was just about to step out
the door when I saw Oenothea on her way home with a
brazier of live coals. Quickly jumping back, I pulled off
my cloak and stood there nonchalantly in the doorway as
though waiting for her to return.

Dumping the hot coals over a heap of dry reeds, she
piled a few sticks of wood on top and apologized for
having taken so long. Her neighbor, she explained, had
refused to let her leave until she'd had the customary two
or three friendly glasses of wine.

"Now then," she said, "what have you been doing while
I was gone? And where are the beans?"

Thinking that my rout of the geese deserved at the least
a few words of praise, I described the battle in detail and
concluded by triumphantly producing the dead goose, the
sight of which I thought might console her for the loss
of her beans. But when she saw that dead bird, she let out
such a squawk that for an instant I thought the house
had been invaded by a second flock of geese. Unnerved
by all this outcry and puzzled to know what was so terrible
about what I'd done, I asked her why she was angry and
why she seemed to think that goose deserved more pity
than I did.

[137] Furiously slapping her hands together, she cried,

157

"You monster, don't you dare say another word! Do you know the sacrilege you've committed? You've murdered Priapus' pet goose, the favorite of all the married women. And don't suppose it's not a serious matter. If the magistrates find out, it's up on the cross you go. This house was innocent of any bloodshed until you defiled it. Now, thanks to you, any of my enemies who wants has the power to expel me from my priesthood."

❧

"Don't make such a fuss," I said. "I'll give you an ostrich in place of the goose."

❧

Then, to my amazement, she sat down on the bed and sobbed over that dead goose until Proselenos arrived with the things she had bought for the sacrifice. Seeing the dead bird, she asked Oenothea why she was crying and, being told, promptly burst into tears herself, exclaiming over me as though I'd just murdered my father and not some damn goose. Finally I got disgusted. "Look here," I broke in, "why don't you let me pay you for the goose? After all, if I'd insulted you or killed a man, it might be a different matter. But a goose! Here, take these two pieces of gold. With them you can buy yourself some geese, or gods too, for that matter."

At the sight of money, Oenothea melted. "Forgive me, young man," she said, "I was only anxious on your account. You mustn't take it as ill will; it was a proof of my affection for you. But don't you worry your head about it any more; we'll see to it that no one ever finds out. You just pray to the gods and ask them to pardon your sacrilege."

Rich, you journey well. Your money slicks the sea.
Your winds are fair; you sail at will and do not drown
        —though loaded down with money.

And rich, you marry well. Sleep with Danae. Why not?
(Just whisper in her father's ear what he told her
when Jupiter as a rain of gold descended:
        —"Dear, you've married money.")

158

Poet or lawyer, either be: the world's applause
is yours. No matter what you say, or how
                    —nothing talks like money.

Or be a judge. Gavel down your "Guilty" or "Acquitted,"
secure as Servius. The world's not judge of much
                    —except your Honor's money.

Examples enough.
                    The moral is: money money money.
It pays to pray:
                    Jupiter is money in the bank.

❦

Setting a jar of wine beneath my hands, she made me
extend my fingers and carefully rubbed them down with
a purgative of leeks and parsley. Then, mumbling a prayer,
she threw a handful of filberts into the wine, and according to whether the nuts fell to the bottom or floated, drew
her conclusions. I noticed, however, that the empty nuts,
being filled with air, floated, while the good nuts with
meat in their kernels sank to the bottom . . .

❦

She slit the belly of the goose and extracted a fine plump
liver with which she proceeded to tell me my future.
Finally, to remove any remaining traces of sacrilege, she
chopped the goose into small pieces which she skewered
and roasted over the fire. So, instead of the terrible death
to which she had condemned me only a few minutes
earlier, I was served a handsome meal. Between courses
of roast goose, we dumped down glass after glass of good
neal wine . . .

❦

[138] Next, Oenothea brought out a leather phallus
which she rubbed with a mixture of oil, pepper and
ground nettleseed and then slowly inserted in my rectum.
Pitilessly sprinkling my thighs with the same mixture,
the old hag . . .

❦

159

Mixing the juice of watercress with god knows what exotic herb, she spattered my penis with the stuff and brushed the lower part of my abdomen with a branch of green nettles . . .

❦

Despite the fact that the two old women were completely drunk and almost frantic with desire, they tried to take the same road, chasing me down the street and shrieking, "Thief! Thief! Stop him!" I finally escaped, but I had run so furiously that my poor feet were badly cut and bleeding all over . . .

❦

XX

INTERLUDE WITH CHRYSIS

❦

"Chrysis, who once despised you as nothing but a slave, has now decided to share your present lot even at the cost of her life."

❦

"What loveliness did Leda have, or Ariadne, that they could be compared to Circe? The beauty of Helen and Venus is nothing to hers. Why, had she appeared when Paris was judging the three goddesses, had he seen her whole enchanting beauty, he would have thrown Helen over and the goddesses into the bargain. O gods, to kiss her, to hold that heavenly beauty in my arms once more! For then my manhood might revive, that part of me that now lies drugged and dead with some enchanter's spell would rise once more. Then no humiliations would hold me back. Then beat me, thrash me, O my lovely: I would not feel it. Throw me out the door: you play, you tease. Only let me return to your good graces once again . . ."

❦

[*139*] I wore out the bed with my restless writhing, thrashing about as though I held in my arms the living ghost of my lost love . . .

🌸

Not me alone does fate, implacable, pursue.
On others too the grinding rage of heaven falls.
So Hercules was hounded from his home to bear in pain
the angry goddess' grudge. So Pelias once knew
the spite of Juno; Laomedon, unknowing, fought
his fate. Two gods oppressed the beggared Telephus,
while great Ulysses learned of Neptune's sea a life,
its bitterness, and rage.
                         So now, upon me too,
Priapus' restless hatred falls, hounding me on,
over land and sea, on and on, relentlessly on.

🌸

I asked Giton whether anyone had come to inquire after me. "No one today," he told me, "but yesterday a rather pretty woman came and chatted until I began to get bored by her forced conversation. Then she warned me that you had committed a great crime and that you'd be tortured like a slave so long as the person you've injured persists in his complaint."

🌸

I was still grumbling when Chrysis burst in, threw her arms around me passionately, and cried: "O passion of my life, my dream, my only joy! Only death itself will ever quench the flame of my desire."

🌸

One of the new slaves suddenly ran up and told me that Eumolpus was furious because I had taken two days off from my work without leave. So I'd better prepare a good excuse. But as things looked now, it wasn't likely that the master's fury would be satisfied by anything less than a flogging . . .

🌸

XXI

PHILOMELA

[*140*] One of our inheritance-hunters was an extremely respectable matron by the name of Philomela, a lady whose ample charms in younger days had enabled her to come into several large legacies. Now old and faded, however, she made it her practice to offer her daughter and son as wards to childless old men with money, and in this way managed to keep her talents green and flourishing into the second generation. So it was not long before she came to pay a visit to Eumolpus, and after warmly praising his uprightness of life, his largesse and conspicuous humanity, commended her children to his care. He was, she declared, the only man on earth who could be depended upon to give her darlings daily instruction in firm moral principles. In short, she proposed to throw these children entirely on Eumolpus' mercy: his guidance and instruction was the only portion she could give them before she died. True to her word, she promptly left her very pretty daughter and her adolescent son there in the bedroom with Eumolpus and hurried off to the temple on the pretext of thanking heaven for this fulfillment of her dearest hopes.

Eumolpus—whose frustrations had reached such a pitch that he was on the point of making me his Ganymede—lost no time and immediately invited the girl to a lesson in ritual buttock-thumping. But he had told everyone that he was gouty and cursed with a bad liver, and unless he maintained this fiction, he ran the risk of giving the whole show away. So, in order to sustain his story, he ordered the girl to sit down on his lap and test for herself at close quarters the full extent of that "uprightness and largesse and conspicuous humanity" her mother had just commended so warmly. Then he told Corax to slip under the bed, plant his hands firmly on the floor, and stroke the cadence for him by heaving with his buttocks. Corax carried out his orders to perfection: a slow, smooth stroke, every thrust so timed that it coincided exactly with the girl's expert twisting and writhing. Then, as the lesson neared its conclusion, Eumolpus shrieked to Corax to quicken the tempo. Corax promptly obeyed, humping away like mad, while Eumolpus swung there in mid-air, bouncing and swaying back and forth between the servant and the girl, for all the world like a human seesaw. The first lesson over, Eumolpus immediately began the second, much to our own amusement and also his own.

Meanwhile, fearing that my long inactivity had left me out of shape, I approached the brother who was eagerly following his sister's gymnastics through a chink in the door. Sophisticated boy that he was, he made no objection, but once again the god's hostility frustrated my rising hopes . . .

❦

XXII

RESTORED

❦

"There are other gods still more powerful," I explained, "and it is they who have made me a man once more. Mercury himself, the god who guides our unborn souls to the light and leads the dead to hell, has taken pity on me and given me back that power which an angry hand once cut away. Look at me and tell me whether Protesilaus or any of those ancient heroes was ever more blessed by heaven than I am now." With that, I lifted my tunic and displayed myself in my erected glory. Gaping with astonishment and awe, utterly incapable of believing his eyes, he reached out his shaking hands and caressed that huge pledge of heaven's favor . . .

❦

XXIII

MATTERS AT CROTON COME
TO A HEAD

❦

"Perhaps so," Eumolpus admitted. "But Socrates, whom gods and men alike declared to be the wisest man in the world, used to boast that he never looked into a shop and completely avoided all crowds. And it's my belief that our best policy now would be to follow his wise example."

"Very true," I replied. "And certainly no one more richly deserves bad luck than those who envy others their good luck. But how do you think con men and swindlers would ever succeed unless they first got their hooks into a crowd by pointedly displaying fat purses jingling with gold? To catch a fish, you need a baited hook, and you'll never catch a man unless you're prepared to give him at least a nibble of hope."

❦

[*141*] "The ship from Africa with that cargo of slaves and money which you keep promising never arrives. And the legacy-hunters are beginning to lose patience and their generosity is wearing thin. No, unless I'm badly mistaken, Lady Luck is preparing to leave us in the lurch . . ."

❦

XXIV

EUMOLPUS MAKES HIS WILL

❦

"With the exception of my freedmen," Eumolpus said, "all those who come into money by the terms of my will shall inherit only upon satisfaction of the following condition: they must slice up my body into little pieces and swallow them down in the presence of the entire city . . ."

❦

"We know that in certain countries there exist laws which compel a dead man's relatives to eat his body. So rigorously, in fact, are these laws enforced that men who die of sickness or disease frequently find themselves reproached by their relatives for having made their meat inedible. So I warn my friends not to disregard my last wishes, but to eat my body as heartily as they damned my soul."

❦

Eumolpus' reputation for enormous wealth had so completely blinded the poor fools' minds that . . .

❦

Gorgias stood ready to manage the funeral . . .

❦

"I am not in the least disturbed by any fear that your stomachs may turn. They will obey you quite without qualms so long as you promise them years of blessings in exchange for one brief hour of nausea. Just close your eyes and imagine that, instead of human flesh, you're munching a million. If that isn't enough, we'll concoct some gravy that will take the taste away. As you know, no meat is really very tasty anyway; it all has to be sauced and seasoned with great care before the reluctant stomach will keep it down. And if it's precedents you want, there are hundreds of them. The people of Saguntum, for instance, when Hannibal besieged them, took to eating human flesh, and did so, moreover, without the slightest hope of getting an inheritance out of it. And when a terrible famine struck Petelia, the people all became cannibals, and the only thing they gained from their diet was that they weren't hungry any more. And when Scipio captured Numantia, the Romans found a number of mothers cuddling the half-eaten bodies of their children in their laps . . ."

❦

NOTES TO THE SATYRICON

CHAPTER I

Page 21, Line 1. *professors*—Literally, *declamatores*, i.e., professional teachers of rhetoric. During the Republican period in Rome, oratory had enjoyed enormous prestige, and eloquence, whether practiced in the lawcourt or the political arena, was one of the few routes by which a "new man" might rise to prominence and power. But with the end of the Republic and the extinction of political freedom during the Principate, political oratory suffered a permanent decline. Despite this decline, however, the educational curriculum of the Empire remained overwhelmingly centered upon instruction in the techniques of public speaking. In part, of course, this emphasis was practical: forensic training, as we know from the case of Trimalchio's friend Phileros, could make a poor man rich or help him climb to power. But for the most part rhetoric bulked large in the curriculum because it had been hallowed by Republican tradition and the prestige of the great Republican orators; it had become, that is, the "done thing," a badge of social class.

In the circumstances, rhetoric quickly degenerated. Not only did it lack a real relation to the age—an age whose hypocrisy of political power made power of language improbable—but being essentially nothing more than a set of skills itself, it was particularly susceptible to hardening into mere formula. And having no genuine subject-matter, it could not refresh itself; nor could it take refreshment from the seriousness of its students, for they were mostly motiveless. Lacking competitors, moreover, it quickly usurped the curriculum, almost driving literature out altogether except insofar as literature could be made to serve rhetoric. The consequences were far-reaching; for just as rhetoric, once expelled from public life, hardened into artificiality and a sterile academic discipline, so too the usurpation of literature by rhetoric produced no life. And if the typical rhetorical product of the period is the frigid, artificial, banal, and pompous set-piece or *suasoria* of the classroom, the literature of the Silver Age is a desert of rhetoricians tricked out as poets or of lively talents smothered by rhetoric. It is this kind of rhetoric (and rhetorician) which is here satirized by Petronius. Like Juvenal and Martial, Petronius protests with unmistakable animus and wit against the rhetoricians: their absurd pretensions to poetry, the recitations, the hired claques, the frigid mythological epics, the dilettantes without talent, the perversion of patronage, the utter lack of relation between education and life. Characteristically, however, Petronius allows the rhetorician his defense and elides the moral judgment with irony. At least I would suppose that the effect of having the hack Eumolpus condemn the rhetoricians is irony; of Encolpius here one is less certain, but surely he is elsewhere a considerable rhetorician—at least of perversion? The technique would be, I think, Petronian. It is also superb (and self-conscious) rhetoric.   Line 22. *chains*—Prisoners of war were commonly hamstrung as a precaution against escape.

166

Page 22, Line 3. Euripides—Two of the three great tragedians of the Athenian fifth century. Aeschylus is missing, presumably because the sheer magnificence and complexity of his poetic rhetoric made him, for Encolpius' purpose here, an inappropriate example. However, the charge that Aeschylus was obscure was common in antiquity. The notion that Euripides is imprecise and prolix is, of course, essentially a modern, not an ancient, prejudice.   Line 7. poets—The nine lyric poets of Greece were: Sappho, Alcaeus, Alcman, Bacchylides, Arion, Ibycus, Stesichorus, Anacreon, and Simonides (though there are variant lists). Pindar, of course, is the great lyric poet of fifth-century Thebes, while the "Homeric manner" refers to the epic *Iliad* and *Odyssey*.   Line 10. *Demosthenes*—The philosopher Plato (ca. 429–347 B.C.) and the great orator Demosthenes (384–322 B.C.) were incomparably the finest of Greek stylists. It is their naturalness and variety and vitality, their complete freedom from academic theories or pat schemata, that Encolpius is emphasizing.   Line 17. Athens— The Greeks—and the Romans after them—tended to distinguish between a pure and simple style (the "Attic") and a florid and emotional style (the "Asiatic"). Encolpius, of course, ranges himself with the Atticists against what he calls the "flatulent rhetoric" of the Asianists. Presumably, Petronius did likewise, for although he is a master of rhetoric, such rhetoric is normally either parody or irony; elsewhere he speaks of his "pure speech" (*sermo purus*) and a "candid tongue" (*candida lingua*).   Line 23. *Thucydides*— The greatest of Greek historians of the fifth century. The characteristics of Thucydides' style are miraculous speed and concision, a crabbed austerity in the use of effect and figures, as well as a knottiness of texture that makes his language look both roughened and sinewy, almost, as it were, muscle-bound. He is utterly free of any scholastic approach and so individual in his style that his example proved unassimilable by his disciples.   Line 23. *Hyperides* (389–322 B.C.) was an orator of the fourth century whose work survives almost entirely in fragments. A student of Isocrates, he nonetheless strove to keep his rhetoric in touch with colloquial speech. In his day, he was regarded as second only to Demosthenes.   Line 30. *Agamemnon*—A professor of rhetoric and the man who takes Encolpius, Giton, and Ascyltus to dinner with Trimalchio. His assistant is a younger professor (the *antescholanus*) called Menelaus. The point of naming the rhetoricians after the two famous brothers and heroes of the Trojan War is, of course, irony and incongruity. There may be—one cannot be sure— additional irony in making them nominally brothers (see note below, Ch. II, p. 26, *boy* and the hint in Ch. VI on Menelaus' sexual propensities).   Line 42. *lecterns—Pro Caelio*, 17, 41. Line 44. *sponges*—i.e., parasites, from the Greek παράσιτος, a man who eats at the expense of another. These "spongers" are a familiar figure in Latin comedy (cf. the *Eunuch* of Terence) and no less familiar evidently in everyday life.

Page 23, Line 30. *Lucilius*—He (ca. 180–102 B.C.) was the earliest of Roman satirists and probably the inventor of satire as a genre. His work survives today only in fragments, but given the speed with which he composed, his corpus must have been a large one. He was reputed a good but a careless poet, throwing off poem after poem with reckless haste and improvising with great ability.

Line 31. poet—Agamemnon's "improvisation" is little more than a versified version of the stock rhetorical *gradus ad Parnassum*, instruction in how to become a poet. Structurally consisting of eight lines of "limping iambics" followed by ordinary epic hexameters, it is technically uninteresting; but it is probably best read as a parody upon Agamemnon's poetic pretensions and the standard notions of the rhetoricians. The ironies will be obvious. Thus, for instance, Agamemnon's praise of "discipline" and "self-control" clashes with the self-indulgent rhetorical flourish with which the second part of the poem begins. He preaches against cadging dinners, and yet it is Agamemnon who is later described as "an old hand at wangling return invitations to dinner." The curious picture of lawyers relaxing after hours by writing epic poetry is the subject of express condemnation by Eumolpus later.

Page 24, Line 4. Cyrene—A city along the Libyan coast of Africa, renowned as the birthplace of the poet Callimachus and the home of the Sirens.   Line 24. Cicero—The great Roman statesman and orator, was also a practicing poet, the author of a youthful poem on the exploits of Marius, a translation of Aratus' *Phaenomena*, and an epic on his own consulship (*De consulatu suo*) and the Catilinarian conspiracy. The reference is probably to this poem.   Line 28. Helicon—This is, of course, along with Parnassus, renowned as a haunt of poetry. And to arrive at the top of Helicon is to have arrived among the great names of poetry. Helicon itself lay in Boeotia. On its slopes lay Ascra, the home of Hesiod; nearer the summit was the spring of Hippocrene, synonymous with poetic inspiration.

CHAPTER II

Page 24, Line 30. Ascyltus—The companion (and rival) of the narrator, Encolpius. His name is derived from the Greek ἄσκυλτος, meaning "not pulled about," "undisturbed," "unharassed," presumably because, although he is an accomplice of Encolpius' misdeeds and the companion of his adventures, he is rarely the victim or sufferer. He is not, that is, like Encolpius, the persecuted victim of Priapus' anger. The name Encolpius appears to be derived from the Greek, ἐγκόλπιος, meaning "lap" or "crotch." Encolpius, then, is literally The Crotch, the comic Odysseus persecuted over land and sea by the wrath of the phallic Priapus. So, at least, runs one of the common interpretations of the work.

Page 25, Line 1. Agamemnon—He had delivered a *suasoria*, one of the two major exercises in declamation of Roman rhetoric. The *suasoria* itself was a kind of rhetorical showpiece of advice or persuasion, frequently concerned with a crisis in the career of some historical figure. Its complement was the *controversia* or "controversy," a speech on some difficult point of law in a fictitious or quite unreal situation. Among the commoner themes of the *controversia* were those listed by Encolpius in Ch. I, i.e., "pirates trooping up the beach in chains, tyrants scribbling edicts compelling sons to chop off their fathers' heads or oracles condemning three virgins . . . to be slaughtered to stop some plague."   Line 17. town—The location of the action is unknown, despite enormous scholarly ingenuity and argument. The scene must be set, however, in some town along the coast in the vicinity of the Bay of Naples.

The area known today as the Phlegraean Fields, between Naples and Cumae, is probably the most likely situation.

Page 26, Line 9. boy—Literally, the Latin here gives, not "boy," but "brother" (frater). In the sense used here, however, "brother" refers to a homosexual bond between Encolpius and Giton, and this is the normal meaning of the word throughout the work. Because "brother" in English lacks the perverse sense of the Latin frater, I have found it advisable to alter the translation accordingly. This is not squeamishness: it would be difficult, in any case, to misunderstand the nature of the bond between Encolpius and Giton.   Line 19. Tarquin—Lucretia was raped by Tarquinius, the son of Tarquinius Superbus, last of the Etruscan dynasty to sit as king in Rome. Lucretia defended herself to the limit of her ability, and was regarded by Romans as a model of wifely chastity. Her tragedy, according to legend, led to the eventual expulsion of the kings and the establishment of the Republic.
Line 26. gladiator—Gladiators were normally either slaves or convicts. Therefore, for a freeman, such as Encolpius, to have been a gladiator was a disgrace; to have failed in the profession would be the very acme of disgrace.   Line 35. dream-analysis—"Broken bottles" means simply "worthless rubbish." "Dream-analysis" was a common feature of ancient divination and bore little resemblance to modern analytical techniques.

Page 28, Line 4. friend—Literally, "brother." See above, note for p. 26, boy. Relationships become increasingly complex.

CHAPTER III

Page 29, Line 23. song—Literally, the line reads "Even those men who carry the Cynic's wallet and denounce their age have been known to sell the truth for a price." The most famous of all the Cynics was the renowned Diogenes, and the typical Cynical attitude is to adopt the beggar's life on the grounds that the philosophical life is troubled by the possession of money.

CHAPTER IV

Page 31, Line 13. Priapus—The most prominently phallic of all the ancient gods of fertility. He was originally worshiped at Lampsacus on the Hellespont, and from here his worship spread to Greece and Rome. The attribute of Priapus is the phallus, and indeed, as represented in art, he is little more than a very slightly humanized phallus. He is also, as a vegetation god, a deity of the garden, protecting and aiding the sexual processes of nature. What the reaction of the cultivated Roman of the early Empire may have been to his worship, we have no way of knowing; but he seems to have been a figure of fun, broadly but lightly, in a tolerant sense, obscene. He is not, that is, a "great god" with a solemn religious cult, but a minor genius of sexual potency, a domesticated but unreliable lord of lust. Hence, the solemnity with which Quartilla speaks of him here—and Encolpius later—is more an indication of their predilections and natures than of his real power. For Encolpius, "The Crotch," the power of Priapus is absolute. Of the mysteries of Priapus, we know nothing at all; it may be presumed, however, that they were almost entirely orgiastic (in the modern sense of that word).

169

Page 32, Line 6. *dreams*—It was common for the sick or ailing to ask for a cure in their dreams.   Line 27. *curls*—In a free man, long hair was regarded as a sign of foppishness or effeminacy. In a slave, long curling hair was the mark of the *mignon*.

Page 33, Line 37. *Psyche*—From the Greek, ψυχή, meaning "the soul." The incongruity would perhaps be more forceful if we possessed the missing portions of this section.

Page 35, Line 12. *Falernian*—One of the more esteemed Roman wines. It came from the *Falernus Ager* in Campania between the Massic hills and the Volturnus river.

Page 37, Line 3. *passives*—The pun here is of my own invention, since the Latin pun is otherwise impossible to translate. Literally, Encolpius asks Quartilla for an *embasicoetas* (which means, in one sense, a drinking-glass, but, in a second sense, a *mignon*). In her reply, Quartilla plays off the second meaning.   Line 26. *Pannychis*—The name is Greek and means "all night."   Line 34. *yet*—The irony hardly needs to be stressed.

CHAPTER V

Page 38, Line 19. *earth*—Interpretation of this sentence is somewhat difficult and hangs upon the meaning selected for *expectatio liberae cenae*. I have followed Ernout in referring the *libera cena* to the dinner which was provided for gladiators who had to fight on the following day. As such, it contains the possibility of being "one's last meal."   Line 26. *Trimalchio's*—The name seems to be of Semitic origin and to mean "great and rich" or "triply fortunate."

Page 39, Line 19. *Menelaus*—Agamemnon's assistant, the junior rhetorician.   Line 37. *wines*—See above, note for Ch. IV, p. 35, *Falernian*.   Line 40. *toast*—It was Roman custom, when drinking someone's health, to pour some of the wine under the table as an offering to the gods. In this way, one procured the good will of the gods for the proposed toast.

Page 40, Line 21. *dog*—At Pompeii, in the entrance to the so-called "House of the Tragic Poet," there is a splendid mosaic of a leashed dog and beneath it the inscription: CAVE CANEM ("BEWARE THE DOG").   Line 28. *staff*—The *caduceus* of Mercury, the god of trade and Trimalchio's special patron.   Line 29. *Minerva*—As goddess of crafts (and Wisdom?), Minerva conducts Trimalchio to Rome.   Line 36. *tribunal*—The seat to which Mercury hoists Trimalchio is the throne allotted to the Sevirs, i.e., the officials appointed in the municipalities to carry out the worship of the deified Emperor. Election to this office was normally purchased, and Trimalchio was proud of having been appointed without payment.   Line 38. *gold*—They symbolize, of course, a life of gold.

Page 41, Line 5. *beard*—The first trimming of the beard was regarded by Romans as symbolic of a boy's having attained to his manhood and was usually the preliminary to his donning the man's garb, the *toga virilis*.   Line 8. *Laenas*—His gladiator games are otherwise unknown. Their presence here, however, is deliberately incongruous, an exposure of the vulgarity of taste of a man who

170

could juxtapose scenes from Homer with others from mere gladiatorial games. The modern analogy would be the case of that book-collecting millionaire who claimed to specialize in "twelfth-century incunabula and first editions of Zane Grey."   Line 14. *fasces*—In Republican times *fasces* were symbols of authority, borne by lictors (or bearers) in attendance upon a magistrate possessing the *imperium*. The rods signified the magistrate's power of administering a flogging; the ax, the power of life and death. Under the Empire, however, *fasces* were made available even to the Sevirs, each of whom was allowed two lictors.   Line 16. *ship*—The meaning of these brass rams is uncertain. It may be merely that Trimalchio is again guilty of pretentious bad taste, or that he liked this imposing, semiofficial suggestion of naval triumph. As a man who had made enormous wealth from merchant-shipping, he could think of himself as having won some sort of naval triumph. And to get from that to the notion of himself as almost an admiral would not be beyond the limits of *his* ingenuity or pretensions. His only problem is to know how close he can sail to the letter of the law, without incurring its penalties.   Line 19. *cult*—i.e., a *sevir*. Cf. notes above for p. 40, *tribunal*, and p. 41, *fasces*.   Line 27. *December*—The point of this memo would probably be clearer if we knew with certainty the date of Trimalchio's dinner. There are some hints that the date may be sometime in January. If so, the memo must be intended to show Trimalchio's social importance: he is so much in demand that he has to be booked for an invitation almost a year in advance of the date.   Line 30. *colors*—Superstition is one of Trimalchio's most prominent traits.   Line 36. *way*—Romans regarded it as tempting fate to cross a threshold or begin a journey left foot first. Such a step, that is, was *sinister* (Latin for "left") and a bad presage. On the right, however, all was well.

Page 42, Line 9. *trifle*—Expensive because dyed with the famous Tyrian dye. This dye (its color is commonly supposed to have been "royal purple," but judging from modern experiments it comes closer to a rich reddish brown, the color of dried blood) was fabulously expensive and only the very richest could afford it. Petronius' point is that Trimalchio's wealth is on such an astronomical scale that not only does he have a steward who has dependents (*clientes*) so rich that they can present him with clothing worth a king's ransom, but that the steward himself is so fabulously rich that he can, as a favor to his master's guests, forgive the loss of his clothing as a mere trifle.   Line 18. *water*—Three seasons out of the year, especially in Roman times, ice water would be a great luxury. During the Italian winter, however, it is supplied in bitter abundance.   Line 33. *empty*—It is difficult to explain the probable seating arrangements in effect at this particular dinner. The conventional arrangement calls for nine diners (or fewer), but if we assume that two diners shared the same couch or that there were other tables, the difficulty disappears. At dinner each guest was assigned a couch, and the couches themselves were grouped by threes around the three sides of a large table. Dinner was eaten from a reclining position; the diner supported his head with his left arm, elbow on the table, and ate with his right hand. The free side of the table was used for serving and carving, and the table itself must have been lower than the couches where the diners ate. Assuming that supernumerary guests shared a couch with another guest or were seated elsewhere, the following diagram may give a rough idea of Trimalchio's table and the disposition of his guests:

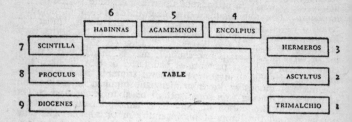

Notice that Trimalchio, as host, takes the seat of honor (1), the upper couch on the right. Normally, he would have sat at (7), next to the guest-of-honor, Habinnas, at (6).   Line 35. bronze —a famous bronze alloy, very highly prized by ancient connoisseurs—including Trimalchio. Its composition is unknown.   Line 41. dormice—Small rodents intermediate between the mouse and the squirrel; they were regarded as a great delicacy in antiquity.

Page 43, Line 2. carried in—Trimalchio's entrance deserves comment. It is primarily the elaborate incongruity of his dress that accounts for the amusement of the more sophisticated guests. Thus, while the close-cropped haircut is typical of the slave or the recently manumitted slave, the broad purple stripe was a privilege permitted only to the Senatorial class. The gold rings, on the other hand, are the prerogative of the equestrian order. Trimalchio, having the right to neither the broad purple stripe nor the equestrian ring, does the next best thing, wearing an imitation steel ring and transferring the purple stripe from the toga to the napkin. Presumably, those who adopted insignia to which they had no legal right could be punished. For this reason Trimalchio specifies that the statue of himself on his tomb is to be shown wearing "five gold rings": the fraud would be unpunishable after death. The tassels may be a sign of effeminacy. The silver toothpick, of course, is sheer extravagance.   Line 34. peahen's eggs—A fabulous delicacy.

Page 44, Line 2. oriole—Actually, the Latin gives ficedula, the modern Italian beccafico or fig-eater, a brilliantly colored bird whose habit of stuffing itself on ripe figs endeared it to Roman epicures. Since the fig-eater is unknown in America, I have translated it "oriole," to which family it belongs.   Line 21. democrat— The proverb means simply that in war (where all men face death alike), social distinctions vanish. Trimalchio, as usual, misapplies his proverbs.   Line 32. Opimius—Trimalchio's attempts to impress his guests commonly founder on ignorance. Here either his chronology or his knowledge of wines is at fault; probably both. Opimius was consul in 121 B.C., and assuming the date of the

dinner is sometime during the reign of Nero, the wine—if Opimian
—could not be much less than 170 years old. Opimian, in any
case, was not a wine which kept well; like any other good Falernian,
it began to deteriorate after twenty years.   Line 40. *skeleton*
—The *memento mori* was a common part of Roman feasts or even
of the decoration of the dining room. We still possess, for instance,
a number of vivid mosaics portraying skeletons with eating-vessels
or food and a moralizing inscription. The point of these mementos,
of course, was: "Eat, drink and be merry, for tomorrow we die."
Trimalchio's memento is, one suspects, rather more vivid than
usual, and the silver joints of the skeleton show the master's touch.

Page 45, Line 13. *food*—In almost all cases, the link between
the zodiacal sign and the food placed upon it is a pun or some
farfetched resemblance. Thus beef is appropriate to Taurus (the
Bull); thus over the Ram (Aries), one finds chickpeas (*cicer
arietinus*), etc.   Line 32. *Pegasus*—The famous winged horse
which Bellerophon rode when he killed the Chimera.   Line
33. *Marsyas*—The satyr Marsyas took part in a musical contest
against Apollo and lost; in punishment, Apollo tied him to a tree
and flayed him alive. The erection, of course, comes naturally to
the Satyr, for the Satyrs were spirits of fertility. Marsyas, however, seems to have been domesticated; at least his statue appears
to have been a frequent gathering place for the whores of ancient
Rome.

Page 46, Line 10. *Fortunata*—The meaning of the name is self-
evident.   Line 36. *Tarentum*—Modern Italian *Taranto*, a city
situated on the instep of the Italian Peninsula.

Page 47, Line 3. *treasure*—Romans appear to have believed that
buried treasure was guarded by an imp or guardian spirit (*Incubus*)
whose distinguishing characteristic was a cap. Anyone who managed
to take off the cap could compel the Incubus to reveal the location
of the treasure. In a very slightly Christianized form, the same
belief is evidently still alive in the Basilicata. At least Carlo Levi,
in his *Christ Stopped at Eboli*, reports that peasants believe that
there are tiny, winged spirits of an extremely mischievous nature
who guard buried treasure. They are called *monacchichi* and are
thought to be the souls of children who died before receiving bap-
tism; their distinguishing mark is a long cape, not a cap, and if
they were caught by their cape, they had to reveal the treasure.
Needless to say, if the *monacchichio* could recover his cape, he
promptly vanished.   Line 19. *Undertaking*—As a profession,
undertaking was, in fact, anything but respectable.   Line 40.
Ulysses—Aeneid ii. 44.

Page 48, Line 4. *zodiac*—The effect of this entire passage depends upon a series of elaborate puns. Consequently, I have made
a rather free translation, convinced that the effect here was more
important than literal accuracy. For those of a literal turn of mind,
I offer the following translation: "This heaven, in which the
twelve gods live, changes itself into as many figures, and at one
time becomes a Ram. So anyone who is born beneath that sign
has many sheep, a lot of wool, a hard head, a brazen front and a
sharp horn. A great many pedants and young bucks [*arietilli*] are
born under this sign. . . . The whole heaven changes into a small
bull [*taurulus*]. Under it are born people who kick against the

pricks [calcitrosi], cattlemen, and those who crop their own food. Under the Twins [Gemini] are born two-horse chariots, oxen, lechers [colei, i.e., men with balls] and those who sit on both sides of the fence. I was born under the Crab [cancer]. Therefore I stand on many legs and own many possessions both on sea and land; for your crab's at home with both. And that was why I've put nothing over the Crab, because I didn't want to endanger my birth-sign. Under the Lion, gluttons and bossy men [imperiosi] are born; under the Virgin come married women [mulieres], runaways, and men who wear leg-irons [compediti]. Under the sign of Libra come butchers, perfumers, and those who sell by weight; under Sagittarius are born cross-eyed men who squint at the vegetables but snitch the ham. Under Capricorn [i.e., goat's horn] you get those poor souls whose misfortunes make them sprout horns, while under the sign of Aquarius [i.e., Water-Carrier] are born innkeepers [i.e., those who water the wine] and men with water on the brain. Chefs and orators [i.e., fish-mouthed men] come under the sign of the Fishes."   Line 44. Hipparchus—Aratus (ca. 270 B.C.) and Hipparchus (ca. 190–124 B.C.) were both prominent Hellenistic astronomers.

Page 50, Line 9. liberate you—The pun here is both elaborate and labored, and I confess to having tampered with the Latin in an attempt to get the right effect. Romans tended to identify their old vegetation god Liber with the Greek god of the vine, Dionysus or Bacchus (also called Bromius, Evius, or Lyaeus, each title referring to a different manifestation or employed as cult-variants). This identification was further supported by fanciful etymology: Liber, that is, is also Latin for "free," and so the god Liber, like Dionysus, was thought to liberate men from their cares. Since Trimalchio's slaveboy is called Dionysus, he must also be Liber; and in being freed (i.e., made liber), he is doubly Liber. But Liber is also the god, and so the implied effect of Trimalchio's action is that of having liberated the god of wine, no mean feat. I have wilfully improvised the words of Trimalchio which follow the liberation and tried to bring the implied effect into prominence. By so doing, I necessarily suppressed what Trimalchio goes on to say, but the pun seemed to me completely untranslatable. What Trimalchio says is this: "I am sure you will all agree that my father is Liber." Trimalchio, that is, claims both that his own father was a free man (i.e., liber)—which he was not—and that the god Liber is his father.

Page 51, Line 4. of course—As an act of kindness, slaves were commonly manumitted in a man's will.

Page 52, Line 22. dark—A conscious mistranslation. The game you could have played with Safinius in the dark is actually morra. Two men put out a number of fingers and each tries to guess the total. The penalty for error is usually a blow. Morra is still played in modern Italy.   Line 42. market—Exaggeration intended to be ironic: he is eating, after all, at Trimalchio's.

Page 56, Line 16. mincemeat—Pentheus, the king of Thebes, was torn to pieces by the Bacchantes (i.e., Maenads, the god-possessed female followers of Dionysus). Cf. Euripides, Bacchae.   Line 35. Tarentum—The suspicion that Trimalchio's geography is weak should not be allowed to detract from the sublimity of the boast.

Tarentum is in the extreme south of Italy; Terracina lies about midway between Naples and Rome. The distance between them would be over 200 miles. The hope of buying up Sicily clearly confirms that Trimalchio has been boasting.

Page 57, Line 2. *court*—Agamemnon appears to have been engaged in a *controversia*. See note above, Ch. II, p. 25, Agamemnon.   Line 15. *Homer*—Trimalchio's learning is somewhat lacking. For the standard version of the story of Ulysses and the Cyclops, see Homer, *Odyssey* ix. The twelve labors of Hercules as such are not, of course, recounted by Homer, though several of them are sketched in or used allusively.   Line 16. *Cumae*—The famous Sibyl who prophesied to Aeneas. It was believed of Sibyls that they were immortal; they shared with men, however, the curse of growing old. Evidently, the Sibyl of Cumae had simply withered away of her own antiquity until she was so small that she spent her days in a jug. In the circumstances, no one will marvel at her wish to die. Cumae was situated on the extreme western edge of the Phlegraean Fields, a few miles to the north and west of Naples, along the sea. The town was very early colonized by Greeks, a fact which probably explains why the boys' question to the Sibyl and her answer are both in Greek.

Page 58, Line 13. *bronze*—On Corinthian bronze, see above, note for p. 42, bronze. Trimalchio's confusion here is almost magisterial. There was evidently a story—the truth of which is explicitly denied by Pliny (*Hist. Nat.* xxxiv)—that Corinthian bronze originated from a chance mixture of molten metals during the burning of Corinth by Mummius in 146 B.C. Trimalchio evidently has this (false) tale in mind, but manages somehow to confound it with the sack of Troy (sometime in the 12th cent. B.C.) and then introduces that poor "swindler" Hannibal from the siege of Saguntum, in place of Mummius at Corinth.

Page 59, Line 1. *balls*—This is the exact sense of the Latin: *putabat se coleum Iovis tenere.*   Line 6. *dirt*—The anecdote appears to have been well known in antiquity. Both Pliny (*Hist. Nat.* xxxvi. 195) and Dio Cassius (i. 57, 21) refer it to the reign of Tiberius.   Line 10. *sons*—Further examples of Trimalchio's erudition. Cassandra, the mad priestess of Troy, has probably been confused with Medea. When deserted by her lover Jason, Medea killed their two sons in revenge.   Line 13. *master*—The text is corrupt. But if Bücheler's proposed emendation [*patrono meo Mummius*] is correct, then Trimalchio is again involved in chronological difficulties. For Mummius, the conqueror of Corinth in 146 B.C., could hardly have left a legacy to Trimalchio's patron, the [Augustan?] Maecenas.   Line 14. *Trojan Horse*—Trimalchio's learning again. Daedalus was the famous craftsman of Crete who constructed a wooden cow for Pasiphae. Niobe, the sorrowing mother of the children killed by Apollo and Artemis, is a far cry from Pasiphae. The Trojan Horse may also be confounded with the Bull of Phalaris; but Pasiphae's wooden cow is a horse of quite another color.   Line 16. *Petraites*—Two famous gladiators of the period. Just as with his entrance-frescoes Trimalchio mingles scenes from Homer with gladiatorial scenes, so with his silver he incongruously jumbles scenes from the arena with mythological motifs.
          Line 35. *she can*—Actually, Trimalchio says that "nobody dances the cordax better." The ancient cordax was a provocative

175

and obscene dance; it was much employed by the Greek comedians.   Line 37. *Syrus*—The actor Syrus is otherwise unknown. The chorus which the servants sang was simply: *Madeia Perimadeia*. The meaning of those words cannot be ascertained.

Page 60, Line 27. *clause*—Trimalchio was excluded as a simple act of respect: his enormous wealth made nonsense of such conventional courtesies.   Line 30. *Baiae*—A famous and fashionable resort lying along the Bay of Naples. To banish a man to Baiae would be the equivalent of banishment to Palm Beach or Bermuda in high season.   Line 44. *farces*—i.e., Atellan farces, a primitive, rather crude variety of early Italian comedy, much in vogue with popular Roman audiences. Normally, an Atellan farce had four stock characters: the stupid father (Pappus), the clown (Bucco), the fool (Maccus), and the wise man (Dossennus). Trimalchio is once more being made to demonstrate his vulgarity. The man who would buy comic actors and employ them on farces would be capable of hiring a string quartet to play him foxtrots.

Page 61, Line 40. *Mopsus*—This is presumably Trimalchio's own contribution to the history of literature, for Mopsus is otherwise unknown and doubtless never existed. However, the text is corrupt.   Line 42. *Publilius*—Publilius Syrus was a late Republican writer of mimes, much esteemed for his collection of moral *sententiae*. Whether the poem quoted by Trimalchio is actually the work of Publilius, we have no way of knowing. My own translation is perhaps somewhat overdone on the side of archaism, but it seemed important to capture the pomposity and bombast which Trimalchio mistakes for profundity. The reader should note that the moral sentiments which Trimalchio finds so edifying in poetry are inconsistent with his own practice.

Page 63, Line 7. *present*—The effect of the following passage is entirely dependent upon a series of (intentionally) poor puns, and literal translation is out of the question if there is to be any attempt to get the effect. My own translation is as close to the Latin as I could come without impossibly falsifying the English. Readers who want the literal meaning are recommended to consult W. D. Lowe, ed., *Cena Trimalchionis* (Cambridge, 1905).   Line 41. *knight*—Ascyltus is evidently wearing the gold ring which was the privilege of the equestrian class.   Line 44. *savage*—A foreigner who became a slave could look forward to the prospect of someday being freed and achieving citizenship. After the fall of the Republic, Roman citizens were not taxed; hence, one of the major inducements to achieve the citizenship was the prospect of relief from taxation.

Page 64, Line 8. *worship*—i.e., like Trimalchio, he is a sevir.   Line 29. *vetch*—For a goat, vetch is good grazing. Hermeros means that Ascyltus is so startled by his torrent of abuse that he looks like a goat who found himself in a field of vetch, i.e., overwhelmed by his *embarras de choix*. Readers may note that there is a real dignity in Hermeros' angry tirade, as well as real social resentment against Ascyltus and his friends.   Line 36. *December*—During the winter Carnival, slaves were permitted the same licence allowed to the free.   Line 36. *freedom tax*—When a slave was freed, his owner was required to pay a 5 per cent freedom tax on his assessed value.

176

Page 65, Line 22. *small*—The answer to the riddle is unknown, despite some ingenious guesses. I have, I confess, slightly tampered with the riddle in order to give it some point in its context.

Page 66, Line 6. *rhapsodes*—Rhapsodists were professional reciters; their standard repertoire was epic poetry, especially Homer. Line 15. *Diomedes*—Trimalchio's garbling of mythology here approaches genius. Ganymede, of course, was the Trojan boy ravished by Zeus; Diomedes was a Greek captain at the siege of Troy. Neither was related to Helen, whose brothers were Castor and Pollux. Trimalchio then confuses Helen's elopement with Paris of Troy and the sacrifice of Agamemnon's daughter Iphigeneia at Aulis. This confusion then leads to Trimalchio's version of the Trojan War, a battle between Trojans and Parentines (meaning either the inhabitants of Parentium or the followers of Paris and probably, in Trimalchio's mythology, both); I have perhaps added to Trimalchio's confusion by translating Parentini as "people of Paros" in order to stress the probable pun on Paris' name. In the end, however, the Trojan War is won by Agamemnon, who surprisingly marries the dead Iphigeneia (it was on the pretext of marrying her to Achilles that Agamemnon was able to get her to Aulis—where she was put to death) to Achilles (who, of course, died before the end of the Trojan War). This leads naturally to the madness of Ajax through jealousy of Achilles, according to Trimalchio (whereas in mythology Ajax went mad because Odysseus rather than himself won the armor of the dead Achilles).

Page 67, Line 8. *saffron*—Saffron was commonly used in Roman ritual. Line 25. *Large Income*—Instead of the usual household gods—i.e., the Lares and Penates who watched over the welfare of the house, protecting births and crops, etc.—Trimalchio's gods represent his commercial deities of good fortune and income. Around the neck of these gods had been hung a good-luck medallion.

Page 70, Line 23. *Apelles*—A famous tragic actor during the reign of Caligula. Line 30. *Croesus*—The same little boy who had preceded Trimalchio's litter in the procession from the baths before dinner. Croesus, of course, was the name of the fabulously wealthy king of Lydia, a byword in ancient times as now for great riches. By calling his slaves Croesus, Dionysus, etc., Trimalchio became *ipso facto*, "master of wealth," "master of liberality and revelry," etc. Line 36. *Bowser*—"Bowser" is my contribution; the dog's name in Latin is *Scylax*, i.e., "chewer," "tearer." Croesus' lapdog is called *Margarita*, i.e., "Pearl."

Page 71, Line 9. *holding up*—Morra again (or possibly a Latin variant of blindman's buff). Line 26. *took him for the praetor*—The praetor is a municipality combined roughly the functions of both police and judiciary. For obvious reasons, neither Encolpius nor Ascyltus is anxious for a collision with the praetor. Line 38. *reserved for the praetor*—the praetor's place would normally be at no. 6, i.e., the "bottom" seat on the middle divan. See note above for p. 42, *empty*.

Page 72, Line 3. *tax*—i.e., the manumission tax.

Page 73, Line 24. *business*—It was customary for men of commerce or business to dedicate at stated intervals a tithe of several tenths of 1 per cent of their profits to Mercury, patron god of trade. Even if we assume that Trimalchio had paid all of 1 per cent for the period, it would have required a profit of at least 1000 pounds of gold to produce a gold bracelet that weighed ten pounds.

Page 74, Line 15. *bring it on*—Another pun. Literally, Trimalchio says: "I could be satisfied with this course, for you have the second tables [i.e., dessert] before you. However, if there's anything good, bring it on. Line 22. *heavy swell*—Aeneid v. 1. Line 26. *farce*—i.e., Atellan farces. See note above for p. 60, *farces*.
Line 41. *branded for it*—Slaves guilty of misconduct (but especially those guilty of running away) were punished by being branded with a hot iron on the forehead.

Page 75, Line 40. *Daedalus*—The famous legendary craftsman who made the wooden cow for Pasiphae and the famous artificial wings on which he and his ill-fated son Icarus attempted to flee from Minos' anger. He was regarded as the inventor of carpentry and of most of its tools.

Page 76, Line 28. *Greens*—In the chariot races at the circus, horses and drivers were distinguished by their colors. At this time there were four colors: Red, White, Blue and Green. But partisanship ran high, and supporters passionately identified themselves with their favorite charioteer and his color. Trimalchio's color is, I would infer, Red. Line 38. *Ephesus*—Otherwise unknown.

Page 77, Line 28. *heirs*—Presumably as a precaution against their selling it. Trimalchio has no faith in the *pietas* of his heirs.
Line 33. *crowded*—In token of Trimalchio's merchantmen.
Line 34. *official dress*—Upon ceremonial occasions the priests of Augustus (i.e., the *sevirs*) possessed the right to sit on a throne (see note above for p. 40, *tribunal*) or judicial tribunal. When seated on this throne, the *sevirs* wore the *toga praetexta*. Line 35. *gold rings*—So far as one can tell, Trimalchio had no right to the gold ring of the equestrian order. Indeed, his very insistence on "five gold rings" after death is fairly convincing evidence of his disability—not to speak of his desire. Posthumously, of course, he may wear the rings with impunity, and Trimalchio typically proposes to go whole hog.

Page 78, Line 2. *over it*—It is sometimes suggested that this touching scene is to be referred to an incident during the dinner, when a slaveboy dropped a silver dish and was punished. Actually, I suspect it is nothing more than a piece of simple funerary symbolism, whose sentimentality would be quite in keeping with Trimalchio's tastes. The broken vase would be the "smashed vessel" of Trimalchio's life, while the boy who mourns him would be the world or the living or Life, etc. Line 6. *Maecenatianus*—Freedmen commonly formed their cognomens from the name of their patron. Thus Trimalchio Maecenatianus would mean that Trimalchio's patron had been Maecenas. From this we have no right to infer that the patron must have been the famous Maecenas, Augustus' friend and chief of state-patronage. The name "Pompeius" would indicate that Trimalchio had also been a slave in the family of the Pompeii. Line 10. *Rome*—Trimalchio boasts, that is, that had he gone to Rome, he could have been enrolled in any of the guilds (or *decuriae*) from which the lower echelons of

178

the civil service were normally staffed. Either from indifference or lack of ambition (!), however, he chose otherwise.

Page 79, Line 31. Menecrates'—A famous citharist during the reign of Nero. (Cf. Suetonius Nero 30).

Page 81, Line 8. Cassandra—Literally, Cassandra caligaria. Cassandra was the mad priestess of Troy; caligaria means "dressed in high army boots," i.e., "masculine, brutal, raving virago."

Page 82, Line 17. emperor—It was not uncommon during the Empire for rich men to list the emperor as one of their heirs. The reason was fear as much as snobbery. Thus, although the snobbish might feel that inheritance established a personal relationship between themselves and the Emperor, the legacy was a wise precaution in an age when the provisions of a will could be set aside at the Emperor's pleasure. The legacy, that is, was little more than a bribe in return for which the other dispensations of the will would presumably be left unaltered.   Line 18. senator's fortune —A senatorial income was classed by law as consisting of at least 400,000 sesterces. It is difficult, for obvious reasons, to translate this figure into dollars; suffice it to say that in Rome it represented an upper-class fortune.

Page 83, Line 17. Apulia.—Apulia would be an understandably desirable acquisition for a man who claimed that he owned property "from Terracina to Tarentum." Apulia (modern Italian Puglia) occupied the heel of the Italian boot. Possession of it would give Trimalchio control of most of southern Italy.   Line 25. Scaurus —Trimalchio is name dropping in order to make an invidious comparison. The family of Scaurus was one of the greatest families of Rome.

CHAPTER VI

Page 85, Line 28. death—An obvious parody of tragic style, though the source is unknown. A very slightly altered version of the same line occurs in Eumolpus' poem on the fall of Troy.
Line 30. fury—The melodramatic tone of this whole incident deserves notice. At least it seems to me that Petronius' penchant for using inflated melodramatic language and mock-heroic situations when dealing with the recurring plights of these perverted lovers has strangely escaped attention. Yet if these incidents are melodramatic—as they so obviously are—we have to ask why. If we do, I think we can see, first, that the continuous ironic self-exposure of Encolpius' narrative is crucial for the total satire, and second, that the very theatricality of his adventures confers on him a "staginess" and romantic unreality that Petronius knew how to exploit. The best example would be Trimalchio's dinner, where there seems to me to be a wonderful tension between the vivid everyday reality of Trimalchio and his friends and the unreality of their marginal, scapegrace, mock-heroic guests—as though the Pickwick Club should suddenly find itself at dinner with three rakes from Restoration Comedy. The incongruity is not merely in character, but the incongruity of realities appropriate to different genres.

Page 86, Line 5. Thebaid—i.e., the fratricidal war between the two sons of Oedipus, Eteocles and Polyneices. Polyneices led an

179

Argive army against Thebes and engaged his own brother in single combat in which both brothers perished. Presumably, the perverted sense of "brother" (see note above, Ch. II, p. 26, boy) is present (as fratricide) in the situation.   Line 35. *leering one*—The theatrical piece alluded to is the *mime*, a farcical little play in which stock characters were employed. The sentiment expressed is a commonplace of ancient poetry; cf. Lucretius De rerum nat. iii. 55 ff.

Page 87, Line 11. *Greek town*—A pointed echo of Vergil Aeneid ii. 664 ff.   Line 29. *lives*—Obviously a high point of melodramatic rhetoric, even for Encolpius. It is difficult to be certain, however, whether the inflation of language derives from tragedy, romance, epic, or mime.   Line 30. *sword*—Probably another Vergilian echo: cf. *Aeneid* ii. 671.

Page 88, Line 7. *Tantalus*—He was represented by Greek poets as one of the great sufferers in Hades. He was afflicted with terrible thirst and placed in the middle of a lake whose waters always receded as he bent to drink. Over his head hung ripe fruit which also withdrew from his grasp. He thus stands for the man who starves amidst plenty.

CHAPTER VII

Page 88, Line 14. *Zeuxis*—He (b. ca. 450 B.C.) was one of the very greatest of ancient Greek painters, renowned for his realism. According to one story, he painted a bunch of grapes so perfectly that birds flew at the picture to eat the fruit.   Line 15. *Protogenes*—Protogenes of Rhodes was a distinguished Greek painter of the late fourth century B.C.   Line 17. *Apelles*—To judge from his reputation, Apelles (*fl.* late fourth cent.) was one of the very greatest of Greek painters. His most famous work was the great *Venus Anadyomene*, or Venus rising from the sea, which he painted for a temple of Cos. The emperor Augustus, however, upon a payment of 100 talents, ordered the picture brought from Cos and installed in the temple of Julius Caesar.   Line 18. *Goddess*—So Ernout, but the reading is uncertain.   Line 23. *heaven*—The "shepherd of Ida" was Ganymede, a Trojan boy of striking beauty, ravished away to heaven by Zeus in the form of an eagle. In heaven, Ganymede became the cupbearer of the gods.   Line 24. *Hylas*—Another mythological *mignon*, beloved by Heracles, with whom he went on the Argo's journey in search of the Golden Fleece. On the coast of Mysia the boy went to draw water from a well, but he was seen by a Naiad who fell in love with him and amorously drew him down into the water. Despite Heracles' searches, the boy was never seen again.   Line 26. *Hyacinth*—A handsome Spartan boy who was accidentally killed during a game of quoits by his lover Apollo. From the boy's blood sprang the flower of the same name. Apollo's instrument was, of course, the lyre.

Page 89, Line 7. *Lycurgus*—The legendary (though perhaps historical) lawgiver of ancient Sparta. His name, like that of so many lawgivers (e.g., Draco), became synonymous with harsh, vindictive cruelty because in a later and more humane age the provisions of his code seemed so comparatively inhuman.   Line 13. *hate*—Presumably because of their talents they are hated by the rich.

Page 90, Line 3. *enemy*—i.e., Ascyltus.   Line 7. *Eumolpus*
—Or, as we should say, the "Sweet-singer."   Line 8. *finance*—
Eumolpus was on the staff of the quaestor, the magistrate in charge
of the finances of a province. By "Asia" is meant, of course, not
the continent, but the Roman province comprising much of western
Asia Minor.   Line 9. *Pergamum*—A rich city in southern
Mysia and the capital of the Roman province of Asia.

Page 92, Line 35. *Democritus*—Democritus of Abdera (ca. 460–
361 B.C.), famous Greek philosopher and scientist, and with
Leucippus, founder of the so-called "atomic" theory, that the world
had been created from the collision of infinitely small particles
called atoms. Called the "laughing philosopher" from his cheery
disposition, he was renowned for his industry and the simplicity
of his mode of life.   Line 38. *Eudoxus*—Eudoxus of Cnidus
(b. ca. 408–355 B.C.), a Greek astronomer, geometer, and physician.
His major work on astronomy (the *Phaenomena*) has been lost,
but the substance of it was versified by Aratus (cf. note above, Ch.
V, p. 48, *Hipparchus*).   Line 40. *Chrysippus*—Chrysippus
(280–206 B.C.) was a Stoic philosopher born in Cilicia and a
disciple of the Stoic Cleanthes. He played an important role in
the formation and development of historical Stoicism. Hellebore
was commonly used as a purgative.

Page 93, Line 2. *Lysippus*—Lysippus of Sicyon, a fourth-century
Greek sculptor of high reputation and ability. In general, it was
his artistic credo that the artist should strive for greater conformity
with nature and he consistently attempted to create a specifically
human, rather than idealized or godlike, beauty.   Line 4.
Myron—One of the most distinguished of Greek sculptors of the
fifth century B.C. His greatest works were the *Discobolus* and the
Cow, both in bronze. Despite Eumolpus' assertion that Myron left
no heir, he appears to have had a son called Lycius, also an artist.
     Line 13. *dialectic*—i.e., the study of the general principles
which underlie a given science or branch of thought.   Line 31.
Phidias—Phidias of Athens (ca. 490–432 B.C.), perhaps the
greatest of all Greek sculptors. He was the architect of the Parthenon, the great chryselephantine statue of Athena, and the statue of
Olympian Zeus.   Line 35. *Troy*—On this poem see the note
on Eumolpus' *Civil War* (Ch. XIV, p. 129, *The Civil War*). In
terms of its subject, note that the *Fall of Troy* is little more
than a *précis* of the first section of Vergil's *Aeneid* ii, and echoes
of Vergilian diction and phrasing occur throughout (cf. Ernout,
pp. 91–94). Despite these borrowings, however, there is real
felicity of statement here and there interfused with stock rhetorical
effects, contorted diction, and some rather frigid antitheses. The
meter of my translation is a loose six-beat movement.   Line
37. *Calchas*—The priest of Apollo who foretold that the siege of
Troy would last ten years.   Line 40. *spoke*—i.e., through the
mouth of his prophet Calchas, telling the Greeks to build the
Trojan Horse. Apollo (with Poseidon) hated Troy, because
Laomedon had refused to pay him for building the walls of the city.
     Line 40. *Ida's*—A mountain near Troy.

Page 94, Line 3. *gift to god*—The Trojan Horse purported to
be an offering to the gods.   Line 8. *Sinon's lie*—Sinon was a
Greek who allowed himself to be captured by the Trojans. Then,

by imposing on the credulity of his captors, he succeeded in convincing them that the Trojan Horse was a harmless offering and could safely be taken inside the city.   Line 30. Tenedos— A small island off the coast of the Troad.

Page 95, Line 2. two boys—The famous statuary group of Laocoön and his two sons in the coils of the serpent presents the scene rather more vividly than Eumolpus' frigid verse with its neat inversions and forced antitheses.

CHAPTER VIII

Page 96, Line 15. brigand—Notice the reversion to mock-tragic or melodramatic language throughout this scene of the lovers' reunion and their make-up. Typically, the scene is concluded with the inevitable and ominous knock at the door.

Page 97, Line 18. acted—The lover's blindness displayed by Encolpius about Giton's motives and character should not be allowed to mislead the reader's judgment. Elsewhere Encolpius thinks Giton too shy to sleep with the little girl Pannychis, and he consistently misunderstands what he thinks is Giton's compassion and consideration for others. At heart, of course, Giton is as meretricious as Encolpius is gullible.   Line 31. Ganymede—See note above for Ch. VII, p. 88, heaven.

Page 99, Line 14. others—See note above for p. 97 acted. Line 17. as you—A parody of Vergil Aeneid i. 605 ff.   Line 18. prosper—Another Vergilian echo: Aeneid ix. 640.   Line 19. beauty—Cf. Vergil Aeneid v. 344.

Page 100, Line 29. farce—We have, that is, Petronius' own word for the theatricality of these scenes: dum haec fabula inter amantes luditur.

Page 102, Line 22. belly—Odyssey ix.

Page 104, Line 32. mind—Parody, I suspect, of a well-known suasoria or of the general technique of suasoriae. For suasoria, see note above, for Ch. II, p. 25, Agamemnon.

Page 105, Line 5. stars—Probably to the Dioscuri, Castor and Pollux, the patron gods of sailors.

CHAPTER IX

Page 106, Line 10. Tryphaena—The name means "licentious," "luxurious." Presumably, if we possessed the lost books, we should know the reason for Tryphaena's exile. It was, however, not unheard of for women—but usually women of very high birth—to be banished for some sort of gross sexual misconduct.   Line 20. Republic of Letters—A not unreasonable rendering, I think, of the pompous Latin phrase: pro consortio studiorum.   Line 31. Hannibal—The great Carthaginian general, arch-enemy of Republican Rome, and a byword—among Romans—for cruel mendacity.
    Line 36. Cyclops—Cf. Odyssey ix.

Page 107, Line 22. passengers—To cover one's head while voyaging was regarded by the Romans as a sign either of sickness or of effeminacy.

Page 108, Line 16. *Menelaus*—The text here is uncertain, and "Menelaus" is a proposed emendation. If sound, it would refer to the way in which Menelaus outwitted the Old Man of the Sea. Cf. *Odyssey* iv. 425 ff.

Page 109, Line 19. *slaves*—Runaway slaves were branded on the forehead with a large *F* (for *fugitivus*, "runaway"). Line 31. *sailors*—It was the custom for sailors, faced with inevitable shipwreck, to make an offering of their hair and beard to the gods of the sea. Hence to shave or cut hair on shipboard seemed to invite disaster and was regarded as ill-omened.

CHAPTER X

Page 109, Line 35. *Priapus*—The nature of the relationship between Lichas and Encolpius is explained by the identity of the god seen in the dream. For Priapus, see note above for Ch. IV, p. 31, *Priapus*.

Page 110, Line 5. *Epicurus*—Epicurus (ca. 342–270 B.C.) was a celebrated Greek philosopher and the founder of the philosophy known as Epicureanism. Basing his work largely upon the atomic theory of Democritus, Epicurus proposed a system of ethics in which the avoidance of pain was regarded as the highest good. In general, Epicurus is somewhat austere as regards pleasure, but later popularization of his theory made him a proponent of hedonism. While the bias of Epicureanism is strongly against religious superstitions, Eumolpus' reference here is somewhat obscure.

Page 111, Line 20. *scar*—Cf. Homer *Odyssey* xix. 473. Ulysses' childhood nurse, Euryclea, recognized her master from an old scar on his leg. Line 41. *Porch of Hercules*—Obviously a reference to a lost portion of the work. Nothing is known of this episode.

Page 112, Line 14. *defense*—The shift to legal rhetoric is unmistakable.

Page 113, Line 37. *eyebrows*—According to Pliny (*Hist. Nat.* x. 67), contact with a salamander causes total loss of hair.

Page 114, Line 33. *implacably on*—The pomposity of phrasing is deliberate, designed to set off the ludicrous battle in the clichés appropriate to poetic descriptions of decisive engagements. The technique is typical of Petronius, as indeed to any satirist with a sense of the real advantages of juxtaposing sharp disparities of subject and style. Line 45. *tragic role*—Again Petronius supplies us with the literary genre—tragedy—which underlies the parody: *audacius tamen ille tragoediam implebat.*

Page 115, Line 11. *bride away*—i.e., the abduction of Helen of Sparta by Paris of Troy which caused the Trojan War. Line 12. *hacks*—Medea, while fleeing from Colchis with Jason and the Golden Fleece, was said to have chopped her brother in pieces and thrown him overboard in order to delay her pursuers.

Page 116, Line 2. *inquiries*—The terminology is, of course, a spoof or parody of the complicated language and provisions of formal treaties.

183

CHAPTER XI

Page 118, Line 9. *Ephesus*—An important Greek city on the coast of Asia Minor, and under the Romans the administrative capital of the province of Asia. The story of the matron of Ephesus is one of the most famous episodes of the *Satyricon*, and from the twelfth century to the present it has been used as the basis of innumerable plays, poems and *novellae*. The latest of these is Christopher Fry's charming *A Phoenix Too Frequent*.   Line 32. *crucified*—Crucifixion was the commonest form of capital punishment in the ancient world, and was usually reserved for the worst types of criminals or the very lowest orders of society. Indeed, one of the major obstacles in the way of Roman acceptance of Christianity was precisely that its founder had been crucified, i.e., had died the death of a criminal and a slave.

Page 119, Line 22. *touched*—Aeneid iv. 34.   Line 41. *love*—Ibid. iv. 38.

Page 120, Line 43. *passengers*—Another incident from the lost sections of the *Satyricon*. Hedyle is probably Lichas' wife.

CHAPTER XII

Page 122, Line 19. *ship*—Presumably, these were emblems of the goddess Isis which Encolpius had stolen.   Line 37. *Fates*—The tone exhibits the rhetorical afflatus of Greek romance in which scenes of shipwrecked lovers appear to have been a commonplace.

Page 124, Line 8. *sea*—Encolpius' apostrophe on the death of Lichas deserves, I think, close scrutiny. At least what appears to begin as a standard rhetorical showpiece on the theme of the mutability of human fortunes and the vanity of ambition suddenly takes on real power of speech and perception and closes with an extremely unconventional attitude to death—unconventional, that is, to a Roman. At least so I read the Latin and have tried to translate it.

CHAPTER XIII

Page 125, Line 27. *Croton*—(Modern Italian Crotona) was originally a Greek colony on the southern coast of Italy, but became a great city after the defeat of rival Sybaris in 510 B.C. It had, however, suffered terribly in the Pyrrhic and Hannibalic wars, and its days of prosperity were over before the Republic ended.

Page 126, Line 9. *wills*—Legacy-hunting was one of the stock targets of Latin literature, and moralists and satirists abused it roundly. (Cf. Horace *Sat.* ii, 5; *Juvenal* v, 98 and x, 202; the younger Pliny, *Epistle* ii).   Line 27. *scenery*—The Latin is specifically theatrical: *largior scena*.   Line 37. *villa*—Reference to another lost episode of the work.   Line 39. *Mother of gods and men*—i.e., Cybele, the Asiatic earth mother. As a personification of the earth, she stood as the giver of all good things to man.

Page 127, Line 45. *Corax*—Or, as we should say, the "Crow."

CHAPTER XIV

Page 128, Line 12. *art*—Cf. Horace *Epistle to the Pisos*, 24.
Line 32. *shun it*—*Odes* iii. 1, 1.

Page 129, Line 3. *felicity*—Horatii *curiosa felicitas*. The phrase
is justly admired, and I confess to having used a rather cumbersome
periphrasis since an equivalent concision in English without real
loss of meaning seemed to me impossible. *Curiosa* implies elaborate
and painstaking care in composition, while *felicitas* in conjunction
with *curiosa* suggests not merely felicity of effect but that ease and
apparently fortuitous formal rightness that is—in great poetry—the
consequence of sustained practice and sheer technical virtuosity. No
phrase could better describe that quality of practical effortlessness
and formal perfection so characteristic of the best of Horace.
Line 24. *fact*—Another elaborate periphrasis for a clause of remarkably condensed Latin: *sed per ambages deorumque ministeria
et fabulosum sententiarum tormentum praecipitandus est liber
spiritus, ut potius furentis animi vaticinatio appareat quam religiosae
orationis sub testibus fides.*   Line 28. *The Civil War*—This
poem is probably the most difficult crux of the entire *Satyricon*, and
I present my translation of it with considerable uncertainty and
diffidence. The central problem, of course, is that of knowing just
what purpose Eumolpus' lengthy epic effusion is meant to serve;
and I confess myself unsatisfied by the customary explanations but
unable to suggest a satisfactory alternative. I suppose the customary
view of the poem is that it is a parody or satire of Lucan's *Pharsalia*.
But this seems unsatisfactory in several ways. For despite the real
resemblances between the two poems and some unmistakable repeti-
tions, most of these resemblances are merely trivial or casual echoes
of phrasing, and as such hardly sustain a theory of forceful parody.
Yet Petronius elsewhere shows himself a superb parodist. On the
other hand, it may be, as Ernout suggests, that Eumolpus was
reviving the criticism that Lucan had sacrificed poetry to history
or rhetoric. On this view, Eumolpus' poem will have been intended
as a kind of model of epic in the classical Vergilian manner, and
the frequent borrowings from the *Aeneid* perhaps support this
theory. But this argument is—at least literarily speaking—weakened
by the fact that Eumolpus patently fails to convince us either of
his own powers of poetry or of the rightness of his own notions
of epic structure. The poem, that is, fails both as a parody and in
its own right; for despite some remarkable internal felicities of
phrasing and effect and one extremely forceful speech, the poem is
unmistakably mediocre and its structure weak and rambling. Given
this fact, the translator's job is both difficult and thankless, for
he must work with a parody so limp as to be no parody at all or an
epic model so trite and unconvincing that it would be dishonesty
to improve upon it in English. Worst of all, it is intolerably long.
My own solution has been a kind of compromise. Thus, to satisfy
the possibility of parody (either of Lucan or contemporary epic
theory), I have made my Eumolpus talk like a third-rate Ezra
Pound; for Pound's *Cantos* are perhaps the best-known of contemporary attempts at "epic" and their very looseness of structure
and their phrase-cadenced rhetoric easily lend themselves to broad
parody. Moreover, in a real sense, Eumolpus and Pound share

common ground in their poetic attitudes to their own individual worlds and societies. Both, that is, are obvious types of the *laudator temporis acti*, praisers of the past and *ipso facto* decriers of the present, and both employ the stock Jeremiad-rhetoric of the professional moralist and the easy examples of contemporary corruption. They deal, in short, with a hackneyed set of sentimental perceptions, and though Pound can contrive real poetic power from his, neither poet can claim much credit for either originality or quality in his working historical perceptions. Indeed, Eumolpus' sixty-line prologue is little more than a trite pastiche of two hundred years of Roman professional moralizing and historical sentimentality. But if its author were alive today, he could only be, I think, a lesser epigone of Pound, incontrovertibly minor as a poet, but by dint of long imitation of his master thoroughly versed in Pound's weaknesses as well as his strength. Or so at least it seems to me. Beyond that point resemblance ends, and for what I have done I can only plead that I have tried to make the poem interesting in its badness. For unadorned mediocrity has no interest, and not even Pound himself could—without totally rewriting it—make this poem good in its own right.

Ideally, of course, Eumolpus' epic should be translated into an English epic convention whose rhetorical effects—periphrasis, ornament, antithesis, inversion, epigram, and an appetite for the grotesque or gory—more or less match the Latin. But the only equivalent English style capable of being so parodied would be an Elizabethan rhetoric grafted onto Miltonic epic. And this seemed to me, upon consideration, unsatisfactory. For a parody of dead epic would interest no one except perhaps the academic scholar. Moreover, Petronius is surely parodying a contemporary style, and therefore, it seems to me, any equivalent translation must also parody a contemporary English convention. The difficulty with Pound, of course, is that his rhetoric is of a generically different variety from Eumolpus', and that the specific object of Petronius' satire must therefore be somewhat lost. But faced with the choice of employing an archaic (and suitably rhetorical) epic manner and a modern convention based upon a different rhetoric, it seemed to me that the modern choice was the necessary one. I do not expect scholars to understand the translator's difficulties, but they should be aware that other than severely scholarly reasons must sometimes determine the translator's unhappy necessity to choose between literal accuracy and the general rightness of effect.

Page 130, Line 18. Hammon—A shrine in the Libyan desert.
Line 24. fangs in demand—i.e., for use in the amphitheaters.
Line 34. eunuchs—The custom of castrating young boys in order to secure a good supply of eunuchs was widely practiced in the ancient world. Though Asian in origin, it quickly spread to Greece and the West. Epheboi (from the Greek, ἔφηβος, young man) is a deliberate intrusion à la Pound of my own. Elsewhere I have similarly introduced a number of phrases in Latin, some original, others taken from the text. Their meaning is normally given, in the Poundian manner, in context or translated directly.
Line 39. perversion everywhere—The reader should pointedly compare this whole passage with Eumolpus' attitude toward Giton in Chapter VIII. Throughout the Satyricon, a great deal of the irony depends upon the reader's understanding and recognition of pointed disparities between practice and profession. Whatever may

be the weakness of the *ad hominem* argument in logic, in satire it is priceless.

Page 131, Line 11. *the scare*—I have simply anglicized the Latin *scarus*, evidently a species of wrasse, a fish much prized by Roman epicures.   Line 13. *Lucrino*—Lake Lucrino, near Baiae in the Bay of Naples, was famous for its oysters.   Line 15. *Phasis*— A river near Colchis on the Euxine. It was renowned for its pheasants in antiquity.   Line 20. *Quirites*—i.e., "countrymen," Romans.   Line 34. *Cato*—Marcus Porcius Cato, the Younger (95–46 B.C.), after his death the accepted personification of the ancient Republican virtues, and particularly renowned for his moral incorruptibility and his unswerving allegiance to the conservative values of the Senatorial order. His famous suicide at Utica had the effect of making him a martyr, and throughout the early Empire he was regarded as the last of the great Romans. But despite his famous incorruptibility, his moral and political intransigence had the effect of polarizing Roman politics and of rendering any compromise impossible. Thus, he himself was as responsible as the demagogues he hated for the Civil War which led to the suppression of Roman liberties in the dictatorship of Julius Caesar. The reference to Cato's rejection here probably means his defeat by Vatinius in the elections for the praetorship.   Line 39. *mos maiorum*— Literally, "the custom of our ancestors" or, as we should say, "tradition."

Page 132, Line 1. *house*—The line is taken bodily, of course, from Pound's famous *usura* Canto. The translation, however, is almost literally exact: *Nulla est certa domus, nullum sine pignore corpus.*   Line 10. *together*—The allusion is probably to the famous conspiracy of Catiline (ca. 90–63 B.C.). Catiline belonged to an impoverished patrician family and his conspiracy was committed to a general cancellation of debts.   Line 17. *Enyo*— The goddess of war.   Line 19. *Crassus*—Marcus Licinius Crassus, a member with Caesar and Pompey of the so-called First Triumvirate in 59 B.C. In 55 B.C., Crassus received the province of Syria and in an attempt to win military glory, he was killed by the Parthians at the battle of Carrhae in 53.   Line 19. *Pompey*—Gnaeus Pompeius Magnus (106–48 B.C.), the Triumvir, was murdered by Ptolemy of Egypt shortly after the battle of Pharsalus in 48 B.C.   Line 20. *Caesar*—Gaius Julius Caesar (ca. 100–44 B.C.), the Dictator, murdered by the conspirators Cassius and Brutus in Rome in 44 B.C.   Line 26. *Parthenope*— The old Greek name for Naples. The "fields of Dicarchis" (or Dicaearchis) is a poetic periphrasis for Puteoli (modern Pozzuoli). Dicarchis was the legendary founder of Puteoli.   Line 32. *Solfatura*—He appears to mean the region now designated Solfatara, though in ancient times the whole Phlegraean Field was noted for its extensive volcanic activity. The chasm was reputed to have been the place by which Aeneas entered the lower world (*see Aeneid* vi. 236 ff). Cocytus was one of the legendary rivers of the classical underworld.   Line 41. *Father Dis*—The Latin equivalent of the Greek Pluto, lord of the dead and Hades.

Page 133, Line 33. *Sulla's sword*—A reference to the great proscriptions and reign of terror carried out by Sulla (138–78 B.C.) against the followers of Marius in 82 B.C.   Line 37. *Tisiphone* —One of the three Furies. Her sisters are Allecto and Megaera.

187

Page 134, Line 10. *strewn*—A poetic reference to the battle of Pharsalus (48 B.C.) in which Pompey was defeated by Caesar, and the battle of Philippi (42 B.C.) in which the army of Brutus and Cassius was routed.   Line 11. *fires*—A second reference to the battle of Pharsalus. Pharsalus was situated in Thessaly.
Line 11. *blood*—A poetic way of describing Caesar's campaign in Spain against the followers of Pompey (49 and 45 B.C.)   Line 13. *desert bounds*—A reference to Caesar's Egyptian campaign.
          Line 14. *Actium*—At the battle of Actium in 31 B.C. Antony and Cleopatra were decisively defeated by Octavian (later called Augustus). Octavian ascribed his victory to the favorable intervention of Apollo on his behalf.   Line 19. *Charon's*—The ferryman of the classical hell.   Line 24. *Styx*—The greatest of the legendary rivers of the underworld.   Line 31. *brother's*—i.e., Jupiter, god of the lightning.   Line 37. *Cynthia*—Goddess of the moon.

Page 135, Line 13. *Greece*—According to legend Hercules had crossed the Alps after his killing of Geryon. Hercules' "servitude" is a reference to the labors imposed upon him by Eurystheus.
Line 30. *Saturn*—i.e., Italy, the famous *Saturnia tellus* of Vergil.
          Line 35. *war*—Caesar's excuse for beginning the Civil War was the decision of the Senate—passed at the insistence of his enemies—that he must yield his Gallic command and return to Rome as a private person before he could be allowed to stand for the consulship. This, of course, would have exposed him to lawsuits and accusations on charges of malfeasance by his enemies, whereas as consul he would have been exempt from prosecution. Hence the senatorial decree was a virtual ultimatum, acquiescence in which must almost certainly have meant the end of Caesar's political career. But by common Roman standards, Caesar could have claimed that his "honor" had been flouted and justifiably move to war against his enemies.   Line 40. *storm*—A reference to Rome's perennial fear of a Gallic invasion. In 390 B.C. the Gauls had succeeded in sacking Rome, and Caesar represents himself as having staved off the Gallic menace through his Gallic campaigns.

Page 136, Line 3. *mercenary men*—Presumably, this is an allusion to the gangs of toughs hired by the demagogues Milo and Clodius and used to bully their opponents.   Line 22. *raven*—The raven, as Apollo's bird, was regarded as prophetic.   Line 33. *ground*—This whole passage dealing with Caesar's crossing of the Alps has been strongly influenced by Livy's famous description of Hannibal's crossing (xxi. 36 ff.)

Page 137, Line 16. *returning*—Hercules, according to legend, had liberated Prometheus from his imprisonment in the Caucasus.
          Line 19. *doom*—A reference to the defeat of the earth-born Giants by Zeus; the Giants had attempted to scale Olympus.
Line 22. *Palatine*—i.e., the Palatine Hill in Rome.   Line 29. *sanguine Germano*—The pun is impossible to translate well. The Latin phrase, *Germano sanguine*, means not merely "with German blood," but "with related blood," i.e., with civil war.   Line 41. *fear*—The whole passage shows a marked resemblance to Lucan *Pharsalia* i. 490 ff.

Page 138, Line 12. *fathers*—Cf. Vergil *Aeneid* ii. 707.   Line 26. *Pontus*—A reference to Pompey's victory (66–63 B.C.) over

Mithridates of Pontus.   Line 28. *Hydaspes*—A river in India
where Alexander the Great had defeated Porus. Pompey's campaigns
had never, of course, taken him to the Hydaspes, but the effect
of the suggestion is to liken him to a Roman Alexander.   Line
30. *pirate-scourge*—In 67 B.C. Pompey had completely crushed the
Pirates who infested the Cilician coast.   Line 36. *twin consuls*
—The consuls were C. Claudius Marcellus and L. Cornelius
Lentulus Crus (49 B.C.)

Page 139, Line 15. *Erinys*—i.e., the Fury.   Line 15.
Bellona—Another goddess of war, the equivalent of Enyo. See note
above, p. 132, *Enyo*.   Line 16. *Megaera*—Another of the
Furies.   Line 33. *Venus*—Julius Caesar claimed to be de-
scended from Venus through her son Aeneas.   Line 34. *Pallas*
—Or Minerva; she was also a goddess of war and strategy.
Line 34. *Romulus*—The son of Mars, the god of war.   Line
35. *sister*—i.e., Apollo and Diana.   Line 38. *Hercules*—
Pompey, because of his travels, was felt to resemble Hercules, and
so Hercules stands beside him here. Earlier, it will be remembered,
Caesar's descent into Italy was likened to Hercules' return from
the Caucasus. The inconsistency is typical of the poem. Tiryns
was the reputed birthplace of Hercules.

Page 140, Line 24. *law*—Marcellus was a Pompeian and consul
in 49 B.C. His brother, also a Pompeian, was responsible for the
law which required Caesar to lay down his command and return
to Rome to stand for the consulship in person. Hence the injunction
to "hold the law."   Line 26. *Curio*—C. Scribonius Curio was
a passionate supporter of Caesar; during the critical months before
the outbreak of civil war, he acted as Caesar's agent in Rome,
checking the Pompeians wherever possible.   Line 27. *Lentulus*
—Lucius Cornelius Lentulus Crus, consul in 49 B.C.   Line 33.
Epidamnus' shore—Pompey attempted to organize his troops and
entrench himself near Epidamnus in Epirus during the early days
of the war.

CHAPTER XVI

Page 142, Line 2. *Chrysis*—The maid of the lady Circe; she is
here speaking to Encolpius on behalf of her mistress.   Line 24.
rows back—According to the Lex Roscia (67 B.C), the fourteen
rows in the theater immediately behind the Senatorial section were
allotted to the Knights (i.e., *Equites*), the influential moneyed and
commercial class of ancient Rome. Hence to go beyond the fourteen rows of the Knights would mean that Circe looked for her
lovers among the lower classes.

Page 143, Line 18. *Praxiteles*—The great Greek sculptor (born
about 390 B.C.). Among his more famous works were an Aphrodite
(of which the Venus de' Medici is an imitation), a group showing
Leto, Apollo, and Artemis, and the Apollo Sauroctonos.   Line
21. *Paros*—An island in the Aegean, famed in antiquity for the
whiteness of its marble.   Line 22. *Doris*—The reference is
presumably to another vanished section of the novel.   Line
29. *Danae*—Jupiter's amatory metamorphoses are a commonplace
of ancient love poetry. As a bull, he carried off Europa; he appeared to Leda as a swan and to Danae in a shower of gold.

Line 39. *sister*—The relationship (like "brother") is again an amatory one.

Page 144, Line 17. *Circe*—Cf. Homer *Odyssey* x. In Homer Circe is the daughter of the Sun and the Oceanid Perse.   Line 23. *Polyaenos*—The name assumed by Encolpius at Croton. It is the same name as that which the Sirens gave to Odysseus (*Odyssey* xii. 184), and it is probable that what we have here is a little realistic mock-epic version of the famous meeting of Odysseus and the enchantress Circe. So elsewhere we have Lichas as a mock Cyclops and Encolpius as Odysseus; Giton under the bed is a tiny Odysseus, etc.   Line 31. *Juno lay*—Cf. Homer *Iliad* xiv. 346 ff.

Page 145, Line 36. *Alcibiades*—The Athenian general. The blamelessness of Socrates' relationship with the young Alcibiades was evidently regarded by the ancients as a triumph of self-control; however, the evidence is mainly Platonic and must be treated with reserve.

CHAPTER XVII

Page 149, Line 28. *soul*—This paragraph is an intrusion of a similar incident (though it actually concerns Encolpius' love for the boy Endymion). The intrusion is clearly unfortunate, for it implies—in context—that Encolpius has at last been successful with Circe. Such a development would clearly make nonsense of the entire succeeding incident (Ch. XVIII).

CHAPTER XVIII

Page 150, Line 19. *let it drop*—A burlesque of epic style. Cf. Vergil *Aeneid* ii. 479.

Page 151, Line 6. *hang down*—These lines are taken bodily from Vergil, and the incongruity between their original contexts and their use here is clearly deliberate. The first line and a half in my translation (which uses four lines to translate the three of the Latin text) come from Vergil's *Aeneid* vi. 469–470 and describe Dido's reception of Aeneas in Hades. The last two lines are made up of two Latin hemistichs, the first from *Eclogue* v. 16, the second from *Aeneid* ix. 436. It should be noted that the effectiveness of these lines depends upon acquaintance with their original context. It is in this sense that Petronian irony is literary and sophisticated.   Line 18. *heart*—Cf. Homer *Odyssey* xx. 17.
    Line 25. *Cato's*—Cato represents the ascetic and censorious puritan mentality, just as in Eumolpus' poem he represents the old Roman republican virtues.

Page 152, Line 8. *perfector*—These Latin words do not occur in the original. I have ventured to intrude them because they seemed to me a reasonable periphrasis of the original (*et hoc vitam dixit habere* τέλος), and because the Greek tag at the close of the poem obviously demanded translation somehow. τέλος is a technical term from Greek philosophy, meaning the ultimate goal or final purpose. Throughout the poem I confess to having taken liberties, but for the most part these seemed to me legitimate expansions of the meaning of the Latin.

CHAPTER XIX

Page 152, Line 25. *Lesbos*—A large island in the Aegean where Priapus must have had a cult.   Line 26. *Hypaepa*—The name of a small town in Lydia.

Page 153, Line 3. *need*—An echo of Vergil *Aeneid* vi. 91.
Line 20. *night*—The pollution would be regarded as ill-omened.

Page 154, Line 9. *Oenothea*—The name means "wine-goddess," an obvious reference to her tippling habits.   Line 41. *Phoebus* —Poetic hyberole for the sun.

Page 155, Line 5. *Circe's*—Circe changed Odysseus' crew into swine. See *Odyssey* x.   Line 7. *Proteus*—The Old Man of the Sea; he had the power to assume the shape of anything he wished.

Page 156, Line 15. *Hecale*—According to legend, Hecale was an old woman who received Theseus hospitably.   Line 16. *Callimachus*—Perhaps the greatest of the Hellenistic Greek poets. Among his more famous works was a (nonextant) epic on the story of Hecale. As a native of Cyrene, Callimachus is poetically "Battus' son," since Battus was the legendary founder of Cyrene.

Page 157, Line 4. *Stymphalian*—One of the feats of Hercules was his encounter with the great carrion birds who haunted Lake Stymphalus in Arcadia. By banging loudly on metal pots, he succeeded in driving them away.   Line 6. *Phineus*—The legendary king of Salmydessus in Thrace. He was punished for his brutality to his sons by having his dinner table attacked by Harpies. It was the custom of the Harpies to foul or fly off with Phineus' food every time he sat down to table. In the end the Harpies were driven away by two of the Argonauts.

Page 158, Line 34. *father's ear*—Acrisius, according to legend, was king of Argos. He was forewarned that his daughter Danae would bear a son who would destroy him, so he locked Danae in a brazen tower to prevent her marrying. Zeus, however, descended to her as a shower of gold, and in due course Danae gave birth to Perseus who destroyed Acrisius.

Page 159, Line 5. *Servius*—Servius Sulpicius Rufus, a contemporary of Cicero, and a famous jurisconsult. I have omitted here the name of Labeo, an Augustan jurist, on the grounds that it simply doubled the obscurity of the reference for the modern reader and added little.

CHAPTER XX

Page 160, Line 14. *Ariadne*—Famous beauties of mythology. Leda was the mother of Helen; Ariadne was the daughter of Minos of Crete, beloved by Theseus and then by Dionysos.   Line 19. *bargain*—Paris of Troy sat as judge in the famous beauty contest between Hera, Aphrodite, and Athena. He awarded the famous golden apple to Aphrodite after she had promised him the loveliest woman in the world, i.e., Helen.

Page 161, Line 7. *grudge*—Hercules was persecuted by the vindictive anger of Hera (cf. the *Heracles* of Euripides).   Line 7.

Pelias—He incurred Juno's hatred by killing his mother's step-mother at her altar. In his old age, anxious to restore his youth, he allowed himself to be cut to pieces by his own daughters at the suggestion of Medea.   Line 8. *Laomedon*—King of Troy, received the help of Apollo and Poseidon in building the city walls. He then cheated them of their pay.   Line 9. *Telephus*—The son of Hercules and Auge. Brought up in ignorance of his birth, he later married his mother, the priestess of Athena. According to another story, during the Trojan War, Telephus tripped on a vine tendril put in his way by Dionysos and was nearly killed by Achilles' sword. Thus the two deities who oppressed him would presumably be Athena and Dionysos. But this is uncertain.
Line 11. *rage*—Ulysses was persecuted by Neptune (i.e., Poseidon) and driven to wander for many years before he finally came home to his native Ithaca.   Line 14. *relentlessly on*—Cf. Vergil *Georgics* iv. 11: *Hellespontiaci servet tutela Priapi*.

CHAPTER XXII

Page 163, Line 17. *Protesilaus*—He was permitted to revisit earth after death. Encolpius, that is, has been resurrected.

CHAPTER XXIV

Page 165, Line 14. *Saguntum*—Besieged by Hannibal, it finally fell (219 B.C.) after an eight months' siege.   Line 18. *Petelia*—Besieged by Rome in the third century B.C. But the reference is uncertain.   Line 21. *Numantia*—In Spain; it was captured by Scipio after a long blockade in 133 B.C.